Pride Publishing books by Remmy Duchene

Tempted to Touch
The Smell of Camellias

Shivers
Ciro
Osaki
Koi

IntoXication
So Into You
Faded Into You

I0680720

INTOXICATION
Volume Two

Lost in You

Fallen into You

REMMY DUCHENE

IntoXication Volume Two
ISBN # 978-1-78686-342-3
©Copyright Remmy Duchene 2017
Cover Art by Posh Gosh ©Copyright December 2017
Interior text design by Claire Siemaszkiewicz
Pride Publishing

LOST IN YOU

Prologue

It'd been so long since the Takao's moved away from Japan in order for the business to work. Though they did not reside in the country, Ko Takao's father, Nobu Takao, insisted on them keeping a great deal of their traditions, which included the death ceremony. So, after his death, Ko had performed the usual ceremonies he was obligated to under his culture. Ko had carried out the Matsugo-no-mizu himself by using clean cotton swabs, dipped in water to wipe his father's lips. His father had told him when it was time. Though the nurses had stood on the other side of the bed and had tried reassuring his father to simply rest, Nobu had been adamant. Death had been near and after a while Ko had sensed it, too.

Right after his father's passing, Ko had forbidden anyone to touch the body. He had covered the shrine Nobu had mounted in an extra room of the house with white paper. On the bedside table beside his father, Ko had removed the lamp and replaced it with incense, a candle some lotus flowers — his father's favorite — and a sharp knife.

Over the front door, he had hung a white Japanese lantern. It was a sign that someone had passed inside the house and back in the day had been mostly for family and friends who'd walked by. Since Ko's mother had died when he had been a mere eight years old and his father's family were all gone, there really hadn't been anyone to tell. But it was tradition.

For twenty-four hours, Ko had kneeled by his father's bed like a dutiful son. He'd clasped his hands in his lap and focused on his father's face. Nobu Takao had been a man of many talents but subtlety wasn't one of them. He had spoken his mind and had demanded what was right. Sometimes, Ko had thought his father hadn't loved him. But as he'd gotten older, he had realized his dad hadn't known any better.

At the end of the day, he had offered incense, had said a small prayer and had risen to carry on with the rest of the ceremonies. By then, someone had called Thaddeus, who had shown up with flowers. When Thaddeus had hugged him, Ko's legs had given out under him, for it had been a while since he'd eaten. Without a word, Thaddeus had walked him into the kitchen, sat him in a chair and offered him a warm mug. Ko had slowly sipped, allowing the sweet flavor of peppermint to permeate his body.

Thaddeus hadn't said how sorry he had been for Ko's loss—Thaddeus was the closest thing he had to a brother and Ko knew Thaddeus understood that Ko never wanted to hear those words. They had sat together in silence until Thaddeus had made him a grilled cheese sandwich and a glass of lemonade.

The days had drifted by slowly between Nobu Takao's passing and the actual cremation. With that final step, Ko had left for Japan. His father's final wish had been to be taken home. Though Thaddeus had wanted to go with him, Ko had had to decline. It had been one of those times where he had to do something on his own.

After scattering his father's ashes around his mother's grave, Ko returned to his hotel room and fell to his back on the bed. So many emotions surged through him all at once and he wasn't sure what to do with himself. Confusion pulsed in his head, his body ached with exhaustion and a sobering sense of loss and grief descended on him like a sudden rainstorm. Tears spilled down the corners of his eyes and lodged in his ears but he just couldn't stop sobbing. After having his father for so long, Ko was now truly alone in the world and it hurt far more than anything else ever had or probably ever would.

In his daze, he rummaged through his pocket for his cell and called Thaddeus—roaming charges be damned.

"Hello?" Thaddeus' sleep-filled voice came over the line.

"Hey," Ko said, his voice breaking. "I'm sorry to call so late but I…"

"It's okay, man. Really. I'm glad you called. How are you?"

"I don't know." Ko blinked, trying to clear the tears from his eyes. "I feel as if the world is ending."

"That's to be expected," Thaddeus said. "I really wish you'd let me come. I understand why you refused, but still. I really wanted to be there for you."

"You were—I mean, you are. Sometimes I get jealous of Ravi."

"Jealous? Why?"

"He has you in all the ways that matter," Ko admitted. "I've never thought of sleeping with you — that's not what this is about. But you're kind and strong and everything I'm not. You're everything I've wanted."

"Come on, Ko. That's not you talking."

Ko allowed his mind to ponder Thaddeus' words for a silent breath. In the end, he merely shrugged and nodded. "It is." He paused as he glanced down at his trembling hands. "Why hold back now, right? You're just going to die, anyway."

"Ko —"

"For the first time in a long time I'm very lucid," Ko continued, as if Thaddeus had said nothing. "All I'm saying is the way you are with him is what I could use in my life right now. Look at all the changes — Dad's gone. I'm here by myself, expected to do what will carry his company through to the next— Damn. I almost said to the next generation."

"As in your children?"

Ko shook his head. "Forget I said that. I just would like somewhere to run to, you know?"

"I get it now. Don't worry. Your time will come."

Ko smiled and sat up. Large tears rolled down his face and plopped onto his thighs. "I don't think so, Thaddeus," he said softly. "Some people are cut out for love and others aren't. Some of us were destined to wander this planet alone, chasing after love, always glimpsing it in the distance but never catching up. And that's okay."

"You don't really mean that. Let me come to you."

"No. You have other things to consider now, Thaddeus. I'll be back soon and you can yell at me all you want."

"Is that Ko?" Ravinder's sleepy voice came from the background. "Want me to pack a bag for you?"

"No!" Ko said. "He can't be advocating this! Listen, I'm just going to get a glass of wine or something, then sleep. They say things always look better in the morning, right?"

Thaddeus chuckled. "Right. But if I don't hear from you tomorrow I'm getting on a plane, got it?"

"Thad —"

"Yes or no, Ko. It's not up for debate."

Ko sighed. "Got it."

After hanging up with Thaddeus, Ko wandered into the bathroom to wash his face and hands. Once he had some sense of pulling himself together, he ordered room service then flopped onto his bed to go through all the paperwork the lawyer had given him after his father's passing. Apparently, his dad hadn't wanted the reading of the will to wait too long. The last thing Ko wanted to deal with was the division of his father's worldly goods. He'd give it all back if he could have his dad now. But, unfortunately, that wasn't how things worked. After so many years of having his father by his side, Ko now had to think about walking the rest of his days alone. It was a daunting concept. For even though Ko and his father hadn't always agreed, Ko had gotten to learn his father's way of saying 'I love you' and most times it had seemed cold and distant, but it had been something.

With his father's death, it was as if a part of Ko was gone, too. But Ko knew he had to do what the Japanese often say. *Kishi kaisei* — wake from death and return to life.

Chapter One

Kishi kaisei.

How in the hell am I supposed to do that – huh, Pa?

"Seriously, Ko. You are not paying attention."

Ko Takao inhaled deeply and tore his eyes from the women in bright-colored saris, walking together along the narrow lane. He'd been in India for three weeks but he still wanted to cry each time he thought back to burying his father. After Nobu's death over a month before, he'd been putting off the trip and hiding in his house while he'd made arrangements for his father's burial. But soon, Thaddeus Masterson and his husband, Ravinder, had flown into Bathsheba and all but kidnapped him.

He cleared his throat. He could tell Thaddeus that he was in fact listening, but knowing his friend, Thaddeus would only follow it up with 'then what did I just say?'

That was a trap Ko knew very well.

"Sorry," Ko said instead. "I didn't mean to drift off like that. What were you saying?"

"You okay?" Ravinder asked.

Ko shook his head. "I don't know." He exhaled long and hard while rubbing his palms along his thighs. "There are so many things running through my head."

"Like what?" Ravinder asked.

"The design for your suits for one."

"If it's too much, Ko, you don't have—" Thaddeus began.

"Oh, knock it off, would you?" Ko snapped. "I'm designing the suits now. Shut up about it..." Ko glanced out of the window quickly before looking at Ravinder and Thaddeus. "Sorry. I've just been feeling inadequate lately."

"How so?" Thaddeus was the first to speak.

"I'm not ready for this. Running Hansamu wasn't my dream."

"What was your dream?" Thaddeus asked.

For a moment, Ko thought about it. But he could come up with no clear answer so he merely shrugged and turned his gaze to the procession of beautifully clad women. After another round of food, the three exited the small restaurant on the roadside and wandered back to the house. As much as he'd like to run all the way there and toss himself into the air-conditioned interior, the humidity weighed Ko down. That, coupled with the food they'd just devoured, was like swimming upstream through molasses.

Heat waves rose from the asphalt, making the humid air around them even more stifling. Ko hated the heat— hated the way it made his head go dizzy when he stepped outside. Then to make things worse, within seconds, his sweat had his shirt clinging to his back. He disliked the smell of the heat—fire mixed with other scents he couldn't quite place. But as he glanced around, Ko could honestly say the beauty of India and its people outweighed the smell and humidity.

Finally back home, he excused himself and immediately took a shower. He then wandered the air-conditioned house shirtless. Though it frustrated him to be wearing any clothing at all, Ko had to respect the fact it wasn't his place. Some iota of modesty was required.

While Thaddeus went on a business call, he made himself useful in the kitchen by spreading his new designs for Hansamu on the island and studying them. Ko had no clue what he was looking for but something was off. Absentmindedly, he tapped his pencil against the side of his head. The label's sales were through the roof and that was how his father had always kept it. The pressure now was to keep the company going at the size his father had always wanted. Hansamu was to remain small but giant in reputation and quality. Whenever his father had seen clothing lines filing for bankruptcy, he'd always shaken his head and muttered, *'Baka wa shinanakya naoranai.'*

Ko smiled at the memory. "You can't fix stupid, indeed."

Staring at the face of the model currently leading the charge for the company, Ko sighed. The same disappointment that had clouded his judgment after his father had announced who the model was filled him once more. The model was handsome with a nice body but he looked nothing like an everyday man. He wasn't the kind of man Hansamu represented. No, the first thing Ko needed to do was find a new face. He turned the picture over so his mind could work, then went back to adding little things to his sketches. For a while, he managed to forget the enormity of the responsibilities now sitting on his shoulders. In the silence of the house, Ko merely went back to what he'd loved doing—creating.

Thaddeus had asked him what his dreams were, and sadly Ko couldn't remember. So much of who he was and what he did was tied up in a company his father had started. He'd lost himself within the ranks and the nightly meetings. With his thoughts once again jumbled, Ko gave up on work and went looking for Thaddeus. Though his best friend was still on the phone, Ko took a seat on the large sofa and impatiently waited for Thaddeus to finish.

"Okay, you have my attention," Thaddeus said, a smile grazing his thick lips. "What's the matter?"

"I feel restless, unworthy—"

"Whoa! This again? Unworthy? Of what?"

"My father's legacy."

"Ko—"

"I mean," Ko continued as if Thaddeus hadn't said a word. "He leaves me with this empire and I'm supposed to carry it on and make sure it stays in good standing. Damn. It's a lot."

"I get it." Thaddeus walked around the desk to sit beside him. "And you know Ravinder and I are here if you need a hand. Between the two of us, I'm sure we could give you more help than your father would know what to do with."

Ko sighed and dragged a hand over his face. "Yeah. Both of you have your life to deal with right now. Shouldn't you be looking into kids?"

Thaddeus smiled. "We are not Darius and Feng."

"So, you don't want kids then?"

"Of course. But since we've been married just two years, we've barely had time to be together. Between us staying on at Rajput longer than we were supposed to, me starting an actual firm and Ravi building his company, we've been crazy busy. We haven't spoken at length about children yet."

"Well, if you don't mind me saying, you're getting old."

Thaddeus laughed. "I could say the same for you."

"Me?" Ko sputtered as if Thaddeus had said something so blasphemous it warranted bulging eyes and a gasp. "Nah. Husband and kids are not in the cards for old Takao. I've tried."

"Maybe you should try again. It has been a while since I've seen you with anyone."

"No. Love isn't for the Takao men. Mom left Dad for some politician when I was four. He raised me on his own. He never dated after that. I guess Mom leaving the way she did really tore a piece off him."

"I know the story. And yes, your father was hurt and I don't think he could have risked it again, especially with a child he had to look out for. But that doesn't mean you won't find a lover who adores you." Thaddeus eased back into the seat. "If an old dog like me could find someone, why not you?"

"Because karma is a son of a bitch."

"I thought karma was a woman."

Ko groaned and stood. "I'm going for a walk."

"Maybe you could see if Abhay wants to go out tonight or something. He would make a pretty decent wingman."

"No. He hasn't seen Priya in almost six months. I'm sure there are better things he'd like to do tonight. And besides, I need alone time to think. I'm trying to figure out a way to get a new face for Hansamu. The one we have isn't quite right."

"When you say 'new face'…"

"The current model we have heading the line isn't—I don't know. I don't like the way he looks. He doesn't represent the men the line is for—that the brand is for. Dad didn't like it, either, but it was a last-minute thing and he didn't have a chance to do an extensive search to find the right fit."

"Well, maybe you could try Jackson."

"Who is that?"

"Jackson Stark?"

Ko arched an eyebrow. "You mean Kent Stark's son? How old is he? Seventeen?"

"Yeah. Like nine years ago." Thaddeus laughed. "He's twenty-six now."

"I don't know if he's grown into those jeans I saw him in the last time," Ko scoffed. "He was this lanky kid. It's been a while since I've seen him. What's he been doing?"

"He went to university for business and graphic design. Now he's working for Darius. He designed and produced *Together We Rise*."

"As in, the video game?" Ko asked.

Thaddeus nodded.

"Seriously?" Ko fell back into his seat. All thoughts of going for a walk were gone and he couldn't get enough information, it seemed. "You're kidding."

"Why?"

"I love that game!" Ko said. Of course, he knew if he met Jackson he'd probably never admit to it. "It's so...so...real."

Thaddeus nodded. "Yeah. He started the concept for a project in university but nothing ever came of it because he had to focus on school. Once he was finished, Darius made him come up with a full proposal for it, including a business plan, then went over it. Apparently, he liked what he saw because *Together We Rise* is now one of the highest-grossing video games of the last two years. I think he's working on a follow-up but I'm not big into video games."

Ko nodded. "All right. I'll take a look at him."

Thaddeus went back behind his desk and tapped away at his keyboard. He turned the laptop so Ko could see the screen. What he saw caused his eyes to widen. The last time he'd seen Jackson was at the launch party of Thaddeus' new security software. He barely remembered the kid, but back then he had been skinny with big brown eyes, large hands and a smile that seemed to encompass his whole face.

Not the man on the screen.

Ko stared silently, allowing his eyes to trail over Jackson's face. His smile was still as big as ever but didn't look so out of place as before. Jackson Stark seemed to have grown into himself with a sleek, muscular body, and wide shoulders that held the Hansamu design perfectly.

"He's wearing one of Daddy's suits," Ko managed. His voice cracked only slightly. Hopefully Thaddeus would see it as emotion over the loss of his father and not arousal.

"Yeah. So, what do you think?"

"I'd have to see him without his shirt," Ko said before he could stop himself. "The underwear shots will have him shirtless."

Good catch!

"Well, I could make a few phone calls. Not sure if he can take time off from Stark right now, but since you're going home in a week, anyway…"

"Yeah." Ko cleared his throat and stepped away from the screen. "I can have a meeting with him. It would save me time and money to have go-sees set up and the flood of models coming into the office. Ugh."

"Awesome. Let me talk to him first, okay?"

Ko nodded. "I'm going to head out for that walk. Give you and Ravi some time alone. I'll be back."

"Ko, you don't have to…"

"I know," Ko said. "I need the air."

It was a lie and even if Thaddeus sensed his bullshit, he didn't call Ko out on it. Ko didn't need the kind of air India had. But since he'd been to India he always seemed to be with Ravinder and Thaddeus. He knew they'd missed each other, that they needed time to be alone together—even though they hadn't said so. Besides, Ko hated being a third wheel and he sometimes got a little jealous of the love he saw between Thaddeus and Ravinder.

Shoving his fingers deeply into his pockets, he exited the large gates to the Mastersons' Raja property and turned left. He wandered down the long outer driveway then headed right along a freshly paved street. Before Thaddeus and Ravinder had bought the house, the street had been nothing but dirt and gravel. Thaddeus had paid to have the road paved so he and his fiancé could have something that wouldn't destroy their vehicles.

With the late evening sun bearing down, the asphalt was soft beneath his shoes and the air was rich with the smell of tar. Deep down he knew that couldn't be safe but he was so far into his mind that Ko didn't particularly care. He was too busy wondering what Jackson Stark looked like underneath that suit. Ko was curious about stripping off Jackson's clothing with his teeth and watching that dark flesh come to light.

"Son of a bitch," Ko muttered, drawing his shoulders up to his ear and quickening his steps. "What in the hell is wrong with me?"

He received no answers to that except a cow mooing from somewhere to his left. Squinting, he turned his head in that direction, trying to see the animal. All he saw were small houses littering the landscape, along with huts, long since empty.

Finally, he came to a roadside bar. Indian music blared from a television set on an upturned bucket on the front stop step. He peered over and realized the sounds were coming from what appeared to be a Bollywood movie. Ko had seen his fair share of them since becoming friends with Abhay and Priya Chetan.

Speaking of Priya—Ko stopped to watch the actress gyrate across the screen before stopping to glide her neck left to right as her eyes darted from side to side— Priya would look amazing posing with Jackson. With design concepts dancing around inside his head, he entered the muggy bar and found a seat close to the very end on the far side.

"Soda?" Ko asked.

The man wiggled his neck with a smile. "Coming right up!"

True to his words, the bartender quickly returned with a bottle that must have been in the freezer. He handed over some money and unscrewed it. When he took a drink, the soda was basically a slushie. Ko didn't mind. It worked wonders to soothing his overheated body. He paid no attention to the rumble of at least three different languages happening around him. It didn't matter, anyway, for he understood none of them. Ko nursed on his soda until his bottle was empty, bought three more and headed out. He was tempted to keep walking away from the house but his body just didn't want to do it.

Halfway back home, his cell rang and he picked it up without checking the screen.

"Takao?"

"Hey! Ko!"

Ko groaned. "Hey, Merrick. How's it going?"

"Spectacular. Listen, have you given any thought to what I ran by you?"

"Not yet. I just buried my father and my best friends kidnapped me for a vacation. All business is on hold right now until I get back to town."

"Aw-right, cool. How you doing, anyway?"

Ko hated that. His welfare shouldn't be second fiddle. Still, he said nothing to that. "Better, thanks. Look, I gatta go. I'm in India right now and—"

"Oh, right! Okay, talk to you when you get back."

Ko grunted and hung up. There was no way in hell Ko was going to let anyone design a line of men's thongs for his company. Men had way too much junk to be wearing ass floss. And who thought that was sexy? If you had to wear something like that, just go without!

Irritated, he made his way back into the yard and turned to watch the gate close silently. He then jogged up the front steps, around the side of the house and sat on the pool deck. For a moment, he debated just leaving the others until he was ready to go in. But he figured they'd get warm so he carried them inside and stuck them into the fridge. As he was closing the fridge, he could hear the sounds of lovemaking coming from upstairs. Ko sighed, grabbed a glass and filled it with ice then pulled out one of the beers. After wringing off the cap, he dumped the content over the ice and swirled it around as the moans grew louder. Opting to give them more time, Ko carried his beer back to the deck. He sat with his feet in the water, cold glass in one hand, trying to remember the last time a man thought enough of him to make love to him.

* * * *

When his trip came to an end, India left him more than a little better—physically anyway. Emotionally he was still a bit off. He returned to Bathsheba earlier than he'd told everyone and merely hid out at his place. It was partly because he had an appointment and him partly needing to be alone to breathe and grieve.

The first morning he woke up feeling as if he had been run over by a garbage truck. The jetlag mixed with the messed-up time zone and the alcohol from the plane left him drained. Ko toyed with the idea of hitting the gym but settled for going on a run. The way his body was, he knew he'd wind up dropping a ten-pound weight on his foot or something. The run didn't last very long, half an hour and he was back. That had been a horrible idea, too. Maybe Ravinder was right—he needed to give his body time to heal before he started pushing again.

But it was never that easy—it couldn't be. Ko had to maintain Hansamu and find a way to not get buried under his father's shadow, even in death.

Once he was dressed, Ko stopped long enough to brew some coffee, take a couple of sips, then gathered his keys and wallet and headed out of the door. Thaddeus had given him the heads-up to one of Jackson Stark's shoots and Ko had managed to talk the photographer into letting him watch. It was homework—not because he was super curious about what Jackson looked like while the cameras were flashing. The fact that seeing Jackson's pictures aroused him had absolutely nothing to do with anything.

But even as he sped through the rain-damp streets, he couldn't make himself believe those lies. The photo shoot was at one of Bathsheba's prized historical houses. Back in the day, Burnham had been a plantation house—slavery, owners, the whole nine. But the owner had found Christianity and after years of a tarnished reputation, he had begun fighting for slavery to be outlawed and had used Burnham house as a refuge for slaves seeking freedom. Ko had read all about it on his flight over from India—it wasn't as if he'd had anything else to do.

The pictures did Burnham house no justice. The large structure stood as a testament of time before him as the gates swung wide to admit his car. He slowed to a crawl, keeping his eyes on the property, from the gargoyles on the highest parts of the roof, to the rounded windows and almost ancient walls. The staircase leading up to the massive wooden door was grand and made of stones. Ko wondered how they had managed to move those back then.

Finally, he got himself together and followed the signs to the parking and eased in between a motorcycle and a silver BMW. After quick check of his face in the car mirror, he eased from the vehicle and closed the door while glancing around. Apparently, he couldn't enter through a back door so he hurried around the side. He jogged up to the front door and had to brace his feet to pull it open. Once he was inside, the wonder didn't end. But he was a man on a mission. He finally found the location of the shoot and stood in the back to see what was happening. In the center of the large room was a single chair—like a throne of sorts. The photographer was fiddling with her camera as Jackson entered from a side door. The two talked for a little, then Jackson removed his robe and stood perfectly sculpted, facing the throne. The photographer gave a few instructions and the shoot began.

"More intensity in the eyes," the photographer barked.

Is that even possible? It already feels as if when he looks at me, I'm liable to implode.

"Good!" she hollered. "That's it. That's it!"

Ko was drawn by the change in Jackson's body. Suddenly he wasn't just Jackson anymore but a king — neck elongated, shoulders straight and strong. Every movement seemed like something a man of power would take. Ko leaned his back into the wall, folded his arms across his chest. Jackson rose from the throne and took a step down. He made his way to the foot of the steps, then turned as if he was going back to his seat.

"Beautiful!" the photographer called. "Straighten your back just a tad — yes! Yes!"

Ko couldn't breathe. Jackson had a nice ass.

"Lift your chin a bit," she continued. "Perfect! Now, go to the top. Stand beside the throne, and remember, Your Highness — this is your land!"

That seemed to be the motivation Jackson needed to turn it up a notch. He did as the photographer instructed and the shots that came afterward, Ko knew were spectacular. Then his gaze locked with Jackson's and Ko figured if he hadn't been propped against something he would have toppled over. For that moment, breath wasn't important. The connection he had with the model was all the life support he required.

"I'm Idris Elba and you want to do me!" the photographer hollered.

Ko laughed.

"Yes!" she cheered. "Wonderful!"

In that short time, Ko had done so many deliciously naughty things in his mind to Jackson. In his head, Ko had his young lover tied to the banister at his home and drove into his body from behind like a beast in heat. He had grabbed the rail on either side of Jackson then slammed forward until Jackson was shouting. He had Jackson bent over the hood of a car, leaning against his office desk, spread wide in the sand on a beach somewhere. In that short instant, all the delectably devilish sins one could commit were carried out.

"Okay, we need you to change," the photographer said and Ko could have strangled her with his bare hands.

The hold Jackson had over him broke and he gasped softly before staggering out of the door again. There was no way he could talk to Tasha and Jackson about his plans then. Confusion and arousal mingled inside his head and stormed through his body. The hairs on the back of his neck stood on end as a shiver trailed through him. Ko's heart hammered so loudly, he swore everyone could hear it.

He'd gone too long without a lover. That was the only explanation that made any sense. All the years he'd spent hiding from love, pushing lust away and burying it beneath the obligation to please his father, the need to fulfill all his other obligations, were coming back to haunt him. All he wanted to do was go home to some heated lube, porn and his hand.

After a good self-work session, he'd be right as rain.

Chapter Two

Applause rang out from behind Jackson and whirled around. He arched an eyebrow then smiled before walking over to Thaddeus Masterson. Jackson remembered the first time he had seen the muscular, African-American stud with the contemplative brown eyes and the sinful mouth. He had been a teenager and had almost crashed into Thaddeus leaving Darius' office. Even then, Jackson had known there was something so overly special about Thaddeus, and that night his wet dreams had been even hotter than before. Jackson might even go as far as to say he had a thing for Thaddeus for one misguided moment. He'd quickly gotten over that when he'd found out Thaddeus was taken—soon to be married to Ravinder Raja—one of Uncle Feng's friends.

Years later, Thaddeus was still the kind of man a gay boy's dreams were made of.

Jackson chewed on his bottom lip as the two bumped fists then hugged. "How you been?" Jackson asked.

"Good." Thaddeus nodded. He followed Jackson across the room to where a group of water bottles were lined up beside a pile of towels. "I can't complain."

"I hear you're getting married."

Thaddeus grinned. "That's true. Can you imagine?"

"Well, congrats, man. Ravinder is an awesome sort of guy."

"Thanks."

"How'd you find me, anyway?" Jackson dragged a clean towel over his face then against his neck, then wrung the cap off one of the bottles of water.

"Darius. I stopped by your old studio. The sign outside said it was out of business so I went to your uncle."

Jackson grinned. "Yeah. The Collinses wanted to retire and move to Florida. Their kid didn't want the place so they sold it. They're going to turn it into some kind of ESL school."

"Sad really. The studio has been there for years."

Jackson nodded. "Yeah. The place is older than me. I've been going there since I was six. It was sad to see it go. I toyed with the idea of buying it, but I wouldn't know the first thing about running a business."

"And it would eat into your dancing."

"Exactly. And I think my father would kill me to if I took on anything more. I'm already not sleeping as it is."

Thaddeus grinned. "Well, in that case, I should get to why I'm here."

Jackson eyed him with a smirk. "What's up?"

"I have a friend who owns a highly successful clothing empire," Thaddeus said, sitting on the floor with his back against the wall. He stretched his legs out before him. "His father passed recently, leaving everything in his hands and he feels the face of the line isn't what it should be. He's looking for a new lead model and I recommended you."

Jackson arched an eyebrow. Aside from the Men Tower Magazine shoot, Jackson hadn't done any real modeling in over a year. His work at Stark and his dancing pretty much kept him busy. Still, other than his latest shoot, he'd only done a few shots for Feng, Darius' husband, as a part of Feng's new portfolio. But that didn't really count — did it? "You told him about me? Thaddeus, I don't know, man."

"What do you mean, you don't know?" Thaddeus asked. "You're a good-looking kid. You take care of your body."

Jackson's cheeks burned. "That's not it. He knows I'm — well — gay, right?"

"I don't know if that's any of his business. I'm sure Ko wouldn't…"

"Ko? Ko Takao?"

"You know him?"

Jackson shook his head. He could tell Thaddeus that Ko had crashed his shoot with Men Tower and they'd had a bit of a moment. Though they hadn't said a word to each other and Ko had been on the other side of the room, Jackson had felt something. There had been a certain electricity rushing through his veins at having Ko's eyes on him. Knowing Ko watched him had had Jackson wanting to be devoured by the Japanese hottie, and after the shoot and the adrenaline had worn off, those thoughts terrified Jackson beyond belief. "I know of him." he lied easily. "The label you're talking about is Hansamu."

"Yeah."

"Damn." Jackson had to sit down. He sipped from his water, deep in thought. Would working for Ko be a good idea?

That's dumb. You'll never see him. The only people you'll have contact with will be the photographer and your co-star, if you have one.

Jackson frowned.

Could he really be the face of such a large line? Would his face and body convince men they should be wearing Ko's clothing? Then again, his closet was packed with pieces from Hansamu — they fit like a dream.

"Think about it, huh?" Thaddeus asked. "It would be a great opportunity for you."

"Yeah, it would," Jackson said softly. "It scares me, you know? Being the face of a line of this size."

"You won't be alone. You remember Priya?"

"Beautiful Indian woman — her brother is Abhay, I think."

"Yeah. She's the female lead of the line right now and will continue to be. It seems the public adores her. If you're in, I'm sure she'll love to work with you." Thaddeus stood.

Jackson nodded. "Okay. I'll get hold of you tomorrow and let you know."

"Good. Now, I should go. When I left the car, Ravinder was on an international call to Mumbai. I should take him home so he can get some sleep."

"Give him a hug for me," Jackson said. Over the past few years, he'd become friends with Ravinder Raja since Ravinder was like a brother to Feng Stark.

"I will. And you're coming to the wedding, right?"

"Of course. I think Uncle Darius would disown me, otherwise."

Thaddeus laughed then turned to leave. He stopped while digging into his pocket. He pulled out his wallet, retrieved a card and handed it to Jackson.

"Thanks. Have a good night."

"You, too, Jackson."

Jackson remained where he was standing a moment longer. Modeling wasn't what he wanted to do with the rest of his life. Dancing would last only until his body decided not to corporate anymore. His education to make video games would only be as useful as long as his ideas were fresh and there were people in the world who loved gaming. This gig wasn't going to last a lifetime. It was another thing to give him some exposure, to put his face out there so people knew him as just Jackson Stark and not Darius Stark's nephew or Kent Stark's son. He wanted to be known for what he accomplished.

Finally, he unglued himself and gathered his things. He got dressed and left the studio, heading east on Elgin Road toward the center of Bathsheba where he lived in a one-bedroom condo. He had bought it two years ago after finishing university and right before he'd scored a job with Darius' company. Dancing was a lucrative racket if you could find the work.

He was barely through the front door when his cell phone rang. He dumped his keys on the kitchen island then picked it up.

"Jack, listen," Charlie Stone said excitedly. "There is a call out for a principal dancer for The Orangutans. It's one day of shooting and the pay is the usual, on a Saturday. You want in?"

"What kind of question is that?" Jackson asked. "You know it!"

"Sweet! I'll let Paul know."

"When you say Paul…"

"The rapper from the band."

"I've known you for years. When did you get on a first name basis with Paul Shankar?"

Charlie laughed. "You know me, man. I get around. Listen, what you doing tomorrow night?"

"I have a few concept ideas to finish up but I can get that done tonight. Why?"

"I need a chill night."

"I hear you. I want to talk to you about something. You got a sec?"

"Always."

Jackson poured some orange juice, rummaged through the freezer for ice and dropped as many cubes in as he could. When the glass was almost overflowing, he bowed forward and drank the excess then added another ice cube. "So, you remember Thaddeus Masterson?"

"Thaddeus…Thaddeus…don't think so."

"He's engaged to Ravi."

"Oh! Yes!" Charlie said in a Barry White-esque voice. "That tall drink of hot chocolate. How could I have forgotten him?"

Jackson laughed. "Down, boy. That tall drink of hot chocolate is getting married soon and is officially off the market."

"Oh, you're no fun."

Jackson crinkled his nose and took a drink from his glass. "Anyway. Apparently, Ko Takao is the new owner of Hansamu and he's looking for a face for the line. Thaddeus recommended me."

"Hot damn!"

"I know! I told him I'd think about it."

"Think about it?" Charlie asked, shock evident in his voice. "Boy, what's wrong wit-choo?"

Jackson chewed on his lips. "Say what now?"

"What's to think about? This is no doubt a lucrative deal. So that's some major cash in your pockets. You can save for everything from that."

"I know. But it seems big, you know?"

"Well, you wouldn't be human if it didn't scare you, so I think you're right on track. Take it. Do your thing and enjoy it. You're young and sexy…"

"Sexy?" Jackson asked. "So why did we break up?"

Charlie cleared his throat. "You stopped wanting me."

For a moment, Jackson said nothing. He licked his lips and nodded needlessly. "I guess that's an important part of a relationship, right?"

"Yeah. The love isn't enough without the other stuff. They say love should be everything but love without attraction isn't real. Love without carnality, without wanting, isn't enough."

Jackson agreed but didn't voice that. "Well, for what it's worth, I'm sorry."

"Don't be. If you fall out of love with someone it's not because you're a douche. Your heart is the asshole."

Jackson laughed. "I'm glad we can still talk, Charlie. I'm glad I didn't lose you."

"I'm glad you didn't lose me, either. I am a whole lotta awesome."

"Check out the ego on this guy!"

Charlie chuckled. "Ego nothing, man. I'm just sayin'."

"Yeah, yeah."

"I'll see you tomorrow night," Charlie said. "Oh, and if you're still clear as mud on this whole Hansamu thing, talk to your dad or Darius. They know this guy better than you and can give you some insight on his friends. Or even talk to Ravi."

Jackson promised he'd sleep on it then take Charlie's advice if he was still unclear on what to do the next morning. After all, he had promised Thaddeus an answer soon. Still drinking from his juice, he climbed the stairs, deep in thought. The conversation he'd had with Charlie about why they'd broken up was still fresh in his head. It wasn't that he didn't love Charlie. No, Jackson would always love Charlie. But his friend didn't want children. In fact, Charlie had nothing good to say about kids. When he had realized that, Charlie was no longer sexy in Jackson's eyes. There was nothing more attractive than a man with kids. Jackson wanted children—a whole army of them if he could handle it. He smiled.

There were other reasons why he'd seemed to stop wanting Charlie but the kids situation was the one hurdle Jackson just couldn't get over.

With a sigh, he set his half-full glass on the bedside table next to his alarm clock and peeled off his clothes. He bunched up each article in a small ball and made a three-point shot to the laundry hamper in the corner under a large window. Jackson managed to get everything in except his boxers. He shrugged with indifference before he walked over, picked it up and dropped it into the hamper.

"Guess my jumpshot needs a little work," he muttered and chuckled.

* * * *

Bright and early the next day, Jackson reported to the office. He had a few things he had to finalize before his second game could be released on time from Stark Enterprises. The first game, *Together We Rise*, had done so well, Jackson still thought it was all a dream. He didn't have any more space on his mantel for awards. Proud, he leaned back in his chair and took a moment to bask in the happiness that radiated through him in that moment. But he didn't spend too much time on that. *Together We Stand* had to be bigger, better. The characters had to be more in depth, the graphics crisper. Everything about the sequel had to outdo the first.

In the beginning, the critics had said he had gotten the job only because he had Darius Stark's DNA in him. After the game's release, the stories changed to his success being beginner's luck. Jackson would be damned if he proved them right.

So far, the beta testers were enjoying *Together We Stand*. There were a few things Jackson had to take back to the drawing board but he didn't see doing that as an issue. Even after the first game had been out, it still had a few tweaks he would have liked to get done. He'd worked closely with the beta players since they were there to make sure the game had been put together right and the community would enjoy it.

If Jackson was being completely honest, he was more than a little frazzled about the whole thing. Everything had to be done in the next two weeks. The launch party was quickly approaching, but before then, they had an ad campaign to put together, followed by a round of press and conventions. Though he wouldn't be doing the promotion circuits, he still had to meet with the voiceover actors and the rest of the team who did face the public to show off the games.

Needless to say, everything had to be perfect.

He gathered the tablet, exited his office and hurried down the hall to Darius. The door to his uncle's office was open and though Jackson could hear voices, he stuck in his head. "Dad?"

His dad laughed and waved. "Hey, son. How's your day?"

Jackson hurried over to hug him. "Good. I was coming to pick Uncle Darius' brain but I can come back."

"No need." Darius rose to close the door. "Sit, would you?"

"Dad." Jackson took a seat beside his father and set his tablet on Darius' desk. "What brings you here?"

"Can't a guy come visit his brother and his son without everyone suspecting him of having ulterior motives?" Dad asked, eyebrows raised.

"Um…no," Jackson said.

He laughed out loud. "That's exactly what your uncle said. What is it with you two?"

"We're realists?" Jackson asked.

"No, what the two of you are, are asses."

Jackson chuckled. "Seriously, what's up?"

"Nothing. I just wanted to see you," his dad said. "I mean, I don't want to take things for granted, and over the last little while you seemed to be so busy. I figured I'd pop in, see that you're breathing, that sort of thing."

"Jesus, Dad, I'm sorry."

"No need."

Darius sat on the front of his desk and watched them. Jackson offered him a small smile. He thought back to the last few weeks, and though he had seen his dad, he couldn't remember the last time they'd been in the same room together.

"And things are about to get crazier," Jackson said. "Thaddeus offered me a sit down with Ko Takao to model for Hansamu."

"That's amazing news," Dad exclaimed.

Jackson nodded. "I told him I'd think about it."

"What's to think about?" both Darius and his dad chorused.

Jackson shrugged. "I don't know. I guess I don't want to bite off more than I can chew and being gay, that could hurt his brand."

"You do know Ko is gay, right?" Darius asked.

"Yes, but being gay and having a gay face are two different things," Jackson muttered. It wasn't until the words left his lips that he realized just how truly dumb they sounded.

"Well, shit. That's the biggest load of crap I've ever heard," Dad said.

That surprised Jackson. When Darius had come out to Kent, Kent hadn't handled it well. It had been even worse when Jackson had come out. That had put a strain on their relationship but over the years, his dad had made an effort. He was probably still not a hundred percent with it, but he did prove to Jackson that he loved him. "But, Dad!"

"No buts. If you're not going to do this, find another reason, because that one is bullshit."

Jackson turned to Darius for some support but Darius was giving him the same look his dad was. Jackson groaned and nodded. "Okay. The launch of *Together We Stand* is right around the corner and…"

"I'm not saying be complacent," Darius said. "But after the reviews the betas have given you, and the success of the first, this game will practically sell itself. And Violet can be your face at press conferences that you can't make it to — don't worry. This was my dream, remember? We need you to find yours."

Jackson offered a shaky smile. In one conversation, his dad and Darius had taken away all the crutches he had for not accepting Ko's offer. With nothing left, he made a mental note to call Thaddeus as soon as the meeting with his father and uncle was over. He nodded. "Okay then. I guess that's that."

Chapter Three

Ko was barely in his office before Stella Priest entered and flopped into the seat across from his desk. She looked tired, but she always looked like that. Her black and blue hair was tied up in a tight, efficient ponytail and her face wore the least amount of makeup he'd ever seen on a woman—lip-gloss and eyeliner. That was it. It wasn't that she wasn't interested in her appearance. For as long as he'd known her—five years or so—she was always immaculately dressed, but according to her, she was allergic to most makeup out there. Proof came when she'd used what was labeled as 'hypoallergenic foundation' and she'd spent a week in the hospital because she'd broken out in the worst case of hives he'd ever seen.

He dropped his bag on the floor by his chair then sat on the front edge of his desk and folded his arms.

"How was India?" she asked.

"Hot. But nice," Ko admitted with a grin. "You know Ravi and Thaddeus—they just had to get me away from here and I can't say I blame them."

"Awesome. So what's this I hear about you replacing the face of Hansamu?"

"You knew this was coming, Stella." Ko rose to get a bottle of water from the mini fridge. "Want anything?"

Stella shook her head. "I figured things would change. But have you found someone yet? It's not like you can let his contract run out if you don't have a clue of where to find someone." She paused as if to measure her words but Ko was aware that wasn't the case. Stella had little quirks that a person who didn't know her would definitely misread.

He also knew she wasn't finished so he waited.

"Even if you did find someone," Stella continued thoughtfully. "Would you release the guy we have now? And what would you do with the contract for him?"

"He doesn't have much longer left."

Stella consulted her tablet. "A month."

"Right. So we run what we have of him now and when he finishes his contract we give him a good going-away package and move on. His agency will need a little time to find him something—maybe we can talk him into a couple of extra months just so we can get things squared with the new model. It sounds harsh but business is business."

Stella nodded. "That doesn't yet answer the question of did you find someone to replace him. I mean we can't get rid of one face without another."

"I know that. I think I've found the perfect guy." Ko grabbed a folder from his bag and handed it to her. "I'm just not sure if he'll accept." He then focused on removing the seal on his water and taking a drink while she skimmed through what he'd given her.

"Oh, gawd! I hope he swings my way." Stella moaned. "He's a little young but—come to Momma!"

"Down, girl. We're going to wait until he accepts the job and finishes his contract before you set your sights on him. I don't want a lawsuit."

"Dibs!"

"What?" Ko asked, arching an eyebrow. "You can't just call dibs on someone."

"Why not?"

"Seriously?"

"That's not an answer."

"He's not the last piece of chicken at the dinner table!" Stella rolled her eyes. "How else am I going to let my intentions be known?"

Ko groaned but he doubted Stella heard that. She was still busy rifling through the images Ko had managed to get from Darius and Kent.

"All I'm saying is," she said, "once he's finished working, I want some of that."

"And if he doesn't swing that way?"

"Then you definitely have to tap that."

Ko winced. It was hard to hear that kind of talk. No matter how long he'd known Stella, he never got used to how brazen she always seemed to be. Still, he crossed his ankles and took another swallow from the water. "I saw him model for Men Tower a couple of days ago, and damn."

"That good?"

Ko nodded. "The man has skills, and seeing him in these pictures does him no justice. His body is more toned, skin darker and seems smoother. I think all the airbrushing they did to his photos is just a waste of money."

Stella moaned.

"Breathe, Stella. No climaxing on my chairs, please?"

Stella laughed. "Sorry. Couldn't help it."

"Oi." Ko shook his head. "But seriously, I have a meeting with him today. I figure I'd take him out to lunch and talk to him personally. Apparently, he's a little hesitant about doing this."

"Hesitant? Seriously? What's to be cautious about?"

"Being the face of anything is a huge responsibility."

"Did Julia Roberts contemplate Lancome?"

Ko rolled his eyes. He just couldn't help it.

"All I'm saying is that Hansamu may have a small space, but our brand is world renowned. Princes are wearing our lines. Any model would be crazy not to want this — and to have it simply handed to them...?" Stella said.

"Not everyone is like that. Jackson has a job that he loves with people he adores. If he agreed to come on board, it would mainly be as a favor to Thaddeus," Ko replied.

"Uh-huh. And the money — what's that? Chump change?"

"Stella..."

"No. The point I'm trying to make is, the guy needs a good smack to the back of the head to get some sense into him."

Ko knew she wasn't convinced so he gave up. "Clear my schedule for the rest of the day, would you? I have this meeting then I'm heading home. India is still kicking my ass."

"Ain't time differences a bitch?"

Ko laughed. "And the jetlag. Don't forget the jetlag."

"Never." Stella grinned and stood. "I'll clear your schedule. You were supposed to talk to Ivor today..."

"Call him and see if I can have that chat with him before I leave for lunch today. The meeting with Jackson is at one so maybe I could talk to Ivor at eleven-thirtyish?"

"I'll see what I can do."

When he was finally alone, Ko fell into his leather seat and grabbed his bag. He removed some designs he'd been working on and stared at them. It seemed since the possibility of having Jackson Stark as the new face of Hansamu, Ko couldn't stop thinking of sexy new styles for men. Each piece would flow over Jackson's body inside Ko's head and sat just perfectly. He smiled at that thought and set the drawings aside. If he was going to make it to lunch on time, he had to clear a few things off his plate first.

One phone call morphed into a meeting then finally his conference call with Ivor. The Hansamu website needed to be spruced up and Ivor was in charge of that. Ko wanted minor changes, prices to be fixed and to go over the specs for their sale that was coming up in less than a week. Though the sales team — and by team he referred to one person in her office — had everything set up, Ko was paranoid. That call ran a little late and when it finally ended, he had to motor it out of the door. He never liked rushing — that was why he had appointments. Still, he stopped at his place, changed, then headed into the center of Bathsheba. Thankfully, traffic was light. All the tourists were gone and he made it to Bronte's with ten minutes to spare.

Accepting a seat by the window overlooking the mountains, he shed his leather jacket and hung it over the back of his chair.

"Would you like a drink while you wait?" the server asked.

"Yes please. Um — do you have apple juice?"

"We do."

"Can I have a glass? The colder the better."

The young man nodded and left Ko alone. As he was getting settled on his chair, Jackson walked into the place and Ko tried his best not to stare. He picked up the menu and pretended as if he hadn't seen Jackson at all. Though he had the menu up, his brain was counting down to the moment Jackson would be seated across from him.

"Mr. Takao. Your guest…"

Ko lowered the menu and pushed back his chair. He rose to shake Jackson's hand. "It's good to see you, Jackson."

"Don't you mean it's good to see you again?" Jackson asked, releasing Ko's hand.

Ko chewed on his bottom lip, not sure how to take the question. Jackson's voice had dipped an octave lower with the comment, but Ko could have been hearing things. Instead, he smiled. "Yes. I'm sorry to seem like a bit of a stalker. The visit was a business thing, I promise."

"I see."

"Please. Have a seat."

"Would you like a drink to start?" The server wanted to know of Jackson.

"Water, please."

Alone with Jackson, Ko closed his menu and inhaled. He already knew what he wanted — it was the same damn thing he ordered when he was in a pinch and didn't think his stomach could handle anything heavy — chicken Caesar salad.

"I was surprised when Thaddeus told me you wanted to speak with me about your line," Jackson admitted, fingering the edges of his menu. "I mean, aside from Men Tower, I haven't done any real modeling in almost three years."

"Isn't it like riding a bike?"

Jackson smiled.

Ko's heart soared.

"Not really," Jackson said.

The server returned with their drinks and went away.

"Well, from what I saw at the shoot, you're a natural. You follow instructions and you get the job done." Ko took a drink from his glass. "That's all we can really ask."

"Right."

"I don't want to pressure you," Ko said. "But I need to mold Hansamu into my own image, so to speak, and the guy we have is not what I need."

"But me—you need."

Ko trembled. If only Jackson knew. He licked his lips and decided to try again. This time he pulled one of the ad campaigns with the other guy from his bag and slid it across the table to Jackson. "Let's think like the regular man for a second. He works hard. He wants to look like he plays hard, even if he doesn't. Hansamu wants to tell the regular Joe that yes, we can make you look like you walked off the pages of GQ, so we want the right face and body to say that. If you were Tom from Boise, accountant, husband to a soccer mom, father of two-point-five kids, would you want to buy anything this guy's selling?"

He watched as Jackson picked up the poster and stared at it. For a moment neither man spoke. Ko took a breath and leaned back in his chair.

"I see what you're saying. He doesn't seem trustworthy."

"Precisely," Ko said. "I know you don't need the money but it's a good paying gig and it would look good on your resume, I promise."

"And just to put this out there. I'm gay—you know that, right?"

"So am I. I don't see what this has to do with—"

"You said Tom from Boise has two-point-five kids and a wife."

Ko laughed. "It was just a scenario—the first thing that popped into my head. Everyone can wear my suits. Gay, straight. Black, white, humans, aliens—everyone."

"I don't know," Jackson said. "Aliens may need a few more arm holes."

Ko laughed. "Right. But you get what I mean."

"I get it. Okay. Do you have a sample contract?"

Ko tilted his head. "I can have my assistant send one over as soon as tomorrow morning."

"Good." Jackson turned the ad over and pulled a pen from his breast pocket. He scribbled on the back then slid the ad back across the table. "That's my email address. I'm going to have Uncle Darius' lawyers take a look at it, and if everything is on the up and up, I'll take the job—not that I don't trust you. But you can't be too careful, you know?"

"I know, and I understand completely. I'll also have her send you over a breakdown of payment. We don't know what the campaign will be yet, but we already have a female model to work with you."

"Priya?"

"You know Priya Chetan?"

Jackson nodded. "She was at Thaddeus' launch with her brother. Smart woman—after speaking to her, you begin to see the world in a whole new light. It's strange."

Ko laughed. "That's our Priya, yes."

"It would be an honor to work with her."

Hearing that, Ko inhaled deeply and finally relaxed. With business out of the way, they focused on food, and soon they were laughing and chatting as if they were lifelong friends. Ko took that moment and ensured he enjoyed every second. This was as close as he figured he'd get to dating the young stud.

He frowned but hid it with the dessert menu. Though he didn't feel like ordering anything from it, he settled on a double scoop of vanilla ice cream with caramel sauce and crushed, salted peanuts.

Jackson took the picture back from Ko and turned it over to write again on the back of it. This time he smiled when he stopped and slid the picture to Ko. "That's my personal number. Feel free to use it anytime."

Ko flushed and hoped Jackson didn't see it. He was a grown-ass man blushing at some presumable flirtation. *For shame!*

When lunch was over, Jackson stopped to gather something from the hostess. He walked out of the doors to join Ko on the sidewalk with a black helmet underneath one arm.

Jackson Stark just got a whole lot sexier. *Shit.* Ko wanted to groan.

The two shook hands and Ko watched as Jackson jogged across the parking lot to a black motorcycle. He tossed his leg over it and the tightness of his jeans then perfectly accentuated Jackson's muscled thighs. Ko trembled and remained rooted to that spot, staring until long after Jackson had slipped his helmet on, lowered the visor and the cycle had roared to life. Soon, Jackson disappeared in the distance and Ko was left feeling as if he had been stripped naked and licked.

Chapter Four

With a quick stop to check in on the progress of a few things at the office, Jackson headed home. He had a night in with Charlie, and if he didn't hurry, he would most certainly be late. Sure, Charlie was never on time and they often joked that Charlie would be late for his own funeral, but Jackson had things he had to get done first.

As he entered the front door, his cell phone picked up his wireless signal and bombarded him with notifications. There were emails, Facebook updates, Instagram updates — why did he even have Instagram? He never posted anything instantly for he hated everyone in the world knowing where he was at every given second of the day.

"That's what I get for not putting this crap on silent," Jackson muttered. He scanned through all of them as he entered the kitchen, dumped his keys on the island and opened the fridge for a bottle of water — all without looking up. Once the coolness was in his hand, he spared it a glance to ensure it was indeed water, used his hip to bump the door closed, then climbed onto a stool.

There were quite a few emails since the last time he had checked but the one that drew him was from a Stella Priest. The subject heading said *Sample Contract from Ko Takao*. He instantly opened it and scanned it. Everything seemed legit but just in case he forwarded it to Darius' lawyer. After sending Stella a quick reply to confirm he had gotten the contract, he ignored the rest of the messages, plugged in the phone to charge, then put some effort into preparing for his night with his best friend.

He stopped to turn on some music then hummed to himself while putting some beers to cool along with a bottle of wine.

True to form, Charlie was half an hour late and when he finally walked through the door he was speaking on the phone to someone in German. Jackson assumed it was a business thing, hugged Charlie tightly, then headed up the stairs. He was barely at the top when Charlie called his name.

"Where you going?" Charlie asked. "The king is here."

Jackson laughed. "Ass. I still have to shower."

"Oh, okay. I'll be down here when you get out."

"Don't be a dope. Grab a beer and come on up."

"Jack, I—"

Jackson cocked a hip and rested his hand on it. "I thought we were past all this awkwardness."

"Okay. I'm coming. Sheesh. Just stop giving me the Darius Stark glare."

Jackson laughed and continued up the stairs. By the time Charlie entered his bedroom, Jackson was shirtless and digging through his closet for a pair of track pants. He glanced over his shoulder to see that Charlie had climbed into the center of the bed, set his laptop before him and was sipping from a beer.

"How was your day?" Jackson asked.

"Same old. I'm having an issue with one of my international students," Charlie said. "I'm tempted to cut my losses and pray when he repeats the course he'll have another professor."

"Why do you keep beating yourself up like this? You do the best you can then hope it works out."

"I'm an idiot?"

Jackson laughed, pulled his Nike track pants out and shook them. "Finally! Damn—thought I left them at Uncle Darius' again."

Charlie merely laughed.

He took a quick shower and by the time he was finished and dressed, it was well into the evening. The music downstairs had stopped since he hadn't bothered filling the other four trays. He didn't really see the point. Usually after one album finished, he needed the silence to kind of digest what he'd just heard.

The two set to work on dinner.

"So, you met with Ko Takao…" Charlie said, dropping a handful of pasta into some boiling water on the stove.

Jackson, who was busy chopping up some oregano, stopped and chewed on his bottom lip. "Yup."

"Is he as sexy as the media makes him out to be?"

Jackson frowned and went back to what he'd been doing. "I didn't notice."

"Oh, man, you're a liar."

"What? We went for a business meeting. I didn't have time to check out the goods for you."

Charlie sighed dramatically. "Seriously? Was he at least good-looking?"

"Yes."

"Okay then. Continue."

Jackson spared his friend a glance before shaking his head. "I asked him to send me over a sample contract and I'd have Darius' lawyer take a look."

"And?"

"He did and I think it's a pretty great deal." Jackson finished the oregano and piled it to one end of the board before reaching for a tomato. "I personally didn't need them to tell me that but had to cover my ass, you know? Anyway, I'd work predominately for him, and since I wouldn't be able to do any other modeling work until my contract is over, he's paying me one-point-eight for the whole campaign—well technically, it's in money and other benefits but it all adds up."

"One-point-eight—million?"

Jackson nodded as the sharp blade slid through the tender flesh of the red fruit then hit the board. "He gets me for a prolonged period of time and he's projecting this to be huge."

"Damn, brother."

"Right?"

"And there aren't any red flags?"

"No legal ones that I can see. Waiting to hear back from the lawyers, but I don't anticipate anything popping up."

"Damn."

Jackson inhaled.

"Okay," Charlie said. "Why do you still sound hesitant? Is it cutting into your Stark gig?"

"Not really. I can use vacation time for traveling, and as a designer I can basically work from anywhere. I would just have to travel with my computer and all the crap I'd need, but Darius doesn't mind. The contract for Hansamu is for two years."

"Then what's holding you back?"

"I don't know. The other day when I was doing the Men Tower shoot, Ko was there."

"Wait. You didn't tell me this."

"I didn't think anything of it. I mean, we didn't talk or anything. Apparently he spoke to Tasha ahead of the shoot and asked if he could stop by. When I came into the room, I saw him and at first I didn't know who he was. I just figured one of the workers at the place was curious and decided to take a look-see." Jackson rubbed at the back of his neck self-consciously. "Then the shoot began and I could feel his eyes on me. Like he was touching me and shit—it's stupid. Anyway, he just stood there, watching. Then, before he left, I looked up. Kinda to let him know that I could see him."

"Maybe even to tell him you felt him liking what he was seeing?"

"That's an asshole thing to say, Charlie."

Charlie tossed up his hands. "Why? Because you don't think a man wants to know that his advances are noticed?"

"No. Jesus! He's way older than me and I'm not his type."

"How would you know what his type is?"

"I just—I know, all right? After that, he left. I mean, of course there was nothing there. Ko was scoping out the talent he wants to use for his branding. That's all it was but inside my head—it was so much more."

"Fine. If that's all it was, why are you still pussy-footing around accepting this deal?"

"I don't— I'm an idiot."

"Well, I can't disagree with you there." Charlie sighed then continued, "This is a great deal, man. What other model can say they got something like this without even looking? That the owner of the label handpicked them to face the line without auditioning or headshots or any of the regular drama that comes with this world."

Jackson didn't say anything else on the matter. They cooked in silence but Jackson's mind was a flurry of activity. They ate and talked, even watched a movie. Once they were settled in for the night, Jackson laid on his back thinking of Ko Takao and the sadness he remembered in the man's eyes. Well, at first it had been sorrow, but from time to time that had faded and something else had filled Ko's gaze that Jackson couldn't quite put his fingers on. Still, his decision to model for Hansamu should have nothing to do with Ko and more to do with the financial side of things and the exposure rewards that came with the job.

At around three in the morning, Jackson's phone chimed. It was an email from Darius' lawyer stating he could find nothing to make the contract damaging to Jackson. Everything was straightforward and it was his professional opinion that the contract was valid and legal.

"There," Jackson muttered, crawling out of bed to grab his laptop from where it usually sat on his dresser. After booting it up, he sent Ko's assistant an email.

Dear Ms. Priest,
Please advise Mr. Takao that I would be honored to work for him on his new campaign. Please let me know a suitable time that I may come in and have a talk with him.
Thanks,
Jackson Stark

He took a second to spell check his letter then hit Send. When he finally crawled back into bed, Jackson didn't have to toss and turn. He fell asleep immediately.

* * * *

Rain poured over Bathsheba mercilessly. Instead of taking the motorcycle, Jackson was forced to drive his truck. He pulled into the parking lot of Hansamu's headquarters, rooted around in the backseat for his umbrella, then hurried into the building. He still managed to get water in his shoe and his shoulders were wet. Frowning, he set his umbrella on a rubber mat by the security station and rode the elevator up to the seventeenth floor.

The doors opened to a luxury front desk with *Hansamu: Clothing to boost your spirits* written along the front in fancy letters. The walls were packed with pictures of past models—glossy images of beautiful men with too much lip-gloss. Other wall hangings featured past ad campaigns and a few framed reviews of Hansamu clothing.

Behind the secretary's desk was one framed picture that stood out. Jackson recognized the man with gray hair, strict eyes and rigid lips to be Nobu Takao, the former owner of Hansamu. The frame looked golden and robust with Japanese characters carved into it the exterior.

The floor was hardwood—Jackson knew quality flooring when he saw it. He had helped his Uncle Darius and Feng pick out the new ones for their second home in Aspen and considered himself somewhat of an expert in the matter.

There was no one there, which seemed a bit odd, so he took a seat and waited. Soon a woman with black and blue hair, very minimal makeup and a rather infectious smile hurried over, her stilettos clicking on the floor.

"Good morning." She extended a hand. "You must be Jackson Stark."

"That would be me." Jackson rose and accepted her greeting.

"I'm Stella. Stella Priest. We spoke through emails. I'm sorry. It's been a little hectic around here lately," she said. "Come, he's waiting for you. Did you want some coffee or tea? I know the weather is not ideal today."

"No, thank you. I'm good."

"Okay. This way please."

He followed her along a wide corridor with more glossy-looking models on the walls. At the end, there was another golden-framed picture of Nobu. Finally, Stella stepped aside and motioned for him to enter. When he did, he found Ko standing at the window of the office, hands stuck into his designer suit pants pockets, long, black hair in a tight ponytail and his wide shoulders set almost in determination.

"Boss?"

"Mmm?" Ko replied.

"Jackson Stark for you?"

Ko turned and smiled. It was a soft form of mirth that didn't quite reach his beautiful brown eyes. He had the look of a man still in heavy contemplation. Jackson returned the smile and moved forward. The door clicked closed behind them and suddenly Jackson was ensnared in a room, alone with one of the sexiest men he'd ever been blessed to lay eyes on. Though he knew didn't have a chance in hell with Ko, no one could begrudge him a little fantasy.

"It's good to see you again, Jackson," Ko said. "Please, have a seat."

Jackson fell into the sofa like a sack of potatoes and prayed Ko hadn't noticed. He crossed his legs and straightened his back against the leather comfort.

"I see you've come to a decision," Ko continued. "I'm glad you decided to work with us. Our campaign is still in the planning stages and I still need to finalize some things but New York Fashion Week is quickly approaching. We skipped out on it this year but next year we're hoping to hit it bigger and better. In September, we have Milan Fashion Week to look forward to and I'm hoping to have a few pieces to use by then. That means the campaign, or at least teasers of it, has to be ready to go."

"September is three months away," Jackson said. "I'm sure that can happen."

"Yes, but it would be a miracle. You see, rolling out something major in three months would be a fool's errand. I mean, it can happen but I don't want to rush it. I'm talking with the organizers of the MFW into giving us the introduction to the show. We put on a performance, push out a little teaser, make people crave more but don't really reveal anything until next year's New York Fashion Week."

"That's a lot of time from now."

Ko nodded. "Agreed. But I want to do this properly — get the right inspiration. Make sure the designs are fresh and what people want to wear. You see, we don't design for the runway. Hansamu design clothing that people can go backstage, take off our models and wear home. We want clothing that's practical and for everyone."

"I can dig that. So, when do I start working?"

"August — well, that's when your major shoots begin. In a couple of weeks, I should have something put together of where we want to go, themes, that kind of thing."

"Hmm."

"For the time being we're keeping your contract and identity under wraps. For the teasers, we won't be showing your face, just your body. We want your identity to remain a secret until next year."

Jackson laughed. "Is that even possible?"

"I think it is."

"What about those who know my body?" Jackson asked.

Heat flashed through Ko's eyes. Jackson knew what that had been. He'd seen the way Feng looked at Darius when he thought no one was watching. It was the same fire. A smirk danced across Ko's lips. Jackson shook his head and rested back in the seat. Maybe he'd been imagining things.

Of course you're seeing things, dumb-dumb. Sheesh.

"No one knows your body that well," Ko said. "Unless you have a tattoo or a certain piercing."

"No." Jackson felt the wind knocked out of his sails then and he was instantly irritated. "None of those. But I'm not exactly a virgin."

"That's good to know."

Jackson frowned. "What I'm trying to say is, people have seen me naked, so they might guess."

"Maybe not. If they do guess we just evade until the time is right."

"I see."

Ko rose from his chair and walked around to sit on the front of his desk. There was purpose in each step, as if Ko thought of where to place each foot and how firmly. It was something Jackson admired in a man when it came to business. But in other things, Jackson preferred a little bit more...improvisation. He cleared his throat and lifted his eyes from the way Ko's pants fit over his perfectly sculpted thighs.

"Look, Jackson," Ko said. "I want this to be a working relationship we're both comfortable with. I'm not my father and I'm trying my best to make things work the way he liked but with my flair, of course."

"Of course."

"I just— I don't want this to be torture for any of us."

Jackson smiled. "It won't be. When can I see Priya?"

"Soon. I hope. She's currently in Belarus with her brother on vacation. She's due back next week."

Jackson pulled out his personal card and handed it to Ko. "Can you give this to her? She can give me a call whenever…"

"Sure." Ko accepted it. "You're wet. I'm sure we can find something for you to change into."

Not as wet as I'm sure you could make me with that tongue. "That's okay. I'm heading home after, anyway."

"We both know traffic." Ko hopped from the desk and headed for the door. "It's no trouble at all. Come on—besides, this gives me a chance to show you around."

Chapter Five

Ko spread his legs, shoulder-length apart, and hunched down. He dipped into his first squat and when he rose, back straight, he twisted his body side to side. Working out gave him a chance to clear his mind. For the past couple of days, he'd been thinking of Jackson. Maybe giving him a personal tour of Hansamu headquarters might have been a bad idea—in hindsight. After Jackson had left him, Ko had spent most of the day with his head in the clouds, imagining things he had no right to.

He continued his squats and once finished, he went in for his push-ups. Most times he used machines for this but with the way his mind was, he didn't want to space out and drop a weight or something equally as stupid. One workout routine led to another and soon he was jogging on the treadmill. He didn't like that— running for an hour and still stuck in the same place wasn't his idea of fun. But it had been raining a lot in Bathsheba of late and getting drenched wasn't in Ko's plans at all.

An hour and a half later, Ko exited the gym with his bag strapped over his shoulder. The sun hid behind some clouds but the rain had stopped. Feeling a bit daring, he decided to walk the two blocks home.

After freshening up, Ko got dressed in a pair of black slacks, dark blue dress shirt and strung his designer watch around his wrist. He ended by dabbing on some aftershave and glancing at himself in the mirror one final time. Satisfied, he found his keys, wallet and phone and let himself out of the luxury building. For a moment, he stopped and took a deep breath. The scent of impending rain always allured him. Add that with the smell of freshly cut grass and he was positively in heaven. With his mood great, he climbed behind the wheel of his sports car and turned north.

It was late. The sun had run its course for the day and was setting behind one of the mountains in the small city. The sky was a menacing gray as the storm clouds rolled in from the east. Still, Ko wound down his window and rested his elbow against it. He cranked his stereo high and tapped his fingers to the tune.

Once the song ended, he hit the repeat button and nodded. Another thing about a great song, in Ko's opinion, it couldn't be listened to just once.

He sped through the intersection of Dawson and Chance, hung a left and pulled the vehicle up before a nightclub. From the outside, it looked like a gray abomination that rose out of the ground in the middle of a street lined with restaurants. The windows were draped with thick red curtains and the sign outside was so inconspicuous that if one wasn't paying attention he could drive right by it.

There wasn't the usual line out front because it was a private party. They hadn't even advertised it. One of his connections was in a band called The Orangutans and they were previewing their latest video for *Kiss Me, Kill Me*.

Once he parked, he jogged up the front steps and was allowed in by a beast of a man. Spec, as they lovingly called him, was ex-SEAL and was as kind as he was deadly. The two bumped fists then hugged.

"It's good to see you," Spec said. "Sorry about your father."

"Thanks." Ko offered him a smile. "Paul here yet?"

"You know how he do," Spec jargoned. "He was here long before we opened the joint."

Ko laughed. "Yeah I know."

The two touched fists again and Ko made his way into the interior of the elegantly decorated space. For a moment, he stopped to let the pulsing music take him and shove him into the mood to dance. Once his head was bopping to the beat, he descended the three steps and inched across the dance floor, accepting kisses to his cheeks, hugs and bumped fists as he went. Finally at the bar, he leaned in to speak with the bartender who walked over to him the second their gazes met.

"Taka," Kramer Salley said. "You still look good enough to eat."

"As always." Ko's cheeks heated. "I'm not on the menu, Salley."

"Too bad." Kramer stopped to chew on the corner of his bottom lip as he all but undressed Ko with his eyes. "Too damn bad. Whiskey sour?"

"Not tonight. Cranberry with a lemon twist?"

Kramer grinned and nodded. He sauntered off to make Ko's drink and in no time at all, Ko was on the move once more. This time, he ascended four steps, walked around a white column and in through a set of glass doors. Inside, he found Paul Shankar, the rapper of The Orangutans, who he hugged. Then there was

Devlin Marrow, the drummer and Mitchel Daz—the lead vocalist and bass player. He greeted all of them with hugs.

The door opened once more but Ko merely ignored it and fell into one of the seats. He set his drink on the glass table and was getting ready to have a conversation with Paul when Devlin spoke.

"Hey, Ko, meet our principal dancer-slash-actor, slash all round good guy," Devlin said. "Jackson Stark."

Ko's heart stopped.

"We've met," Jackson said, taking a seat and leveling his brown gaze on Ko. "How are you, Ko?"

"Great," Ko managed. "I didn't know you knew the guys."

"Yeah, Paul is a friend of a friend."

"Dev said you were a principal dancer. Are you in the video?"

Jackson nodded.

A man of many talents, Ko thought.

"It was a last-minute thing," Jackson continued. "When I got the call, I couldn't say no."

Ko smiled. "I get it."

"Well, you two," Mitchel said, "break it up. They're about to show the video."

"This is the part that always gets me," Paul confessed. "After all these years."

"I have a feeling it won't get any easier," Jackson said. "But don't worry. Quality music is quality music and there'll always be those of us who appreciate it."

Ko rose and walked to the glass. They all crowded around and stared out across the club at the massive screen that was now counting down from ten. Because they were in the Premium VIP, Ko had a perfect view of the screen. When the beat to the song began, the screen had a bed, rumpled as if lovers had spent the night there. Suddenly, Jackson's partially nude body fell from the ceiling against the bed.

Ko's heart raced as he watched. It took everything inside him not to shove his nose onto the cool surface and pant. Pushing his fingers into his pocket, he took a step back to put some space between himself and becoming a stalker. The video was very hot—from Jackson's toned body moving across the screen with more grace and agility than a man should have, to the curve and flow of his body. Everything about what he was seeing appealed to him and made the attraction he had for Jackson Stark move from blind to almost obsessive.

At the end of the song, the audience cheered. Some whistled, others made monkey sounds, but everyone seemed happy. Though Ko applauded, the turmoil inside him was mounting. How could he see Jackson like that and not want him? What gay man, for that matter, could see Jackson Stark looking so beautiful and not yearn for him?

"What do you think?" Devlin asked.

Ko cleared his throat. "I think you got a hit on your hands."

"You really like it?" Mitchel asked. "You're not just saying that?"

"Don't pay him any mind," Paul said as the crowd began chanting for them to play the video again. "It's a departure from what we usually do but change is good, right?"

The DJ started the video once more and Ko thought he would die. For a moment, he turned to watch Jackson, who was still staring past the glass to the screen. When Jackson glanced over at to him, Ko returned his gaze to the video even though he was liable to combust if he had to see Jackson cradling the other guy's face so tenderly another time. It was a video — the emotion on the screen was all smoke and mirrors — but seeing Jackson that close to another man made him crazy.

Perhaps it was jealousy.

Moving from the spot he'd been glued to, he headed for the door.

"You leaving?" Jackson asked.

"No. Going to get another drink."

"We're in VIP. There's a bar here," Jackson said.

"I just — I needed to talk to Kramer."

"Oh…Okay."

Ko fled the VIP and though he truly didn't want to talk to Kramer again, he couldn't take off now. Frowning, he found the bartender, ordered another cranberry juice then turned to watch the audience. The video was long over and they were now dancing to some other band Ko's brain just couldn't place. He downed his juice and his frown deepened. The way he was feeling required something stronger — something that would burn a trail down his throat and warm his insides. But he didn't like drinking if there was even a remote chance he'd be driving.

Frustrated, he set his empty glass on the bar and faced the crowd once more. This time, Jackson stepped through them like Moses from parting the Red Sea. Ko's heart fluttered, his aroused cock hardened and every muscle in his body tensed. Finally, Jackson was close enough to press a palm against Ko's chest, leaned forward and spoke into Ko's ear.

"Dance with me?"

Ko held his breath. He turned his mouth to the side of Jackson's face, knowing it was a bad idea. Jackson smelled like fire and musk "I don't really dance."

"Are you kidding me? You're friends with Paul Shankar—you dance. Come on."

Unable to resist, Ko agreed and Jackson took his hand and led him to the dance floor. The moment they found a spot, the music changed from pulsing hip-hop to a baby-making slow jam. But Ko couldn't seem to walk away. In fact, he reached for Jackson and pulled him into his arms. He slid a palm downward to the small of Jackson's back and rested his cheek to the side of Jackson's head.

In that moment, Ko closed his eyes and imagined he and Jackson were together, that they were in love. All thoughts that anything sexual between them would be highly inappropriate were shelved, and he gave himself over to being a man with desires for just that moment. He allowed himself to picture them dancing around a bedroom, almost on the brink of making love. Then they would stop, for that was the foreplay, and climax would be too soon. Once they both could breathe again, the dance continued.

For a second, Ko belonged to someone, his heart, his body, every fiber of his being and it was the most exhilarating feeling he'd ever experienced. He held on to it with Jackson's toned body against him. He savored that sensation of belonging as if his life depended on it. He daren't think of what happened when air was able to pass between them once more, when Jackson would let go and he would have to walk away. The only thing that mattered was that Ko was in Jackson's arms, that he experienced what Darius and Feng had, what Ravinder and Thaddeus had found.

When Ko had been a little boy, his father had often quoted the great samurai Miyamoto Musashi in saying fixation is the path to death, fluidity is the path to life. He never had understood it. Having Jackson in his arms revealed the meaning to him like the heated rays of the sun after a cold winter's day. The realization dawned on Ko then that though Jackson didn't know it, Jackson owned Ko's body.

But Jackson would never find out.

Ko would never tell.

Chapter Six

A week after the video release, Jackson slipped back into routine. By the time the week ended, he was finished revamping a few things in *Together We Stand* and shipped it off to the next set of eyes that would go over it again before it even made it to the beta testers. On Saturday, he'd promised to help his father with putting in a new deck on the house. The existing one had been there since before Jackson had been born and was starting to show its age.

When he arrived, his father was nowhere to be seen. He let himself into the house and disarmed the alarm. Once that was out of the way, he removed his shoes and headed into the kitchen to pour himself something to drink then wandered into his father's office. On the wall across from his dad's desk was a picture of Jackson. It was one of the first ad campaigns he'd ever done—for a sports car. It had come out better than Jackson had thought it would, especially since he didn't see himself as particularly handsome. When people had started offering him money to pose for them—for clothes and cars and the like—he had taken the gigs while doing his dancing. A movie company had even offered him quite a large sum to take off his clothes — all his clothes.

Jackson had politely declined but had been secretly flattered.

He took another sip and rested his ass to the front of his father's desk. Slowly, he dragged a lazy palm over the hard surface. With a sigh, he eased forward and wandered around the office, peering at the books. They were all leather-bound and quite expensive. His father didn't mind people touching them and he wasn't the type to force anyone to wear protective gloves. To his dad, books were meant to be read — leather-bound or otherwise. Jackson came across a first edition of Charles Dickens' *A Christmas Carol* and pulled it from the shelf. He skipped to the part where Marley's ghost arrived. It was always his favorite section.

After reading the scene, he set the book back and fell into his father's leather chair. He never had liked the feel of the thing, but swirling it around, the view of the garden at the side of the house took his breath away. It always had, ever since Jackson had been a boy.

But as he'd grown older, things between him and his father had become strained. For one, his dad had stopped him from seeing Darius. Darius was the one man in the family Jackson felt any type of connection to. Darius always understood Jackson, when even his own father didn't. When Darius' guidance had been taken away, Jackson's world had ended. The reason for the breakup of the family, was that his dad wasn't too keen on the whole gay thing. When Darius had come out of the closet, Jackson's father had flipped and all but disowned Darius. It took Jackson coming out for his father to go crawling back to Darius, begging for forgiveness and help dealing with his gay son.

Jackson took another sip and turned away from the picture. After his drink, his dad was still not back so he got comfortable on the sofa. His mind slipped to Ko Takao. Though Ko was his to be his boss in a few weeks, Jackson couldn't help wondering what lay beneath his hard exterior.

Their dance had turned Jackson on. He hadn't been sure Ko would agree to it, but Jackson was happy he had. Even as he lay there, waiting for his father, Jackson got hard. Ko's perfect body was against his —

"Jack? Jack, you here?"

"Yeah, Dad!" Jackson got up and pulled his clothes in place before leaving the office to meet his father in the kitchen. "Hey."

"Sorry I'm late coming back." He poured himself some juice and took a long drink. "Who knew selling a business was this much of a headache."

"Uncle Darius warned you."

"Yeah. I just need some peace, Jack. I don't want to miss any more of your life. Are you seeing anyone?"

Jackson choked on air.

"What?" his dad asked.

"Um...I...um... No. I'm not seeing anyone. Dad, seriously, we don't have to talk about my sex life or lack thereof. I know you were never a hundred percent on board with what Uncle Darius and I are."

"I'm sorry you feel that way. I may have been a moron when this whole journey started, but look how happy Darius is with Feng. How can I still hold any form of resentment or hatred about being gay? That's a love I —"

"Dad?"

"I never found that love with your mother. I mean, I loved her but it wasn't that deep love I see every time

Darius and Feng glance at each other. I'm sorry. I shouldn't be telling you this."

"It's the truth, right?"

Kent nodded.

"Then nothing to be sorry about. After Mom died, you remained single. Why?"

"I don't know. For a while, I figured that would make you happy and keep you safe. After all, there are some weirdos out there, you know? Then after you became an adult it was just easier."

"It's never too late."

"Yeah, right. No one wants an old man."

"Ko Takao is younger than you," Jackson said sarcastically.

His father arched an eyebrow. "The designer and your new boss? Yeah. Why?"

Jackson hesitated. He wasn't sure how much he should tell his father. Though his dad said he was fine with the gay thing, Jackson couldn't be certain. He licked his lips and climbed on one of the stools. "I asked him to dance the other night at the video release party."

"Right."

"And I want him, Dad."

"Jack, he's your boss."

Jackson rubbed his eyes. "I shouldn't have said anything. Let's start working on pulling off the old deck." He eased from the stool and tried to get by his father, but was stopped when Kent grabbed his arm.

"You don't trust me," Kent said. "I'm sorry."

"It's not that. It just feels weird telling my…father…that I am interested in someone that isn't remotely appropriate. I don't even know why I mentioned it. Ko's friends with Thaddeus, so chances are he's all moral and stuff. I'm on his no-go list."

"No-go list? Is this a gay thing?"

Jackson laughed. "No. It's like, for straight men—dating their best friend's sister. That kind of thing."

"Oh, right. Sorry."

"It's fine. Come on, this deck is not going to pull apart itself."

"Okay. Let me grab the gloves and the tools. I had the guys put the garbage container in the backyard so it's easy to get the old materials out."

"Perfect. Trucking it to the front yard would add days to our work."

His dad chuckled. "Gimme a sec."

It didn't take his father long and soon they were dressed in construction gear and were taking their frustration out on prying board and nails from an old build. They worked well into the day, stopped for something to eat before going back and finishing up the demolition.

"I'm exhausted," Kent said. "This was supposed to be a bonding thing for us but I don't know if us building the deck back by ourselves is a good idea."

Jackson laughed. "I'm going to go out on a limb and say it's because neither of us ever built anything in our lives."

"That is true."

"Look, Dad. How about we find something else to bond over?" Jackson laughed. "Like, traveling or building a model airplane. Maybe not something that needs to be structurally sound."

His dad nodded. "I'll start getting quotes on Monday. Did you mean it about us finding something else?"

"Why wouldn't I mean it?"

Kent shrugged. "I don't know. I just— I had to ask."

* * * *

For years, Ko wanted to change his workout routine. It took Thaddeus to help him do that with routines that were constantly changing, evolving. Ko delved into the workout mixed martial arts fighters used to stay fit, agile and strong. With his legs shoulder-width apart, he lowered himself, gripped the two pieces of rope, and got as comfortable as the position would allow. He bent slightly forward to take the strain off his back and made waves with the heavy ropes. With that routine finished, he did burpees followed by push-ups and crunches. He skipped cardio and was moving on to some strength training when he noticed a crowd had gathered at the far side of the gym, staring into the dance room. Curious, he abandoned his training and headed over.

He managed to make his way through some of the bodies to the front and stood there, arms folded over his sweaty chest, staring at the vision before him. He knew Jackson Stark could dance, but holy shit!

His mouth was dry. His palms began sweating even as he unfolded his arms and rubbed them against his thighs. His body burned and all Jackson was doing was moving across the floor as if Julliard was his alma mater. When he stopped, everyone around Ko erupted in applause and whistled. Jackson grinned boyishly, did a few bows and a couple of fake curtsies, which made the crowd roar with laughter and more applause. Ko smiled as Jackson first bowed. Jackson's smile disappeared when his gaze met Ko's. The young man picked up his towel and headed out the other way.

Ko frowned and jogged around the glass partition.

"Jackson!"

"Hey."

"You're running from me."

"Don't flatter yourself." Jackson passed the towel against the back of his neck. "You're my boss. I don't want to spend my private time with you, too."

Those words hurt Ko but he cleared his throat. "I didn't know you could dance like that — even though I saw you in the video."

Jackson smiled. "Thank you?"

"It is a compliment, I promise," Ko said. "Anyway, listen. I have the concept for the first shoot you'll be doing soon. Do you want to grab a coffee and go over it?"

"I..."

"We won't be alone, Jackson. Priya will be there, too."

"She's back?"

"She comes back tonight. So I was thinking on Saturday around four, if you're not busy."

"I don't really have a choice, do I? I do work for you and that's a part of the job."

"Come on, Jackson. Why are you like this?"

Jackson's shoulders rose almost to his ears then fell. "Sorry. It's been a weird morning and I'm waiting to hear back from an audition. I get cranky when I'm waiting on something."

"Maybe you need someone to teach you a little patience." Ko smirked.

Jackson tilted his head. "Many have tried. All have failed."

"That's because you haven't had the right teacher." Ko couldn't help himself. Flirting with Jackson just seemed to be something that came naturally.

"I see. Well, I'm always open to learning," Jackson said, strapping the towel around his neck.

"That's good to hear. So are we on for Saturday?"

"Tell me where and I'll be there."

Ko smiled. "Well, I have an amazing backyard."

Jackson nodded. "Sure. If you text me the address, I'll be there."

"I will. It was good seeing you. I know I haven't been in touch for a little bit but I didn't want to seem as if I was stalking you. Do you always dance here?"

"No, my studio is fully booked so I needed a place to practice and Charlie said I could do it here."

"Charlie?"

"Yeah, a—friend."

"I see. Anyway, I'll see you Saturday." Ko didn't wait for Jackson to reply. Instead, he turned and walked away, feeling like a moron. Obviously, Jackson had a man from the way he'd said 'Charlie'. With a frown, he mentally kicked his own ass until after his workout ended and he climbed into his vehicle. All the way home, each time Jackson came to mind, he forcefully pushed the image to the deepest corner of his mind.

That night, he rested on his back on the deck behind his house and stared up at the sky. It was a clear night and the stars twinkled beautifully above him. The soft, cool air swirled about him, giving him the chance to really breathe. In that moment, he allowed memories of his father to bathe over him. On purpose, he stuck to the good times—though they had been few. Good times like when his father had craved ice cream and they would sit on a chair beneath the sycamore tree in the backyard and eat chocolate fudge ice cream from the same container. That stopped the moment Ko had hit seventeen. He'd kept hoping his father would share a jar with him, but after his seventeenth birthday it had never happened again. As an adult, their quiet father-son moments had been rare. On the off occasion when the two of them had agreed on every aspect of a design, or agreed with the direction a project had been going—

those instances might be reaching, but Ko treasured them.

The shrill ring of his cell phone jarred him from his thoughts and without looking, Ko answered it.

"Ko! It's Thaddeus."

"Hey, Thad. What's up?"

"Nothing. What you doing right this minute?"

"Lying on the deck."

Thaddeus paused. "Did you throw your back out again? I keep telling you we weren't made to bend like that but you never listen."

"Funny." Ko chuckled. "No. It's dark enough to see the stars so I was trying to put a few things in perspective."

"Well, listen, I was invited to a little shinding at a friend's tonight and was told I could invite you. You in?"

"Which friend?"

"Darius and Feng. Feng scored a kick-ass gig with Jaded X Magazine."

Ko sat up instantly. He arched an eyebrow. "Um...I don't know."

"Seriously, Taka? You're not doing anything at home. Let's go out. Besides, it would be good to see you."

"Thaddeus, it's just that— I don't think it's a good idea because I've been fantasizing about Jackson."

Thaddeus went quiet.

"Thaddeus? You there?"

"Yeah." Thaddeus cleared his throat. "You see something you like. I can dig that."

"No. It's a horrible thing."

"Give me one good reason why."

Ko paused to count off his reasons on his fingers. "Well, for one, he's Darius' nephew. Two, I'm his boss. Three, he has a man and four, Jackson is too young."

"He's in his late twenties. You're…thirty-seven. I don't think that's such a big gap."

Ko sighed. "Probably not. But even if the other points are moot, he is involved with someone and I'm no homewrecker."

"Then if he is dating, it shouldn't be a problem. You know what the right thing to do is."

"I don't want to be an extra wheel, man. It feels like shit and I hate it. You'll have Ravi and Darius has Feng and Jackson has Charlie. I'm just going to take a shower and crawl into bed."

"Okay. If you change your mind you know where we'll be."

Ko hung up and flopped to his back once again.

But in the end, he wound up at the damn party, anyway. "Hey, Mr. Stark," Ko said, handing over a bottle of wine. "I didn't want to come empty-handed. Congrats on the new gig."

"I love when people call me that—Mr. Stark." The Chinese man grinned brightly.

"I figured as much," Ko said with a laugh.

"And you. I'm glad you could make it. Thaddeus said you weren't coming."

"I wasn't going to but the silence at home was driving me crazy."

"I know we aren't that close, but if you want to talk…"

"Um, no." Ko thought about it then shook his head. "No, I'm good. Thanks for offering. I will remember that."

Feng nodded. "Thanks for the wine. Come in, there's food in the backyard. Wine is in the cooler in the kitchen, beer in the back, and I think Thaddeus and Darius are around here somewhere."

Ko grinned. "I'll find them." He left Feng and hurried through the living room, then the kitchen and out the back door. He found Thaddeus with Ravinder sitting across his lap, Darius was turning meat on the grill, and Jackson and some man—who had to be Charlie—were trying to get a group of Chinese lanterns to inflate. Ko tried not staring. He tried not being weird about the whole picture and hoped he succeeded. Plastering a smile on his face, he stepped through the door and the others looked up.

"Hey!" Thaddeus cheered. "Didn't think you were coming."

"Yeah," Ko said.

Darius hugged him and handed him a beer. Thankful, he accepted and took a drink. He made his way around to hug Thaddeus and Ravinder but avoided Jackson and his man like the plague.

Chapter Seven

There was something so immeasurably sexy about a man wearing a graphic T-shirt, black leather jacket and black jeans. Ko made the outfit a visual aphrodisiac and Jackson was stuck around loved ones, having to hide his arousal. Jackson barely ate anything. He pushed enough into his mouth so Darius or Feng wouldn't question it, but each bite made him feel ill.

As the night wore on, though he managed to be involved in what was happening around him, Jackson kept his eyes on Ko. He'd tossed bits and pieces into the conversation, pretending all was well so Charlie or the others wouldn't ask any questions.

Each time their gazes happened to meet, Ko didn't so much as smile. It was a stark change from the gym. The light in Ko's gaze no longer existed — that smoldering look of dare that caused Jackson's body to pulse in ways it hadn't before. There was, however, something that fired through the designer's eyes that left Jackson curious and turned on. It was a new kind of desire that promised untold pleasures. Jackson needed that. When their little game of cat and mouse was too much, Jackson rose.

"You're leaving?" Charlie asked

"No. I have to…use the bathroom."

It was a lie. But Jackson didn't want to have another one of those conversations with Charlie. It was jumbled enough in his head and he knew he wouldn't have any answers to the questions Charlie would ask. He wasn't paying much attention and crashed into Darius as he rounded a corner to head up the stairs.

"Whoa! What's your rush?" Darius asked.

"No rush."

"Jack? You okay?"

Jackson shook his head. "I'm fine…just…aroused."

"Okay, you're a growing boy. It happens."

"That's not it." Jackson dragged a hand over his head. Though he wanted to hide in one of the rooms upstairs, he followed Darius into the kitchen. "It's so infuriating."

Darius tilted his head. "Come on. I know you better than most people around. Something is wrong. You can come to me about anything."

"I know, Uncle Darius. It's— I really— This is inappropriate. But I can't help it. Then to add to that, one second he seems like he's flirting with me and then the next, nothing. It could be all in my head. I'm well aware of that. I could have misinterpreted what his actions toward me meant. It happens all the time, right? This whole relationship thing is a pain in the ass."

"Um…"

"I mean, sure he's older than me. But I'm not a kid."

"Jack—"

"And how comes he's so hot and cold? Shouldn't a man his age know what he wants? What do you think?"

"Well—"

"Uncle Darius, I don't get it. Maybe I should just follow my first instinct and leave well enough alone."

"You see—"

"After all, it's not like a man like him would be interested in me, anyway. What was I even thinking getting so worked up about all—"

"Jackson!"

Jackson blinked. "What? Stop yelling at me!"

"Can I get a word in here?" Darius asked.

"Sure." Jackson's cheeks heated. "Sorry."

"Who are we talking about?"

Jackson sighed. "Weren't you listening?"

"Yes, but you just rambled on and on. I couldn't get a word in edgewise and you never mentioned who you were referring to. Let's start over. Who is this man and why is flirting with him inappropriate?"

Jackson walked to the window and stared out to where Ko was laughing at something Ravinder was saying. The whole group seemed to be having a good guffaw so that meant Ravinder was telling a story. "Ko."

"Does he know you're interested?"

"Are you kidding? No way. What would I know about seeing a man like that, anyway?"

"A man like what?"

"He's mature, smart, wealthy beyond my wildest dreams. He works hard and at his age he probably knows what he wants and it can't be me."

"He should be so lucky." Darius sounded irritated. "When did you get such a low opinion of yourself, huh? I thought Kent and I raised you better than that."

"When it comes to regular things, I go for it. But this isn't like getting straight A's in school or hitting the game-winning homerun. This is so much more than all those things combined. I can't."

Darius sighed. "You won't know until you try. Have I told you how I met Feng?"

"At the diner he used to work at."

"Yeah. What I didn't tell you was that he hated my guts the first time I met him," Darius said. "But I was attracted to him. The fact that he still wanted to strangle me even after he found out who I was made that draw to him even stronger and I had to fight to get him alone just so he could see something in me."

"And it worked."

"It worked. Attraction isn't the only thing but it's one of the first things. It needs to be a two-way street and constant. How I got Feng is the exact thing you should not do. Find a way to figure out how he sees you. Maybe after the contract is over you can ask him out to dinner."

"I'm liable to combust if I wait that long," Jackson muttered.

"Well..." Darius' voice was right beside him. "Looks like he's going down to the beach. Now's as good a time as any to have a little chat."

Jackson's heart raced with those words. He watched until Ko disappeared on the path leading from Darius' place toward the beach. For a moment he hesitated but Darius merely grabbed a couple of beers from the fridge and handed them to Jackson.

"You don't even have to speak," Darius said. "Just hand the man a beer."

"I..."

"Trust me."

With a nervous smile, Jackson accepted them and exited the house. He hurried along the path that was lit with Christmas lights Feng had strung along the trees all the way down to the end of the private pier and back. He caught up to Ko just as he stepped off the pier and onto the sand.

"Hey," Jackson said, extending a beer.

"Hey." Ko accepted. "Thanks. Don't think I should be drinking."

"Oh. Sorry." Jackson wrung the cap off the bottle and took a long drink.

The two walked in silence across the sand until they were just out of reach of the water. The moon was like a giant pie in the sky. Though the water was dark and Jackson could only see the waves once they died against the shore, he knew the water was there in the abyss. The sound of the waves rolling in only to draw back always gave him a sense of serenity he didn't get anywhere else but on a dance floor.

"Isn't Charlie going to wonder where you are?" Ko asked.

"Is that jealousy I hear?" Jackson countered.

"Yes."

Jackson chuckled, his face burst into flames and his body trembled. "You're serious?"

"Beating around the bush takes too much energy. I'm older, Jackson. I don't have that kind of time or patience."

"Why? Why would you be jealous of Charlie? It's not like you're interested in me, and why would you be? I'm sure you can get any of those wealthy Wall Street types you want."

Jackson sat in the sand and rooted his toes. For a while, he said nothing. Suddenly he was back in high school again with a crush on Charlie and had no idea how to act or what to say. But Ko wasn't Charlie. Ko wasn't seventeen years old and unsure of his sexuality.

"I should get back," Jackson said, rising to dump the rest of his beer into the sand. The alcohol might be playing a role in the way his mind was feeling. As he tried walking by, Ko stood, caught Jackson's arm and yanked him backward. Jackson turned and crashed into Ko's chest. The force tore a gasp from Jackson's lips.

Ko's vise-like grip against Jackson's arm loosened somewhat but Jackson didn't move. Neither spoke. The sound of the waves blended with a dog barking in the distance did nothing to interrupt what was happening between them.

Instead of trying to get away, Jackson braced his palms to Ko's chest and trembled as Ko's warm breath washed over Jackson's face. Ko smelled like fire and leather, a hot combination on the right man's flesh. Jackson closed his eyes and tilted his head, giving Ko access to his mouth should Ko choose to take it. Their breaths mingled and with each exhalation Jackson's body brushed into Ko's. Electricity crackled around them.

"Tell me you don't want this." Ko's voice hitched. "Tell me to let you go. That this is inappropriate and I have no right."

"I don't want this," Jackson said softly. "Let me go because this is inappropriate and you have no right."

Ko exhaled loudly and instantly let his hand fall away from Jackson's arm. Jackson took that moment to peel his body from Ko, turned on his heels and fled up the path back to the house. When he returned, he merely grabbed his wallet and headed for the door. Charlie caught him half-stumbling down the front steps.

"Whoa! What the fuck?"

"Sorry, but I can't stay here," Jackson said.

"What? Did he do something?"

"No," Jackson whispered, the word leaving a bad taste in his mouth. "That's the problem. We haven't even started working together yet and already I want to jump into his bed. I'm not thinking straight right now."

"Jack, wanting to fall in a man's bed isn't the end of the world," Charlie advised. "It shows you're human and humans are sexual beings. Stop holding yourself up to this impossible standard. Ko is sexy. Any gay man or straight woman would be truly cold if they didn't want him all over them."

"Do you want to fall into his bed?"

"For the night? Yes. He's not really my forever type."

"This is stupid. It's like I'm intoxicated by him and every time he shows a little kindness I go all loopy."

"Again, that's normal."

"He thinks you and I are together."

"You set him straight?" Charlie asked. "Right?"

"No."

Charlie sighed.

"What?"

"He's never going to make a move if he thinks you're involved," Charlie said. "From what I've read about Ko Takao, he's not really old-world Japanese in all things, just some things. High morals are one of those things. What're you gonna do, huh? Run away every time he enters a room?"

"It has crossed my mind."

Charlie shook his head. "Go back down there and set him straight about you and me. Then, tell him what you're thinking."

Jackson took a breath then hugged Charlie tightly. At that moment, the front door opened again and Ko stepped through. He offered them a tight smile.

"Goodnight," Ko said, passing by and heading straight for a dark sports car.

"Ko!" Jackson called. "Ko, wait."

"I'm sorry. I have to go. But see you Saturday."

Jackson jogged after him and caught Ko just as he opened the car door to climb in. "You and I need to talk. Can I treat you to lunch tomorrow?"

"I…" Ko glanced to where Charlie was still standing now on his phone. "I don't think that's a good idea."

"We need to clear up a few things before we start this job. Meet me at Coalminers at twelve?"

Ko said nothing.

"Please?"

"Okay. Twelve." Ko entered the car and Jackson stepped back so he could close the door. He didn't so much as honk but reversed from the driveway.

Jackson remained there. He didn't know for how long, but at some point Charlie finished his call and was standing beside him.

"You didn't tell him, did you?"

"No."

"Why not? Jackson, he was right there."

"He needs to breathe right now. I invited him to lunch tomorrow down at Coalminers. Hopefully he'd have enough time to think by then."

Charlie sighed. "Hopefully he'll show up."

"That, too."

Chapter Eight

The next morning was Friday. The sun shone brightly through every window in Ko's place. He stood for a moment to stare across the vast landscape at the mountains in the distance, wanting to feel as large and out-of-the-world wonderful as he imagined they did. But in the back of his mind, Jackson lurked like a specter.

Usually Ko would use the first few hours to hit the gym but if he was going to make it to Coalminers, he had to skip that. Then, to make matters worse, he received a call from his photographer that she was in the hospital and had to cancel with him. Thankfully, she hadn't signed the contract yet but he still had to find a new photographer.

Groaning, he wrapped a towel around his damp hips and grabbed his iPad. He Facetimed Stella and she leaned in to eye him.

"You didn't sleep last night," Stella said

"Of course I slept."

"Nope. The bags under your eyes tell the story as plain as the nose on your face." She sat back. "What's going on?"

"First, Audrey can't do the shoot. She's in the hospital right now and even though she didn't tell me what's happening, I'm going to assume it's bad."

"I'll look into that."

"Send her some flowers for me."

"Okay. Tasha Simpson is a good one, too—she shot Jackson Stark for Men Tower."

"I remember." Ko nodded. "Get a hold of her. Find out if she's available for the dates we need her. She might want to use a different concept for the shoot, I don't know."

"Those are easy enough. What's the next issue?"

"I think I have a thing for Jackson— No, wait, let me rephrase that. I know I have a thing for him."

"So he does swing your way! I knew it!"

Ko glared at her.

"What? I'm happy for you. Aww, come on now! Please tell me you've made your intentions known!"

"What is this? The eighteen hundreds? Forget I asked that. Look, last night I almost crossed the line. Then I saw him outside with his boyfriend and I lost my mind. I don't even know why I'm going to see him today. I don't need the added temptation of seeing him outside of a professional setting."

"No. What you don't like is not being in control."

Ko wanted to scream. Instead, he rubbed his tired eyes and yawned. "Listen, do those things for me. I have a couple more things to get done before I need to head out for lunch. Did you hear back from Ivor?"

"Yeah. I just got off the phone with him. He's starting the updates today."

"Perfect. I noticed we haven't gotten any more complaints, but I still need the bugs worked out."

Stella nodded. "Well, have fun on your date."

"It's not a date."

"Me thinks—"

"If you say thou protests too much I'm going to strangle you."

Stella giggled. "Now, now, Mr. Takao. What would Buddha do?"

Ko crinkled his nose at her but couldn't help laughing. "Go away, Stella."

"Right away, sir."

Even as the tablet went back to his screensaver, Ko was laughing and shaking his head. Sometimes Stella could be a little vulgar but he couldn't see his life without her. Feeling refreshed, he got dressed in a pair of blue jeans and a black dress shirt. Working from home didn't mean he was less busy. In fact, the phone calls were forwarded to him so he had to deal with them anyway. The emails never stopped coming and neither did the headaches of dealing with people who wished to work for Hansamu in whatever capacity, though they weren't remotely qualified.

Giving up on those for the day, he set his sights on the scholarship he and his father had been talking about developing. He didn't think it would be so complicated but there was a lot of research and proposal writing involved. So far, he had finished the first draft but a few paragraphs stood out as clumsy and raw. Before he knew it, time had gotten by him and he was definitely going to be late for lunch with Jackson.

Ko hurried out of the door, his leather jacket over his arm. Then it was a mad dash across town to Coalminers. Finding parking was another pain in the ass but he managed to snag a space from a blue sports car. He found Jackson at one of the private tables overlooking the mountains.

"I'm sorry I'm late. I was working from home and time just kind of got away from me."

"It's fine," Jackson said. "Please, sit."

Ko hung his jacket over the back of his chair and took a seat. He ordered a mimosa then laced his fingers in his lap. Jackson seemed as though he hadn't gotten any sleep either. His dark eyes were slightly red and he didn't seem like the same man Ko had seen at the Kingly photo shoot. That look on Jackson worried him more than he cared to admit.

"So, you wanted to talk to me," Ko said. "What about?"

"Straight to the point, huh?"

"Remember what I said about beating around the bush?"

"Right, sorry. First, Charlie and I aren't together — well, we aren't together anymore."

Ko pressed his lips into a thin line.

"I mean, we dated but that was in high school. We broke up in college because…because…we broke up because we wanted different things."

"I see. You seem pretty close for exes. All the guys I've broken up with or who've broken up with me I want dead."

"I know that's how people think it should be. Charlie and I didn't have a bad break-up. We both agreed to walk away from dating but there was nothing wrong with our friendship."

"You were friends who had sex going back to being friends — how did your other boyfriends handle that?"

"They didn't. When they heard Charlie and I slept together they ran for the hills. I guess if you were smart you would, too."

Ko shook his head. "I'm a grown man, Jack. I do what I please."

"Right."

"But there is a thought of you sleeping with Charlie again," Ko said. "Any man who had a brain would worry about that."

"Then that man and his brain don't trust me, and if that's the case, we can't be together."

"But what if this man and his brain thought you were very sexy and would like to get to know you?"

"Then this man…"

"And his brain…"

"Of course." Jackson nodded. "Would have to get over me and Charlie sleeping together. Man and brain would have to accept that Charlie is my friend and he's not going anywhere. And that if this man doesn't know that when I'm with him, he's the only man giving it to me, then he needs to go to hell."

"With his brain."

"Right."

Ko pressed his lips into a thin line.

"Anyway," Jackson continued, "last night, I just told you what you wanted to hear because I figured it would make you feel better. It would leave you with no regrets, no guilt of what I knew was coming."

"What was coming?"

"You were going to kiss me. And men like you would immediately apologize and run. It was probably for the best, anyway."

"Men like me?"

"Yes. Moral men. Men who like it in one position and think it's against God to do it remotely different. Men who will get wild in bed then ask for forgiveness. Men like you."

Ko chuckled. He waited until after the server brought their drinks, took their meal order and left again before he said anything. "And you think I'm vanilla in bed?"

"I don't think you are. I know you are."

"How?"

"I can just tell."

"Come on, Jackson, that's not an answer."

Jackson frowned. "Fine. You're always proper, Ko. The way you speak, dress, walk—last night on the beach, I know you wanted me. I could tell, especially when your voice cracked. But you didn't just take what you wanted—you gave me and yourself an escape. All of it tells me the only thing missing is drinking tea from one of those tiny cups with your pinky sticking out. I don't mean to offend you. It's just what I think."

"And we're all entitled to our opinions."

"But you're still offended."

"No." Ko took a sip from his drink and set the glass back on the table. "We have a meeting tomorrow with Priya at my place. After she leaves, why don't I show you just how vanilla I am?"

Jackson's Adam's apple danced.

"Like I said, you have your opinions and you're entitled to them. The questions now become—are you all talk, Jackson? Or can you put your body where your mouth is?"

Chapter Nine

Being at the airport on any day was a pain. But as Jackson stood at the glass window of the Bathsheba International Airport and stared out at the Boeing cruising toward the gate, his heart raced. He was about to be a grand uncle in his twenties. But that wasn't what scared him. Once this little boy made it into Darius' and Feng's arms, Jackson's life would be changing for the better—he hoped. He found it strange how much he loved a child he hadn't even met yet. Though Darius and Feng had traveled back and forth between Bathsheba and China numerous times in the adoption process, Jackson had always been too busy to join them.

He turned to look at Darius who was pacing one way then the next.

"Uncle..."

"Mmm?"

"You're wearing a path into the floor."

Darius laughed. "I'm sorry. I'm nervous."

The reunion between Darius, Feng and their little boy, Oliver, was a beautiful one that left Jackson smiling so hard he thought his face would be stuck that way. He hugged the ten-year-old tightly, for though they had yet to meet face to face, the two had played numerous games of chess online. That had been Feng's idea to get the two acquainted.

Afterward, though Feng and Darius invited him over so they could have dinner, Jackson declined. He figured they needed time as a family and he should go home and get some work done, anyway.

On the ride to his place, he wondered if he'd ever be as happy as he had seen his uncle that day. Sure, he was content with his life at the moment, but his future looked lonely and dreary, and that sent a cold tremor through him. Jackson entered the lift and pulled the doors closed and locked. The freight elevator took him and his motorcycle up to his penthouse and he rolled the cycle into the sunroom. He'd had it tricked out so he could have a place for his bike.

Once parked, he made a sandwich and reported to his office in order to start working on his new game. But after a couple of hours, he had nothing.

Jackson crumpled another piece of paper and chucked it behind him. He couldn't concentrate on building his third game. Sure, the second game still had to be released, but he couldn't wait until then to begin the third and final game in the series. First the title wasn't coming to him. *Together We Rise*. *Together We Stand*, and now what? *Together We Fall* — not encouraging. *Together We Die* — morbid. *Together We* — What the fuck?

Nothing made sense.

Frowning, he gave up and walked away from what was left of his notebook. Maybe he needed alcohol. Some singers couldn't write great tunes unless they were drunk or stoned off their asses. That could be his issue.

Lost in his thoughts that had gone from the video game to his impending meeting with Ko, Jackson made his way into the kitchen and began prepping dinner. Though he wasn't sure what he was in the mood for, he began making an omelet. Breakfast for dinner and there was nothing anyone could do about it.

"That's right. That's how I roll."

He laughed out loud to himself and reached for the ground pepper when his doorbell rang. Jackson shrugged, dumped some pepper into his palm and tossed it onto his eggs. He only answered the door after he covered the pepper and set it back on the rack. Charlie hugged him and walked into the condo.

"Hey, brother!" Charlie said. "You haven't answered your phone all day. What is going on?"

"What do you mean? I've been working."

"Uh-huh."

The two entered the kitchen and Jackson went back to cooking.

"And now you're making breakfast for dinner."

"I'm an adult. If I want to rim a man for dinner, I'm allowed to."

Charlie laughed. "Whatever, man." Charlie grabbed water from the fridge and climbed onto a stool. "So, the reason I've been calling you non-stop all day is to find out how things went with Mr. Takao at lunch yesterday."

"I told him everything," Jackson said, whisking the eggs with the spices. "He was okay with that. Then I put my foot in my mouth."

"How did you do that this time?"

Jackson pressed his lips into a thin line as he poured his egg mixture into the hot skillet. He chopped up some onions and chives and dropped them in then

turned to face Charlie. "I kinda insulted his sexuality —
well, his prowess, I guess you can say."

"Hoo boy."

Jackson laughed and refocused on his food. Once he
had it on his plate, he began a second omelet for
Charlie. Though his friend had to be talked into it, soon
both of them were seated at the dinner table eating and
sipping on wine. They ate in silence and Jackson was
happy Charlie didn't ask him any more questions about
Ko. They subject switched to video games, something
that wasn't as dangerous as the things he wanted Ko to
do to him. A few times he almost blurted out what Ko
said. But each time that soft, husky voice flowed over
those words inside his head, Jackson spent most of that
energy trying not to moan.

'Can you put your body where your mouth is?'

That had been Ko's question, hadn't it? Did that mean
Ko wanted him?

Long after Charlie headed home and Jackson was
alone, long after the night passed into morning, the
question still vibrated through Jackson's head like a
mantra. He tried clearing it by going for a run but an
hour and a half of hoofing it brought no peace. When it
was time to head to Ko's, Jackson toyed with the idea
of bringing a gift bag with lube and condoms but
decided against it. He was still a little on the fence about
Ko's flirting.

When he arrived at Ko's, he noted that the house was
beautiful. The front had a perfectly kept and healthy
garden. Jackson pulled off his helmet to get a better
look around. The street seemed quiet as if the loudest
thing to ever pass along its banks was Jackson's Suzuki.
A part of him felt bad but another part shrugged. They
needed a little noise to shake the demons.

"Jackson?"

He turned toward the voice and found a smile. "Hi, Ko. Sorry. I was just taking in the surroundings."

Jackson climbed off the cycle, and with his helmet under his arm, he jogged up the front steps and passed Ko into the house. After removing his shoes, he followed a feminine voice with Ko close behind him. Ko's eyes were on him. He moved his hips a little more than usual, straightened his back a little more and made sure his posture was correct.

"Jackson Stark as I live and breathe!" Priya cheered, dumping her cell into her pocket.

He grinned and extended a hand to her but she hugged him instead. Since she'd started working for Ko, Jackson could hear her English had gotten much better. "How are you?"

"I am well. A little tired from vacationing with Abhay, but I cannot complain."

"I'll bring out some snacks and something to drink," Ko said.

"Let me help you," Jackson offered.

"That's all right," Ko said. "I got this."

He nodded and returned his attention to Priya "So we'll be working together."

"Yes. Isn't it amazing?" Priya asked, her eyes bright with promise and wonder. "I'm excited. It has been a while since I have had a co-star. I am happy it will be you. You did accept, right?"

"Haven't signed anything yet, but yes."

"Good."

Ko returned then and set a tray on the table. Though he had declined help before, Jackson reached over to assist in unloading the tray. Once they were all seated, juice and cookies in front of them, the three got down to business. Jackson was stunned to hear that Tasha would be shooting the campaign due to an emergency with the other photographer, but he wasn't going to complain. Tasha was an amazing photographer and he loved working with her. Honestly, he'd declined the Men Tower shoot until they'd mentioned her name.

After a while, Ravinder arrived to get Priya — and then there were two. Silence flowed between them, periodically shattered by a dog barking in the distance. They stared across the table at each other and after a bit, the heat was too much and Jackson had to look away.

"I know what you're thinking," Ko said finally.

"You do?"

"Yes."

"Okay. I'll bite." Jackson lounged back in the chair, hanging one arm over the side. "What am I thinking?"

"You're thinking that because I gave you a challenge yesterday that we must have sex today. But that's not what it meant. I was only half-serious about that. You don't have to be scared we'll do anything you don't want and right now I can see that is not what you want."

Jackson flushed. "And you're sure that's what I'm thinking?"

Ko said nothing. He simply tilted his head, his brown gaze burning a sweet hole into Jackson.

Unable to stop himself, Jackson reached across for the side of Ko's face but Ko pulled away. Jackson was disappointed until he saw the look in Ko's eyes as one full of mischief. Not wanting to give up, Jackson lifted one foot to drag his toes up Ko's legs beneath the table. Again, Ko moved back out of reach.

"Are we really still playing this game?" Jackson asked.

"A game?" Ko asked, pushing his chair back and rising. "No, I don't play games. But you will earn what I give to you."

Ko walked away then, leaving Jackson speechless at the glass table. For a moment, all Jackson could do was sit there staring in the direction Ko had gone. Eventually, he managed to pry himself up and stalked after Ko. He found him in the living room, back pressed against the wall. Jackson leaned his shoulder into the doorframe and watched Ko.

"Whatever happens," Ko said, "don't leave that spot."

"Ko I…?"

"Are you running? Do you want to leave?"

"No."

"Then do as I say."

Jackson inhaled a sharp breath. The change in Ko surprised him, yet turned him on. He folded his arms across his chest.

Slowly, Ko moved his right hand up to drag the palm over his chest up to his neck then down to his nipples. Jackson's mouth watered, for though Ko still wore clothes, when he released the buds, they tightened and protruded against his shirt. It was hard to obey Ko, for all Jackson could think of was rushing forward, holding Ko to the wall and chewing on those nipples until they both climaxed. He dropped his arms and dug his nails into the sides of his thighs.

But he licked his lips and kept his gaze fused to Ko, watching the way Ko arched into his own touch, the silent parting of Ko's lips, the fire in his eyes. Everything in that moment left Jackson weak and trembling. He needed to touch Ko, to see if his skin was as hot as Jackson's was quickly becoming.

"Ko…"

Ko slipped a hand beneath the waistband. He was fondling himself. Jackson could tell by the way Ko's fingers bulged in the front of his pants.

"I'm so jealous right now."

"Of?"

"Your hand."

Ko laughed softly but turned away to hide what he was doing.

"Come on, now."

"Touch me, Jackson."

"Is this a trick?"

"A trick?" Ko arched his ass outward and moaned. "No trick."

Jackson darted forward and slipped to his knees. For a moment, he merely stared at Ko's ass, wondering if he was worthy to be that close to it.

"It's not going to bite you," Ko whispered.

"I'm actually..." Jackson's voice cracked. He cleared his throat, reached around Ko's body to undo his belt, button and zipper. Holding his breath, he slid the pants away from Ko's muscular body. He caressed down Ko's thighs even as he pressed his face forward, inhaling Ko's scent and feeling the heat of Ko's flesh through his boxers. "You are so sexy."

"You think so?"

Jackson didn't reply until he pulled Ko's boxers down and almost swallowed his tongue. He knew Ko had a hot body, but seeing Ko's bare ass was something else altogether. He caressed Ko, sliding his palms over Ko's body, loving the soft hairs. Unable to stop himself, Jackson licked at Ko—up his crack to his back. He wiggled his tongue against the flesh and groaned with the wildness that one action caused in him.

"Jackson..."

In reply, Jackson spread Ko before his eyes and unleashed his tongue. He feasted on Ko and every hard, yet sexy sound to escape his prey's body, teased the beast waiting just beneath the surface of Jackson's soul. Ko reached out and pressed the back of Jackson's head. Jackson took that to mean Ko wanted more so he plunged his tongue past Ko's ring. He loved the sensation tongue-fucking Ko sent through him.

"Oh, damn," Ko whispered. "That's it. If you keep that up you're gonna make me…"

Jackson backed off. He scooted to his butt, spread his legs and drew them up to plant the soles firmly on the floor. He glanced up to see Ko watching him intently over his shoulder.

"You wanted me to watch you, Ko. Turn around and stroke that cock for me."

Ko opened his mouth but he said nothing.

"What's the matter, Ko? Thought you were the only one with a little freak?"

"I never expected you to be this…"

"Shhhh." Jackson licked his lips. "This is no time to talk, unless you want to stop."

Ko said nothing and Jackson smiled.

"Give me what I want," Jackson said.

Ko moaned but rested his back against the wall. He wrapped is fingers around his beautiful cock, and to Jackson's pleasure, tugged.

Chapter Ten

Ko's orgasm cursed through him like a tidal wave. Who knew having Jackson watch him jerk off would leave him so wild and yearning? Even as he slipped to his knees and crawled forward, Ko was weak. Still, he couldn't deny that Jackson, seated on the floor, naked with his beautiful cock hard and ready wasn't enough to make him strong again.

Without speaking, he pulled the tip of Jackson's dick between his lips. He lashed it with his tongue then sucked. Jackson growled and buried his fingers into Ko's hair. Sighing, Ko allowed Jackson to push more of his cock in until Ko gagged a little. Still, he merely adjusted by breathing through his nose.

"Yes," Jackson whispered.

With that encouragement, Ko milked Jackson, loving the way Jackson seemed to melt on his tongue. Jackson's body contorted under him even as Jackson's fingers tightened in his hair. He gave up what Jackson's body asked for, enjoying every gasp, every moan, every sweet, tangy drop of pre-cum.

"Ko..."

He lifted his head to meet Jackson's eyes.

"Ko?"

"I'm right here. Tell me what you need, Jackson." He punctuated his words by dropping a kiss along the head of Jackson's cock.

Jackson whimpered. "Fuck me."

"Are you sure?"

"Come on, Ko. You're holding my hard cock in your hands. What do you think?"

"Our bodies lie."

Jackson sighed and began pulling away from Ko. "This was what you wanted, right?" Jackson asked. "To make me like this just because you can."

"Jack…"

But Jackson merely shoved him away and pushed to his feet. He scrambled for his clothes and had them bundled in his arms as he headed for the back door. "I need to get dressed."

Though Ko couldn't see Jackson's eyes, he knew the man was embarrassed. He stopped long enough to haul on his pants but then rushed after Jackson. He caught Jackson, wearing his pants and no shirt, heading down the steps into the backyard.

"Jackson!" Ko called. "Jackson, wait."

"For what? This is obviously a joke to you — teased the little boy until he begs for it then watch him burn."

"Is that what you really think?" Ko paused. "I can fuck you, Jackson. I can give it to you better and harder than you've ever had it. That's not the problem. Want isn't the issue either. Make sure you know what you're asking because once we cross that line there's no going back!"

Jackson whirled to face him. "That's the line you're worried about crossing? Sucking me off in your living room, wasn't it?"

"Shit! I don't know! I've never done anything like this before."

A silent eternity passed between them even as Jackson pulled on his shirt. He walked toward Ko and stopped a mere inch away from him. For a long time, their eyes met and Ko wanted nothing more than to take Jackson into his arms and kiss him until Jackson was breathless and climaxing. But he didn't see passion in Jackson's eyes, just anger and confusion.

"Let's get something perfectly clear." Jackson's voice was hard. "I'm not a child. I'm a grown-ass man who knows what he wants. If I say I want to be fucked, that's what I mean. Don't second-guess it. Don't judge it. Just do it. If you have an issue with that or if you're hesitant, then that's on you."

Ko moaned.

"Now. We're going to try this again."

Jackson walked around him and into the house. He followed behind Jackson, watching the way he navigated the stairs then found the master bedroom as if he had done so before. Standing at the door, he waited while Jackson got naked again.

"Condoms and…" Jackson asked.

"Bedside table, top drawer."

Jackson gathered what they needed and turned to face him.

"Ask me again," Ko said, his voice cracking. Watching Jackson's dick harden made Ko tremble. "Ask me again."

"I don't ask, Ko. I demand what I want—fuck me!"

Ko was no fool. He didn't wait to be asked a third time. This time, when those words left Jackson's lips, Ko peeled off his pants and walked over to Jackson. Gripping his shoulders, Ko spun him away and bent him over the side of the bed. Falling to his knees, Ko shoved his tongue between Jackson's perfect cheeks and licked. Jackson hissed but Ko didn't stop. He didn't let up. Jackson was delicious and ready. His hole quivered and tightened around the tip of Ko's tongue.

"You're so tight," Ko managed before plunging his tongue in again. Though he wanted to play with Jackson, to finger his hole until Jackson had no choice but to submit, Ko's cock was so hard it was almost painful. He needed release and the only person who could do that for him was Jackson. After dressing himself in one of the condoms and sliding his lube-covered fingers over Jackson's hole, he rose to his feet, gripped Jackson's hips and positioned his throbbing dick at Jackson's entrance.

"Ko…"

"Yes?"

"Please?"

Ko sighed and pushed his hips forward. He growled like a beast as Jackson's hot, tight body accepted him. For a breath, he held still. He wanted to slam into Jackson, to feel their bodies collide and to hear Jackson's reaction. But Ko knew once he moved, Jackson's hole would be his undoing.

"Ko!"

The sound of Jackson's strangled plea jarred Ko back to himself and he gritted his teeth. He gave Jackson what he demanded — over and over, slamming his cock as deep as it would go. Each time he did, fire lashed at Ko's body, leaving him delirious with pleasure. He tried his best to hold on, to enjoy ever second, every heated wisp of carnality that flowed between them. But taking Jackson was better than Ko had imagined. Listening to Jackson's rugged breath and his cries for more had Ko whimpering and grinding into his lover.

By the time Jackson orgasmed, Ko was already past the point of no return. The moment Jackson's hole tightened even more around him, Ko merely allowed the goodness of it to cross his eyes and push him over the brink. He came hard inside the condom, still lodged deeply within Jackson's body. A primal sound filled the room and echoed off their sweat-covered bodies. Ko had never had a climax so powerful that he was left stiff yet shaking.

Jackson laughed but his eyes were closed. The sound of their breathing mingled and matched and that surprised Ko. That one, small thing filled his heart close to bursting and he didn't care if he sounded like a needy fool. He'd never had that with a man and it was wonderful. Ko resigned himself to enjoying it no matter how long or how short it lasted.

"Jack…" Ko managed before slumping to the bed on top of Jackson. "Damn…"

"That was much better than running away," Jackson said. "Am I right?"

"Gimme a second," Ko whispered. "I don't think my brain's on."

Jackson laughed and shifted, causing Ko to fall to the bed. They faced each other and for the first time, Ko managed to lay still and stared into a man's face. Even in his lust-induced stupor, Ko could see that Jackson was beautiful. Everything about him turned Ko on, even though he'd just had him.

"This is not right," Ko panted.

"What isn't?"

"How is this even possible?"

"Ko?" Worry filled Jackson's voice. "What's wrong?"

"How could I be ready to go again already?"

A slow smile curled Jackson's lips as he slipped his hand between their bodies to find Ko's dick. He stroked and massaged, turning Ko into a heated puddle.

"Don't complain, Ko," Jackson told him. "If you want to take this ass again, you don't need rhyme or reason — just climb on and go for a ride."

"I'm dreaming, right?" Ko asked. "I have to be dreaming. I've never met a man like you before — so ready, so willing."

"I've never met a man like you before." Jackson leaned in and dropped a chaste kiss to Ko's lips. "So open and ready to bring out the nasty in me."

"I…"

"I love it. I know I can be myself in your bed, Ko."

Ko smiled and caressed Jackson's cheek gently. He knew sleeping with Jackson could blow up in his face — especially when Darius found out. But he couldn't have resisted Jackson if he tried until the world ended.

"You surprised me, Jackson." Ko admitted. "I never expected you to be so freaky."

Jackson grinned. "That's a good thing, right?"

"Why don't you lift that ass of yours in the air for me and I'll show you."

* * * *

Jackson woke up with a start. There was a body behind him, an arm tossed possessively across him and his bed had moved. For a second, he remained motionless, eyes darting around the room, lit up dimly by a fading moon. Then slowly, he began remembering.

He'd kissed his boss — and he'd liked it.

He'd watched his boss jerk off — and he'd liked it.

He'd felt his boss's mouth on his cock — and he'd liked it.

Wait.

Flashes of their bodies tangled in the sheets charged through his head. Every breath, every pass of Ko's tongue on his, every soft touch or hard grab. Yes, Jackson had been thoroughly used by Ko in every breathtaking way possible and he had loved every single second of it.

Licking his lips, he rolled over to look into Ko's face. His almond-shaped eyes were closed but Jackson could still see the fire that raged in them as he had pushed deeper into Jackson. Jackson reached up and eased a strand of hair from Ko's face to reveal a scar just to the right of his nose. Jackson kissed it before he could stop himself and Ko sighed.

"Ko?"

No answer.

In that moment, Jackson could see himself with Ko, waking up every morning like this. He craved that connection with another man but he barely knew Ko— shit, he shouldn't have even spent the night. Cross with himself, he eased out of Ko's arms and left the room on his tiptoes trying to find the bathroom. He could have used the en suite washroom but then Ko would wake up at the sounds and begin asking questions. It seemed Ko could read Jackson better than any other man and that scared Jackson.

He found a bathroom at the end of the upstairs hall— it was merely a sink, mirror and a toilet. Still, he used it, washed his hands before he caught his reflection in the mirror. Sounds of their lovemaking filled Jackson's head. The memories were stark and jarring, and though he began getting hard again, Jackson couldn't believe what he'd done. He had been brazen, demanding what he wanted from Ko and responding with equal wildness and now he felt as if he'd been out of line.

The thought hit him like a punch in the chest and he panted, trying desperately to catch his breath. Then suddenly his heart began racing as if he'd been running a marathon. He scrambled through the house, being careful not to make any sounds. Quickly, he gathered his clothes, found his helmet and left through the back door. Outside, he slipped on his helmet, climbed astride the cycle and pushed the stand off the ground. He rolled the motorcycle quietly down the driveway and a little way down the road before he started the ignition. As he rode through the dew-covered morning, his heart got a chance to settle down. He refocused on everything that had happened the night before and felt ill.

He'd been wild and vocal in Ko's bed. He'd gotten what he had wanted from Ko and it had been amazing. But how could Ko want a man who was capable of that? Jackson pulled into the parking lot of an all-night diner and bought some pancakes and eggs for breakfast. He eventually wound up sitting on Charlie's couch with his friend staring at him curiously.

"Okay," Charlie said finally. "Where's the body?"

"Huh? What?"

"See? You weren't listening! What's wrong?"

"Who said anything is wrong?"

"You show up at my place at" — Charlie checked the time on the DVD player and shrugged — "four in the morning looking like your cat has died."

Jackson set his glass on the coffee table and fell back against the sofa. "I don't have a cat."

"Jack…" Charlie said in that voice that brimmed with strained patience.

"Sorry. Ko and I slept together."

"Woohoo! Wait…no."

"It isn't even the fact that we slept together. It's the way I was during the whole thing."

Charlie got up. "I need alcohol for this."

"Dude, it's four in the morning!"

Charlie returned with two beers and extended one to Jackson. "It's five p.m. somewhere."

"Seriously?"

Instead of answering, Charlie set the extra beer by Jackson's feet, wrung the cap from his and sat again. "Okay, explain."

"You know I'm no slouch in bed," Jackson started. Charlie smirked at him but he ignored the look and continued. "But what happened last night with Ko goes way beyond anything I've ever done or experienced. This morning I woke up beside him and he was so damn handsome and I started thinking — shit, I'm a nester."

"Let's start at the beginning. What do you mean 'goes beyond anything you've ever done'? Did he do something that you weren't — ?"

"No. Nothing like that. He had me…"

"Had you what?"

"Begging."

Charlie went quiet for an instant then burst into laughter.

Jackson glared at his friend with his head tilted to one side. "It's not funny."

"Yes, it is."

"I shouldn't have come here," Jackson said, rising in a huff. "Your ass is an ass."

"My ass hasn't been pounded as good as yours was tonight in a long time," Charlie said, laughter still in his voice. "I'm sorry, all right? Jackson, don't leave. Look, I laughed because — well, because everyone, man or woman, should meet a lover who makes them beg for it. It's one of the sexiest things ever."

"What? Sexy?"

Charlie took Jackson's hand and led him back to the couch. "Listen. Sex isn't supposed to be boring—I'm a strong believer in that. And to find a man who is that good of a lover that you are delirious, brother, that's an awesome thing. It's nothing to be ashamed of. It doesn't make you a slut."

Jackson hung his head. "But I was so…" He sighed.

"Ko Takao can make a man do crazy things. I can tell. He has that body on him and a very, very sinful mouth."

"Hey, down, boy."

Charlie laughed. "Again, not my type. Crap, where was I?"

"Sinful mouth?"

"Smart ass," Charlie muttered. "What I'm trying to say is most of us look for that one person who curls our toes just by walking into the room. You've found that with Ko so why not see where it goes?"

"We only slept together once."

"Once? Or for one night?"

Jackson's cheeks burned.

"Look, bro. You're going to be working with this guy. Don't make it weirder than it needs to be. Go with the flow, relax, don't be rigid and you'll be surprised how things have a way of working themselves out."

Jackson sighed. "It's a little late for that."

"What's that supposed to—? Jack, tell me you didn't just sneak out in the middle of the night."

"Not the middle of the night, per se—in the wee hours of the morning."

"And that's different how?"

Jackson had no answer. In a panic, he grabbed Charlie's beer and drank until he tasted nothing but foam. His throat burned slightly and it left a bitter aftertaste but he didn't care. The moment he'd thought he'd figured out one issue, he'd managed to get himself into another. He'd seen the problem the second Charlie had asked him that question. He'd snuck out of Ko's bed, out of his house and left like a scared child.

"Fuck. Shit. Ass!"

Charlie grunted. "Come on. You can't go anywhere now. At least try getting some sleep."

"Shit."

"It's not too late to fix this, Jack, my man. But you can't do it now. I'm pretty sure it's illegal to be up at this hour."

Jackson sighed and gave in. He made himself comfortable in Charlie's guestroom but didn't get a wink of sleep. When Charlie entered a few hours later, dressed in a navy-blue suit, Jackson felt as if he had sand in his eyes.

"I'm heading out," Charlie said, sitting on the side of the bed. "Shower and shave before you go. You can pick an outfit out of my closet. Don't go home wearing the same thing you wore last night."

"Thanks, Charlie."

Charlie smiled sadly before dropping a kiss to Jackson's forehead. "You're a good man, Jackson Stark. You just have to stop getting lost inside your own head."

Jackson said nothing.

"Talk to Ko. Do not let this fester."

"I won't."

Charlie rose and buttoned his suit jacket. "So what do you think?" He did a turn.

"Very nice."

"Good. I aim to impress today." Charlie beamed proudly. "It's going to be a great day, Jackson, my man. You'll see."

Chapter Eleven

Ko spent his week catching up on work and putting together the schedule for the rollout of the new campaign. Everything from graphic designers to suppliers came across his desk that week. For the most part, it was with the designers who worked for his father. A few of them never really saw Ko as good enough for the job. He knew that because they hadn't been very quiet about it when his father had been in charge. The people who walked into the meeting with him seemed quieter, meeker and that brought out his inner villain smile. It was the first time he'd smiled since he'd woken up to Jackson scurrying about the house. He'd known what had been happening and usually he'd just go back to sleep, not caring.

Not with Jackson. There was something there, something he couldn't ignore. A few times during the week, he'd been drawn to a window and there Jackson was, leaning against his motorcycle, looking so dangerous. And Ko's heart would soar until he heard the engine dying in the distance.

Ko blinked and the outside came back into focus. He searched the grounds below as far as the eyes could see but there was no sign of Jackson or his black and red Suzuki Bandit 1200S. Disappointment flowed through him and he hadn't realized how he had grown to look forward to seeing Jackson — even from so far away.

The sun was barely in the center of the sky. People scattered in all directions in the busy plaza. A few were seated by tables with their sunglasses fused to their faces and cell phones glistening in the sun.

"Okay." Stella's voice caused him to jerk around to stare at her. "What's the matter?"

"Nothing."

"Ko, you jumped, like, six feet in the air just now."

Ko took his chair. "It's nothing. Really. I was thinking, that's all. You know how I get when I'm contemplating something. Being the boss is a lot for me."

"Fine. Sure." She didn't look convinced. "I've sent the schedule to Jackson Stark. Hopefully there won't be any conflicts. He signed the contracts so now all I need is your John Hancock..." She set the papers in front of him, and like an automation, Ko signed them all.

"Is that all?" Ko asked.

"No. That's not all. You look like the walking dead, boss. What can I do?"

Ko smiled at her. "Nothing. I'll handle it."

"Right. But — But if...if I can help..."

"You'll be the first to know, Stella," Ko said, even managing a lopsided grin. "You'll be the first to know."

"Good. Okay. Um — the meeting for you to sit down and go over specs with Jackson and Tasha is set for tomorrow at eleven..."

Why did he even have to meet with Jackson? Obviously the guy wanted nothing to do with Ko. Hopefully he'd still work for Hansamu because it was too late to find someone else. Ko inhaled. Well, Jackson really didn't have a choice in the matter seeing as they had a contract.

"And you're not hearing a thing I'm saying, are you?"

Ko snapped to. "Sorry. Look, I have to go. I need to talk to someone. Call me later."

"But…"

Ko was already out of the door and heading to the elevator. Stella's stilettos clicked behind him but he didn't wait for her to say anything. He jammed his finger against the elevator button and thankfully it opened right away. The ride down was lonely and quiet—the same way he'd felt when he had woken up and Jackson hadn't been there. But he couldn't get attached. Jackson was young and probably hadn't even had his chance to be wild in life. Why would he want to tie himself down with some man who only had three years to go before hitting the big four-oh?

Ko turned his car to the other side of Bathseba and by the time he pulled into the driveway, it was just after lunch. Thaddeus' car was parked behind Ravinder's BMW and that gave Ko some hope his friend was home. Quickly, he eased from the seat and jogged up the front steps.

"Ko!" Ravinder greeted. "How are you?"

The two hugged.

"I don't feel so good. Is Thaddeus around?"

"He's taking a nap but come in. I'll get him."

"No, Ravi, don't wake him."

Ravinder pressed his full lips into a thin line. "Right. Like Thaddeus would agree to that. Come in. I insist."

Ko sighed but walked by his friend's fiancé and into the luxurious interior. He removed his shoes and made his way into the kitchen.

"Make yourself at home," Ravinder said. "Grab a drink or something."

"I'm not really..." But Ko didn't have time to finish. Ravinder was already gone and he was left alone in the kitchen, the space threatened to consume him. Thaddeus found him that way, standing in the center of the kitchen, rubbing his palms on the sides of his thighs.

"Ko?"

He turned but said nothing.

"Taka?"

Ko knew when Thaddeus called him that, his friend was really worried. Finding the energy from somewhere deep inside, Ko lifted his head and smiled. "I'm sorry. I didn't know you were sleeping."

"It's no big deal. Ravi said you looked like hell." Thaddeus stepped closer and held Ko's shoulders. "Let me get us something to drink then you can tell me what's going on."

Ko nodded.

Not long afterward they were both sitting in Thaddeus' office. The large house had two, Ko remembered. "Um, you can't tell Darius or Feng what I'm about to tell you."

"You're scaring me, Ko. What's wrong?"

"I—uh—Jackson and I— Well, we slept together."

"Okay? And?"

"You know how I swore up and down that there isn't a man alive for me and that I had given up on finding someone?"

Thaddeus nodded.

Ko took a big gulp from his juice and set the cold glass on a coaster on Thaddeus' desk. He stood beside his chair and folded his arms across his chest. "I let myself go there, Thaddeus. And now Jackson wants out and I feel like an idiot. I feel —"

"What do you mean he wants out?"

"I don't think he wanted a relationship. All he wanted was me for one night. But uh…"

"That's not what you want."

Ko shook his head. "Of course not. There's a thing in Jackson's spirit that attracts me and I wanted the chance to show him that I could be more than just a passing fancy for him — I could make him happy." Ko paused. His frustration pulsed at his lower back then spiraled through him like sparks of lightning. "Stupid, right?" He faced the window and as he walked by Thaddeus' desk, he dragged a fingertip against it. "I'm not in love with him — not yet."

"Then why do you think this hurts you so much?"

"I wanted to fall in love with him. I was willingly to let my heart go there." Ko rubbed his eyes. "Don't make a big deal out of it, huh? I needed to tell someone before I imploded. I have a meeting with him tomorrow and…"

"You don't know if you can control yourself."

"I guess." Ko rubbed the back of his neck.

"Ko." Thaddeus' voice was soft, warm, almost like Jackson's naked body. "Ko, you wanting more from a man isn't anything to be ashamed or angry about."

"But why this man? I mean, he works for me, for God's sake."

"It happens all the time. Look at me and Ravi. We worked together and it just sort of happened. Now, I can't imagine my life without him. Sure, falling for an employee isn't the ideal situation but it happens more than you think. What's really bothering you, Ko?"

Ko hung his head. His shoulders dropped lower than he ever remembered them falling and a large lump formed in his throat. "When we were in bed, I felt something. There was this...this...ugh!"

"Breathe."

"He made me do things and feel things and I thought even if was a night of doing everything out of order, he would have sensed it too and he would want to see if we could work. What's really wrong is he doesn't even think that."

"How do you know?"

"Because he snuck out early in the morning."

Thaddeus chuckled. "Ravi did that. He did because he thought I would freak out, that I wouldn't want what he had to offer."

"Did you?"

"Look at the ring on his finger, then ask me that again."

Ko smiled. "Right. Sorry."

"It's okay."

Ko faced Thaddeus. "I'm scared, Thad. These feelings inside me for a man I barely know terrify me."

"Love always does."

"Love?" Ko scuffed. "That's like putting the buggy before the horse, isn't it?"

"You say to-mah-to. I say—"

"Blah, blah, blah."

Thaddeus laughed. "Look, the whole Jackson situation isn't that complicated. He makes you feel what I do for Raviner and you've never had that before. You're freaking out because Jackson is so much younger than you and you are acquaintances with his family. It's overwhelming. But, if you treat him with care and respect, his family will get over their apprehension, if they have any."

"And he's best friends with his ex."

"Charlie. Yeah. I know. They broke up because Charlie hates kids and Jackson wants an army of them."

Ko arched an eyebrow. "An army? Dang."

"Yeah, well, he's always had a soft spot for kids," Thaddeus explained.

"You think if Charlie goes back to him and changes his mind on children...?"

"That Jackson would take him back?" Thaddeus asked. "I doubt it. They are way past that now."

Ko nodded and sat again. "Well, I guess we'll have to wait and see how the meeting goes tomorrow. I'm trying to stay positive but it's hard."

"Of course it is. Everything worth having is hard—including the gutter my mind fell into."

Ko laughed out loud before bumping Thaddeus with his shoulder. "Seriously? You just had to go there?"

"Well, duh! I thought you knew me better!"

It was easy for Ko to be around Thaddeus after that. They talked about other things and by the time he hugged Ravinder and Thaddeus and headed for his car, they had plans for a small scholarship for the two students at Bathsheba High who showed great potential in Arts and Computer Sciences. Though that wasn't what he went there for, knowing of another way to give back to the community that had given him so much, took the bite out of his depression.

* * * *

Tracing the stitches on the sofa's arm with a finger, Jackson tapped his left foot impatiently. It wasn't as if he wanted crazy in the luxury waiting area, but seeing Ko again terrified him. And to make it worse, Ko was forcing him to wait. It felt as if this was Ko's way for getting back at him, and Jackson—even though deep down he knew he deserved it—just couldn't take it anymore. He gripped the arm in a way to keep himself seated.

Wait five more minutes, Jack. Just five…

He was on his feet before he even realized it.

"Excuse me," Jackson said, walking to the secretary's desk. "How much longer is the wait?"

"I'm not quite sure at this point." She glanced down at the phone on her desk. "He's still on the line."

"What about if you just knocked on his door and let him know I'm here?"

"It doesn't work like that."

"This is ridiculous. Where's Stella? Can I speak with Stella? I've been sitting here for forty-five minutes. I have things I could be doing."

"Sir, I don't think—"

"Don't think!" Jackson snapped. "Do."

She glared at him but Jackson didn't care. He didn't back down and soon she was on the phone with Stella. The secretary barely had the phone back in the cradle than Stella approached him from a nearby office.

"Jackson, come this way, please," Stella said. "Ko is trying to hammer out the details for something in Japan. In the meantime, you and I can chat."

Jackson smiled but if he were being honest, he'd admit he didn't want to talk to her. He didn't have to be a genius to know that he was in a lot of trouble with Ko. It wasn't as if he wanted to run. The truth was Ko would have been the first authentic relationship he would have had with a lover if he hadn't run away like a coward. Still, he went through the motions shooting the breeze with Stella. Thankfully, it didn't take long before Tasha entered and Jackson melted to her side. She was familiar and predictable to him. Though he never knew what would come out of her mouth next,

Tasha had never given him a reason to withdraw into himself.

"I'm going to see what's keeping Ko." Stella excused herself.

Jackson cleared his throat and rested his forehead on the large desk. It was cool and hard under him. Still, he stayed in that position, tapping his head slightly against the surface.

"Who's eating your butt?" Tasha asked.

"No one—that's the problem."

Tasha laughed. "I know you're pent-up, but giving yourself a concussion is not going to help."

Jackson sat up with a moan. "I fucked up, Tas. I fucked up royally and I—"

"Sorry for the hold up," Ko said, stepping into the room with Stella on his heels. "The world seems to be going at light speed and I'm caught in the middle."

Jackson kept his eyes on Ko but not once did Ko return the connection. He sat at the head of the table, in a black Hansamu suit that held his toned body perfectly. He set down his tablet on the table and undid the buttons on his jacket. "After careful consideration, I've decided to push the launch of the new campaign to next year. Right now, rolling it out this year would make everything rushed and I don't like sloppy. If we're going to do this, we must do it right."

A lump formed in Jackson's throat and his head throbbed slightly.

"In the meantime, we're still aiming to release teasers for New York Fashion Week this year, Fashion Empire Toronto this year and a couple of other places."

"So you still need me?" Tasha asked. "The teasers don't really need a photographer."

"On the contrary." Ko slid a glossy folder across the desk to her. "Here's a new plan. We may have to change your contract and renegotiate a few things but do you think it's workable? Will it fit your schedule?"

Tasha read what was in the folder for a quick moment then smiled. "I can do this."

"Good."

"What about me?" Jackson's voice sounded small and quivering.

"You'll be working with Tasha for the most part over the next few weeks to create the ground teasers. Then once January rolls around, you begin again with Priya." Ko seemed all business when he spoke. Though he looked at Jackson, his eyes gave nothing away. "We still have spots to last us until the major reveal and that will give me more time to work on a few new pieces for the line."

The business talk took an eternity. Most of it went over Jackson's head for he couldn't seem to focus. When it was over, he remained where he was until he was alone with Ko. But the designer didn't seem to want to stay, for he rose and gathered his things.

"Ko, wait."

"Wait for what?" Ko asked, taking long strides toward the door.

Jackson rushed forward and braced his back against it, blocking Ko's path. "We need to talk."

"I don't think we have anything to say to each other."

"You can't really believe that!"

Ko sighed. "I believe action speaks louder than words, Jackson. You've made it perfectly clear this — us — is not what you want, and even though I was pissed off at first, I understand. Really."

"What do you understand?"

Ko stepped away and put the large desk between them. He folded his arms across his chest and leaned into the wall. "I get you work for me and we shouldn't have done what we did." His voice was cold, strained. "I understand that I'm too old for you." Ko leveled his stare on Jackson. "I get I'm not the kind of man you saw yourself with for the long-term and I get what we had was only for the night."

Jackson looked away.

"What's the matter, Jackson? Can't handle the truth?"

"You don't know what you're talking about." Jackson didn't move from his spot at the door. "You're full of shit...and...and...you don't know what you're talking about!"

"Don't I? I know I woke up in the early hours of the morning to the man I spent hours before making love to, scurrying about in the dark then leaving without a word."

"You— You were awake? Why didn't you say something?"

"What did you want me to say?" Ko unfolded his arms. "Beg you not to leave? Besides, saying something would have only delayed what was happening. I'd rather rip off the Band-Aid, hurt, then move on."

"Ko."

"No."

Jackson rubbed his palms up and down his thighs a few times. He tried speaking but his tongue stuck to the roof of his mouth. After swallowing, he managed to dislodge it. "I didn't leave because I only wanted you for a night! You're wrong and you have no clue!"

"I don't? All right." Ko's shoulders rose then fell. "Why don't you enlighten me?"

Before Jackson could say anything else, Stella stuck her head into the boardroom with a smile. "Ko? Emma from New York Fashion Week is on three. She said you guys have been playing phone tag today?"

"Thanks. Tell her to give me a minute."

Stella nodded, hesitated then stepped from the room and closed the door again.

"It doesn't matter anymore," Ko continued. "I was the idiot who thought there could have possibly have been a thing between us—that there was a spark that could lead to something. I'm the needy son of a bitch. It's not your fault. I should've known better. I'm old enough. Look, I have to go."

"Ko, we still have to…"

Ko shook his head and wrenched the door opened.

"Please…Ko…"

But the man merely stepped through and closed the door behind him. The bottom of Jackson's chest fell out and for a moment he just stood there, shaking and alone. But that shock wore off quickly enough and was replaced by a rage he didn't think was at all possible. He hadn't gotten a word in to explain himself. If Ko thought Jackson was just going to walk out and not say his piece, Ko had another thing coming.

Jackson smoothed his hands over his sides, lifted his chin and wiggled his neck from one side to the next. He counted from one to ten backward and forward then took a few cleansing breaths. Once he could get his feet to move, Jackson let himself out of the boardroom and followed the hall until he got to Ko's office. Even though Ko was on the phone, Jackson took a seat across from his desk.

"One second, Emma." Ko covered the receiver with a palm. "I thought we already said what needed to be said."

"No. You said what you had to say and you didn't give me a chance to say much. So, go ahead." Jackson lounged back in the sofa and crossed his legs. "I'll wait until you finish your phone call. Because one way or another, you and I are working this shit out."

Ko didn't look impressed. His jaws tightened and fury filled his steely brown gaze. But Jackson didn't care. He simply lifted his chin a bit higher as Ko glared at him.

"Emma? Are you going to be free in about twenty minutes? Okay...right. Can you give me a call when you're out of your meeting? There's something in my office I have to tend to. Thanks." Ko hung up and eased back in his seat, his brow eyes menacing as he dragged his fingers through his hair. "What do you want from me, Jackson?"

"I want you to hear me out."

Ko's shoulders rose and fell but he made no move to get up. "You left me, Jackson."

"And you let me go..."

"This isn't getting us anywhere." Ko shook his head. "I have work to do."

"Do you remember what happened when we made love?" Jackson asked.

"Yeah. You left."

"No." Jackson rested his elbows on his knees and leaned forward. "That was after we made love. I meant during..."

Ko gave him a one-shoulder shrug.

"I did things — said things..."

"Jackson, I'm going to need you to make sense because I haven't been sleeping well so my brain is not firing on all cylinders right now."

"I-I...I was insatiable. I begged you, begged you!"

Ko tilted his head to the side. "Um...I'm not sure I follow where this is going."

"I was completely out of control! You had to have seen that. I was behaving like I was depraved and I know men don't find that kind of thing sexy in a partner who they want to have a real, deep relationship with."

"Hold up." Ko rose and walked around his desk. He sat on the edge and folded his arms. "You're telling me you left at that ungodly hour because you thought I'd be ashamed because you begged me to fuck you?"

Jackson turned his head away.

"Jesus Murphy, Jackson! That is nothing to be ashamed of and anyone who tells you different is a fucking liar! Jackson, look at me..."

Slowly, Jackson met Ko's gaze.

"I'm too old for shy." He climbed off his desk and kneeled before Jackson. "The man I take to my bed must know what he wants and demand it. If he wants my mouth, he must be able to take it. If my man's a slut, as long as he is that in my bed alone, then all is right with the world. Besides, I was there with you, remember? Didn't you see how turned on I got from all of it?"

Jackson sighed. "I've made a mess out of this whole thing, haven't I? I kept thinking you're mature and you don't want some guy who gave it up so..."

"Listen to yourself." Ko's voice was softer than it had been before. He caressed Jackson's cheek gently.

Unable to stop himself, Jackson closed his eyes and pressed his face into Ko's palm.

"You're making yourself crazy." Ko was close now, his hot breath bathing Jackson's other cheek. "Let's clear the air right now. Your body excites me and the things I wish to do to it may scare you. But if you were to take off all your clothes right now and bend over that desk, it wouldn't make me think less of you. In fact, I wish you would."

Jackson smiled.

"Was that a smile, Jackson Stark?"

"No."

Ko laughed. "Promise me the next time you feel like this, you'll say something."

He opened his eyes and met Ko's stare. "I promise. Does this mean I'm forgiven?"

"Not quite yet. You've left me with your scent on my sheets and your body in my mind," Ko whispered, pushing upward for Jackson's mouth. "I think it's time you put out this fire you've started."

Jackson trembled. Ko had missed him — he knew it. "And how can I do that?"

"Well..." Ko kissed him, a deep, searing kiss that curled his toes. "You can start with those beautiful lips around my cock."

"You're so sexy when you talk dirty. It makes me hard."

Ko grinned and kissed him again. "That's the plan. So, do we have a deal?"

"What kind of question is that? Of course we do."

Chapter Twelve

Ko handed control to Jackson and followed his lead. With their mouths fused together, Ko rose with Jackson. Somehow, Jackson spun them around and shoved Ko to the sofa. Ko moaned. He stared up at Jackson, memorizing the lines of Jackson's handsome face, his lips that were slightly parted and a little swollen from their kisses—everything about Jackson left Ko wondering how he'd managed to get so lucky.

Slowly, Jackson went down on his knees and pushed Ko's legs apart. Without breaking eye contact, Jackson undid Ko's belt, then his zipper and button. Ko licked his lips and held his breath as Jackson stuck a hand in, wrapped long, warm fingers around his now rigid cock and pulled it from the confines of his pants and boxers. Ko moaned.

"Tell me what you want, Ko," Jackson whispered between licks of Ko's dick. "Tell me how you like it."

"Slow," Ko said through gritted teeth. "Hard. Wet."

Jackson smiled then lowered his head. He pulled in the tip in, lashed his tongue over it before sucking hard, yet slow. A rumble filled the room as Ko wrapped his fingers against the back of Jackson's head. As if they had minds of their own, Ko's toes curled in on themselves even as his eyes crossed and rolled back into his head. He'd never been sucked that well before and though he wanted to tell Jackson so, Ko couldn't find the words.

Each time Jackson pulled him deeper down his throat, Ko's body jerked as sparks of electricity surged through his core. He looked down on one of those odd moments when he could pull his mind from the daze and caught Jackson's eyes.

"Baby," was all Ko managed, for Jackson sucked him deep again while massaging his balls. "Yes, darling."

Jackson lathered Ko's whole shaft, leaving it wet and glistening, only to impale his mouth on the dick again, slurping all the wetness away. He hummed against the head, grazed it with his teeth then sucked the sting away. Ko's hands slipped from the back of Jackson's head and fell to his sides. It was like he had no power to lift them. He was sweetly frozen, his body being pushed closer and closer to exploding, and he didn't care. He craved that big finish, that rush of adrenaline that would course through him. Knowing Jackson was the one doing this to him sent his heart racing faster and his cock twitching in Jackson's grasp.

"Cover the head," Ko gasped. "Just the head."

Jackson followed instructions.

"Now, suck—damn, Jackson! That's it."

Ko allowed his very soul to be carried away by Jackson. From his scent, to the beauty of him on his knees before Ko, left Ko trying desperately to hold off on climaxing. But the more he tried, the more control he lost.

"Don't do that," Jackson said, his voice soft before he licked a finger and pushed it under Ko's body for his hole.

"Jack..."

Jackson didn't stop. He inserted the finger slowly and Ko's eyes widened. It'd been so long since he'd been penetrated, he'd forgotten how good it was when done right. He moaned, lifted his hips from the sofa and surged down again to get Jackson's finger deeper. That was his complete undoing, having Jackson finger him while sucking his dick.

"You like getting fucked, Ko?"

"By you...baby, harder, please."

Ko ground his hips down, taking Jackson's finger as deeply as he could get it just as Jackson's tongue passed over the now tender head of his cock. With a soft whimper as a warning, he watched through a blurred daze as Jackson lifted his head just in time for Ko's spunk to go flying. Ko trembled, jerked his hips up and off Jackson's finger but he couldn't control where his cum went. He growled and reached down to still Jackson's hand that was still jerking him, for he knew he'd combust if Jackson continued.

Instead of backing off, Jackson covered Ko's dick as it sent cum everywhere, sucking every last bit out. "Oh, fuck, Jackson. So good."

Ko sat forward, pulling his cock from Jackson's grasp. He expected Jackson to spit but he watched as Jackson's Adam's apple danced.

"Open your mouth for me," Ko said.

Jackson did.

"You're so sexy right now."

Jackson laughed. "Wasn't I sexy before?"

"You know what I mean." Ko gathered Jackson up and into his arms. Covering Jackson's mouth with his own, Ko could taste himself, hot and musky on Jackson's lips. He deepened the kiss, enjoying their closeness even as he realized there was no turning back now. They'd just done something more intimate than sex and Jackson hadn't once hesitated.

As he reached his palms down to cup Jackson's perfect ass cheeks, Ko pulled back his head. "I want to take you home so bad."

"But, Mr. Takao. You must be responsible. You are at work, after all."

Ko chuckled. "I think we've crossed that line a while ago."

"Maybe. But if you go back to work, I'll make sure I'm waiting for you when you get home."

Ko moaned his disappointment. He wiped a splat of cum from Jackson's chin with his thumb. "I hate it, but you're right. I have one more phone call to make then I will try and get home to you."

"I like the sound of that."

"Of what?"

"You coming home to me."

Ko caressed Jackson's cheeks. Without replying, he kissed Jackson again, throwing his whole self behind it. "You should clean up."

"Sure," Jackson said.

But Ko only released him after another kiss. He pointed Jackson to his private restroom then sat back to fix his clothes. He was aroused again and it hurt pushing his cock back into the confines of this boxers and pants but it wasn't like he had a choice. Frowning, he grabbed some Kleenex and cleaned up the mess he'd made.

"Do you see what you did to me?" Ko called through the bathroom door, dropping the used papers into the garbage.

"I enjoyed that."

Ko smiled, letting himself into the bathroom. He washed his hands then leaned his shoulder against the doorframe to watch Jackson rinse his mouth. "I'll be coming home to you, Jackson Stark."

Jackson grabbed a fresh towel and tapped his mouth then kissed Ko. Ko smirked when Jackson reached into his pocket and Ko leaned back. Jackson held up Ko's keys and jangled them.

"Get your mind out of the gutter," Jackson said. "House key?"

"Sure, baby." Ko took them, removed his house key and handed it to Jackson. "Make yourself at home and I'll be there as soon as I can."

"Good. I'm going to head home and get a few things."

"Not too much clothes—I prefer this beautiful body bare."

Jackson cuddled into Ko's chest. He trembled and Ko wrapped his arms tighter around him. "Are you cold, darling?"

"No. Just not used to this—a man calling me baby or darling. You did that earlier and it drives me crazy."

"Good crazy or bad?"

"Good. How would you say it in Japanese?"

"*Dārin*."

"Doesn't sound as good."

"I prefer *koibito*."

Jackson lifted his head. "And that is?"

"Sweetheart."

"Hrm—well, tonight when you fuck me deep and hard, I want you to call me that again with fire in your voice. I'll decide if I like it better then."

Ko chewed his bottom lip, thinking of that, but released Jackson. He knew if he didn't they'd be tearing each other's clothes off and he had no condoms or lube in the office.

When he was finally alone, Ko couldn't focus on work. Even though he got through his next meeting and managed to make some decisions, it was hard. At the end of the day, he rushed out of the office and sped down the street. He stopped to pick up some takeout. When he got home, the house was quiet. If he hadn't seen Jackson's motorcycle outside, he would have thought Jackson wasn't there. He walked through the house and found his lover, lying naked on his stomach, fast asleep in the master bedroom.

He sat on the edge of the bed and caressed a palm down Jackson's back and over the slope of his ass. For a silent breath, he simply stroked Jackson with his fingertips then his lips. Ko reached into the bedside table for condoms and lube. Though he'd wanted to eat first, food could wait. He saw something much more delectable lying in his bed. Ko kneeled at the foot of the bed, opened Jackson's legs and palmed his ass cheeks. Unable to stop himself, Ko spread those supple cheeks and licked at Jackson's hole. He growled in heat as his cock rose to attention at his first taste of his lover.

"I'm home, baby," Ko said.

Even in his dream, Jackson knew Ko's touch. From the soft caresses of a fingertip to the powerful, all-consuming stroke of Ko's tongue. It passed over his puckered hole softly at first, like a whisper on the wind. Then, it demanded entry, sought to be satisfied, and Jackson woke, shouting Ko's name and trembling. But it hadn't been a dream. Ko's palms were hot against his cheeks, as his tongue dipped deeper and deeper.

"Ko."

"I'm home, baby," Ko whispered between licks.

Jackson sighed loudly and rooted his ass upward, giving Ko better access. Stuffing his face into the pillow did nothing to silence the screams of pure pleasure that escaped his lips like a river overflowing its banks. It all became too much so he pulled away from Ko's mouth and turned over. Instead of letting him go, however, Ko tugged at the sides of his own shirt and discarded the fabric behind him. He then climbed to the bed and started all over again by kissing Jackson before trailing his mouth down Jackson's body.

"I want to tell," Jackson whispered as Ko dragged his tongue down Jackson's abs. "I can't keep us a secret. I don't want to keep us undercover."

"Then tell."

"It can't be that simple."

"Sure it can." Ko stopped and lifted his head so their eyes met. "Claim me as yours."

"You want me to do that?"

"Not if you don't think it's true."

Jackson smiled. "You're mine," he whispered, pulling at Ko's shoulder so their mouths could meet. "I'm yours—you're mine. Mine. Mine…"

They kissed, tumbling on the bed, one on top then the other. Their cocks hard and crushing against each other, Jackson whimpered and tried snaking a hand between them. Ko simply caught it and pressed the hand over Jackson's head.

"Do you want my cock, Jackson?" Ko asked between kisses.

"Yes."

"Where?"

"In me…"

"Can you still beg me or are you ashamed?"

Jackson groaned. His heart hammered as the memory of what had happened the first time they'd made love swam through his mind.

"Are you…ashamed to be wild in my bed?"

"Ko, please…"

Ko climbed astride him and began undoing his belt. Jackson watched, mouthwatering, eyes fused to Ko's body.

"Tell me, when you talk to Charlie about what we do, can you honestly tell him how wild you are in my arms? Or is it a secret?"

"How do you know what Charlie and I talk about?"

Ko didn't reply right away. Instead, he took his dick from his pants, licked his palm and stroked his palm. Jackson just about climaxed at how sexy that was to him.

"You two are best friends, isn't that what you said?"

"Can we not talk about Charlie right now? You're killing the mood."

Ko smirked. "Not for me." He used a finger to gather some pre-cum from the head of his cock and extended the finger to Jackson. Unashamed, Jackson wrapped his lips around it and sucked. Ko moaned.

"Yes," Jackson said, pulling back. "I tell him the truth."

"So you can tell me what you want?"

Jackson nodded. "I want you to fuck me." He reached for Ko's cock and shoved Ko's hand away. Jackson took over stroking the hard muscle, loving the way it pulsed, hot and throbbing in his palm. "As hard as you can."

"Good boy." Ko's voice cracked.

Jackson was so far gone, he wasn't sure how it happened. The world could end and he wouldn't care. All he wanted, all he *needed* was to have Ko so deep inside him, their bodies would be one. When Ko finally filled him, Jackson had to hold his breath, close his eyes and bite down into the pillow beneath him. The harder Ko rode him, the wilder he became.

The first time they had made love, it had scared him. This time, he remembered what Ko had said and let himself go. The first inkling of his undoing started from the tips of his toes before surging to the pit of his stomach.

"Ko…"

"I'm here." Ko nibbled at Jackson's shoulder while driving into him from behind. "Give me what I want, *koibito*."

That word, that perfectly placed word stirred something inside Jackson. He wasn't sure why but his whole sweat-covered body trembled before sparks pulsed off his heart. He surged to his knees, arched his body and gave in to the light that courted the lust inside him.

He had no power to warn Ko. He simply shouted his joy, reached across for one of Ko's hands and dug his nails into the flesh. He broke for Ko, into a million different pieces of light. Jackson allowed it to radiate through him, sending powerful spurts of cum against the sheets beneath him. He shook uncontrollably, whimpering, shouting and pleading all at the same time.

"You are so sexy when you come," Ko whispered, dropping kisses all over Jackson's back.

Jackson moaned. "Your turn."

They switched position, Jackson on his back with his legs spread. Ko found his hole again, but this time he pumped slowly. With their gazes locked, Jackson played with Ko's nipples — pinching them, grazing them with his nails.

"Jackson, if you don't stop that I — "

"That's what I want," Jackson whispered. He licked his lips. "Let me taste you again."

Those seemed to be the magic words. Ko tossed his head back and all the muscles in his body tensed beautifully. When he came, the condom bulged inside Jackson's body but he didn't mind. In fact, he sat up, wrapped his arms around Ko and pulled him down to the bed. Together their bodies shook as they tried catching their breaths.

Time passed.

Slowly…

"Was Charlie your first?" Ko asked.

Jackson swallowed. "Again with Charlie."

"Last question, I promise."

"Yes, he was."

Ko shifted against him and Jackson tightened his arms around him. The fear of losing Ko did something to him — terrified him.

"Don't go…"

"I'm not going," Ko said. "I'm not as young as I used to be and my leg is cramping."

"Oh!" Jackson quickly released him and moved over so Ko could have space on the bed.

Together, they settled in once more.

"I used to be jealous of him — Charlie, I mean."

"Oh, yeah? Used to?"

Ko nodded. "Yup. I know that even though he was your first, I'll be your last."

"You seem sure of yourself."

"I am." Ko pushed to his elbow to steal a kiss.

Chapter Thirteen

Leaving Ko's, Jackson had a ton of thoughts swirling nonstop through his mind. But no matter how many of them there were, they all boiled down to one irrefutable conclusion. Ko wanted him — not just for his body or his work with Hansamu, but wanted him. And he could dance around it all he liked but eventually, if Ko's and Jackson's hearts had their way, he would have to tell his father and Darius and Feng.

Jackson yearned for Ko, too. After they'd made up, fear still curled his insides. He spent the next two days alone with Ko, learning about him, making love and simply enjoying each other without the outside world intruding. But Ko's touches had overpowered the trepidation Jackson had experienced. Every kiss had brought Jackson further and further out of the darkness of his head that he wanted to yell their budding relationship to the world.

'I want to tell,' Jackson whispered as Ko dragged his tongue down Jackson's abs. 'I can't keep us a secret.'

'Then tell.'

'It can't be that simple.'

'Sure it can.'' Ko stopped and lifted his head so their eyes met. 'Claim me as yours.'

'You want me to do that?'

'Not if you don't think it's true.'

Jackson smiled. 'You're mine,' he whispered, pulling at Ko's shoulder so their mouths could meet. 'I'm yours — you're mine. Mine. Mine...'

Glancing over his left shoulder to check on traffic, Jackson switched lanes to avoid the congestion caused by one blocked-off.

'Claim me as yours.'

That was the sexiest thing any man had ever said to him. With those words, Jackson had had to give himself to Ko all over again. Strange, he was weak when it came to Ko and his advances. But the strength Ko gave him with just a look left Jackson speechless every time.

Jackson climbed off the motorcycle and removed his helmet. He looked up at the sky and frowned. Pretty soon he would have to take the pickup out of storage and get it serviced, for winter was coming. With a mental note to himself, he jogged up the front steps. The second he opened the door, Oliver barreled into his body. Jackson laughed and returned the hug.

"Papa never said you were coming," Oliver said in his accented English. "I'm glad you're here."

"I missed you, too," Jackson said, walking his new grand-nephew into the living room where Darius was sitting with Feng. He hugged them both before turning to Oliver. "Ollie, could you give me a moment to talk with your fathers, please?"

Oliver looked hesitant but nodded. He accepted a kiss to his head from Feng before skipping from the room, dragging a teddy bear after himself. Jackson rubbed his palms on his thighs and fell into the sofa beside Darius. He never imagined telling his family about himself and

Ko would be so hard. Coming out to his father had been damn near impossible and it had taken him sneaking a shot of tequila from Kent's liquor cabinet to do it. This was almost the same intense sensation, only this time he couldn't drink because he rode his motorcycle.

The silence in the room was only momentarily interrupted by Feng's camera whirring.

"Something on your mind?" Darius asked, setting his book aside. "What's wrong?"

"Nothing is wrong. Well, not really."

Darius didn't seem convinced.

"I haven't told Dad this yet," Jackson said. "And I still don't really want to say anything to anyone but you all should know before you find out from some media outlet or another."

"Jack?" Feng said softly. "What's going on?"

"Um..." Jackson licked his suddenly dry lips and took a deep breath. "Ko and I are seeing each other."

"Ko?" Darius arched an eyebrow. "As in Takao, Ko?"

Jackson nodded.

"Oh...kay." Feng moved to sit on the coffee table before them. "Why are you nervous about telling us this?"

"Well, Uncle Darius — you and Ko run in the business circles and I know he's a little bit older than I am, but I..."

Darius cleared his throat, his expression unreadable. "Tell us why this is important to you."

"Well..." Jackson hadn't expected that. He'd walked in imagining them hitting the roof when he told them and forbidding him to see Ko. He'd been prepared with a whole different speech. He leaned back into the couch and rubbed his eyes. "I've dated a little since Charlie, Uncle Darius, you know that. But none of these guys made me feel anything. Before I even met Ko he set something off in me that scared the hell out of me. I mean, our eyes met across a theater and it was like he was caressing me and…"

"Go on." Feng's voice trembled.

"We've just met. And I'm not saying I'm in love with the guy, but so far he's given me more happiness than any other lover and I—"

"Lover?" Darius interrupted. "Does this mean you slept together?"

"Yes." Jackson buried his face in his hands. "And I ran the next morning because I was scared of what he'd think of me for doing that so soon. But then we had a talk and he wants there to be something between us."

"So, what's the final word then?" Feng asked.

"We want to date. I mean, we need to have a steady foundation, one that is built on more than mind-blowing sex. He wants us to get to know each other first."

"And what do you want?" Darius asked.

"Him," Jackson whispered, lifting his head to smile at his uncles. "I just…want…him."

Darius smiled and hugged Jackson from the side. "You've grown up, Jack. I'm proud of you for going into this with your eyes open. I'm not best friends with Ko, but from what I hear, and from the kind of man he's been around us, he seems like a good one. You're right, a worthwhile relationship, a strong one, is to be built like you would a house. If you put a house on a sky foundation, all it will need is a little wind and it will topple over."

"But if you dig into the earth, and you make sure those load-bearing walls are set deep down and firm," Feng continued for his husband, "then not even a hurricane can take it down. And trust me, relationships are hard."

Jackson nodded. "We aren't in any rush, really. I mean, with my work at Stark's and my modeling for Ko's new campaign starting early next year, we will more than have our hands full. But we both promised to make time for each other."

"That's a good place to start. It may not even be a dinner out or trips abroad. Something as simple as a bath together or a glass of wine in the backyard." Feng reached over for Darius' hand. "Trust me, it all adds up."

Speechless, Jackson hugged both his uncles and left the room to find Oliver. But just before he was out of ear shot he could hear Feng ask, "How proud are you of that kid?"

Darius laughed. "I don't have words to say just how much…"

With a smile, Jackson jogged up the stairs to spend some time with Oliver. He figured he was going to need to do that before he faced his father. Sure, Kent was on board with the whole gay thing but how would he react to Jackson dating a man so much older? Jackson exhaled long and hard then stepped through Ollie's bedroom door. He found his grand-nephew setting up the board for a game of chess.

* * * *

Long after Jackson kissed him and darted from the house, Ko managed to pull himself out of bed. Though they'd taken a few days to be alone, he was still tired. Perhaps once they got the first teasers out, he could convince Jackson to go away with him. Ko did own a cottage close to the Bathsheba mountains.

Checking the time, he groaned, and without making the bed, he quickly darted into the shower. It took no time at all because he was running behind to meet Stella for lunch. Luckily, traffic wasn't bad and though he was late, it could have been worse. Ko fell into the chair across from Stella and tilted his head. She stared at him with a look that told him she knew something was up but couldn't quite put her finger on it.

"Can I start with a drink for you, Mr. Takao?" The server had materialized out of nowhere.

"Yes, water for now, please. Make it very cold."

"Very good."

When they were alone again, Stella set her eReader to the side and rested an elbow on the table. "Something is different about you."

"I guess you'll find out sooner or later."

"What?"

The server arrived with the water and they gave their meal orders to save time and to stop the interruption. Ko took a long drink from the glass then set it back on the table. "Jackson and I are seeing each other."

"When you say seeing... Friends-with-benefits?"

Ko shook his head. "No. This is serious. Remember when I was dating Ivan and I told you the guy's good-looking but had no clue — that he didn't make me feel a spark and I thought it didn't exist?"

Stella nodded.

"With Jackson, all he has to do is look at me with those brown eyes and I'm on the brink of an orgasm."

"Dang..."

"I saw him model for Tasha before I hired her. I figured it was a great idea to watch him in action first, and from the moment our eyes met across that space, I knew I wanted him."

"Dang."

"Can you say something else?"

Stella laughed. "Listen, don't be your usual self. Don't be scared of this. I've been searching all my adult life for that thing and I haven't found it yet."

"No. For once in my life I'm ready. I'm really, truly ready to give myself to a man."

Stella smiled and lifted her glass in a toast. "To finding that something to make us want to orgasm with just one look."

"I can definitely drink to that," Ko admitted with a laugh. He took a sip from his water.

They got through lunch and the work they needed to and, long after Stella left him at the table, Ko remained where he was, ordering a dessert of caramel carrot cake and a cup of tea. He was halfway through the cake when a familiar face caught his attention.

"Kent!" Ko waved. "Hey."

"Ko Takao, as I live and breathe." Kent walked over with an extended hand. "How are you?"

"I'm good." Ko shook his hand. "You here for a business lunch?"

"No," Kent said, looking around for a moment. "Was supposed to be on a date but I think I've been stood up."

"I'm sorry, man," Ko told him. "Would you like to join me?"

Kent glanced around. "Well, sure."

When they were seated, Ko motioned for the waiter and after Kent placed his order and Ko asked for another tea, it dawned on him that he was sitting across from who he hoped to be his father-in-law. Ko smiled just as the nerves kicked him.

"I heard about you working with Jack," Kent said. "How's that going?"

"We don't start anything major until next year but he has a couple of shoots coming up for the teasers." Ko moved his mug out of Kent's arm's reach and cleared his throat. "I wanted to talk to you about something."

"All right."

"It's about Jackson and I…"

Kent nodded with a smile. It was almost as if he knew what Ko was going to say. "When Jackson came out to me I didn't handle it well. Hell, I almost lost him and my brother. But now, all I want is for him to be happy."

"So, you know?"

"That you're sleeping together?" Kent asked. "He didn't tell me, if that's what you're wondering. I gathered that from the way you said 'Jackson and I'. As long as my son is happy, Ko, I got no problem."

"Are you sure? Do you have any questions?"

"I'm sure. I've learned a long time ago that my son will find someone to be with sooner or later. I've had time to play around with the idea and I find it makes me lightheaded with happiness. Jackson means everything to me."

"I understand. I figured because of my age and…"

"Does Jackson have anything against how old you are?"

Ko shook his head.

"Then why should you? And better yet, why should I? I'm not the one sleeping with you."

Ko laughed. "Well said. I figured Jackson would be telling you sooner or later, but with my life and the media…"

Kent's meal arrived and they sat together in silence for a moment. The only sound in their immediate circle was Kent's fork periodically scratching his plate.

"I didn't plan it, you know?" Ko had been compelled to explain. "I mean, I met him years ago at that launch, you remember?"

"Yeah. That's when I met you, too."

"And then I saw him again and— I don't know."

"These things…"

"Sorry to bother you, Ko…"

Both Ko and Kent glanced up. Stella was back and she seemed flustered.

"Stel? What's the matter?" Ko asked.

"My car won't start," she told him. "I don't know what is happening, especially since I just had the dumb thing serviced. I called the tow truck, but you know how busy they claim to be."

"I will—" Ko began.

"Let me take a look," Kent said, rising before Ko could. "My brother and I took a few courses and I know a thing or two about cars."

"Could you?" Stella asked, smiling brightly. "If you don't mind, that is."

"Not at all…"

Both of them hurried off as if Ko didn't even exist. He laughed and leaned back in his chair. He figured he'd wait a little while, give Stella some time to figure out a way to get Kent on a date, then head out to make sure the two of them were good.

But Ko didn't have to go outside, because soon Kent returned, wiping his fingers on a piece of paper towel.

"I got her running," Kent said, sitting. "She should take it to her mechanic because it sounded a little hinky. The engine, that is."

Ko nodded. "So, when's your dinner?"

Kent laughed. "Tomorrow night. It's just a thank you for helping her out."

"Right." Ko sipped from his tea. "I saw the way you two looked at each other. Don't get nervous. Stella is a fantastic person. She's been dating again, trying to find Mr. Right, and so far, she hasn't had much luck."

"Men are dumb."

Ko laughed. "I can't disagree with you there."

They finished lunch and Ko headed across town to Stark where he knew he'd find Jackson. A secretary showed him to Jackson's office and he knocked on the door.

"Come in."

Ko let himself into the room and closed the door behind him. For a moment, he simply stood before the desk, watching Jackson type furiously away at his keyboard. "Hey, baby."

"Ko!" Jackson flew around the desk to hug him tightly. The two kissed, their tongues swirling around each other's. "We should stop. My office is not soundproof like yours."

Ko moaned. "More's the pity. But all right. I have something to tell you."

"Okay."

"I just had lunch with your dad."

"I thought you were eating with Stella."

"I did. Then she had to leave and I stayed behind to have a piece of cake," Ko explained. "Your dad was there…"

"Right—his date! I forgot about that. I wonder how it went."

"You didn't hear it from me, but his date didn't show up. But we got to talking and one thing led to another and I told him about us."

"Ko, you shouldn't have done that."

"I know and I didn't plan it that way. Why are you upset? I thought you'd be happy he knew."

Jackson cradled Ko's cheeks. "I am happy he knows. I just wanted it to come from me, you know?"

"Yeah."

Jackson kissed him once, then twice. "So how did he take it?"

"Surprisingly well. All I had to say was 'Jackson and I' and he smiled. I tell you, it took a weight off my shoulders because I was prepared to fight with him, to prove to him that even if I don't deserve you now, one day I will."

"What makes you think you don't?"

Ko shrugged. "I don't know."

"Don't you start getting cold feet on me now…"

"I won't. I promise." Ko walked to the window and looked out. There was a partial view of the mountains on one side and the city on the next. "Once your launch is over and the shoot for the teasers are out… Can I interest you in, maybe, a weekend away with me?"

"Is that a trick question?"

Ko laughed. "No trick. I would like to have you all to myself, helpless in my bed."

"Ko…" Jackson moaned and approached him. "The answer is yes."

"Yes to going away or yes to being helpless in my bed?"

"All of it." Jackson tangled his arms about Ko's neck. "The answer will always be yes."

Epilogue

The snow was cool under his back. The temperature had long since dipped and the mountains around Bathsheba became covered in snow. Suddenly the town was full of strange faces and accents. Usually, Jackson enjoyed the vibrant chaos the time of year brought but now, as he lay, staring up into the partly cloudy sky, in the peace of the backyard at Ko's cabin, he wondered how he could go back to being that person. He squinted, trying to see as far as he could, imagining the clouds changing shapes and becoming things from his childhood. But all he saw was Ko.

He closed his eyes and smiled. That wasn't a bad image at all.

"You're going to get sick." Ko's voice was soft from behind him.

But even as his lover said those words, Jackson could hear him grunting to lie beside him. Ko held on to Jackson's gloved hand and squeezed affectionately.

"How long have we been dating now?" Ko asked.

Jackson didn't open his eyes. He was enjoying Ko's hand in his too much. "Eight months next Tuesday."

"Only eight months?" Ko asked. "Wow, I thought it was longer."

"Is that a good thing or a bad thing?"

"A very good thing. They say time flies when you're having fun."

"It hasn't been easy—especially with the campaign and everything that comes with that."

Ko sighed loudly. "And your work with *Together We Fight*."

"I've been meaning to thank you for what you did for me with that." Jackson sat up and turned to face Ko. "You were there and tolerated some late nights…"

"I told you. It was my pleasure. I saw how much you enjoy your work and I never want to be the person to take that away from you."

Jackson licked his lips and leaned closer. "Why? I mean, we didn't have sex for, like, two months. That couldn't have been easy for you."

"No." Ko shifted as if to get more comfortable before speaking again. "It wasn't. But that's what you do when you love someone. I know you weren't shutting me out."

"Some men would have been angry, gone off and cheated…"

"How do you know I haven't?"

That question caught Jackson off guard. He licked his lips again. The cold air seemed to be making them drier than he would have liked. Swallowing the lump in his throat, he gave a one-shoulder shrug. "Because we may have been dating eight months, but I know you very well. Besides, I don't think you could look at me the way you do then go and give yourself to another man."

"And how do I look at you?"

Jacksons stared down into Ko's eyes, searching for the answer in them. Finally, he smiled. "Like you're doing right now. Like you love me more than there are stars in the sky."

A smile traced Ko's lips and that sent a twinkle through Ko's eyes. "I do love you more than there are stars in the sky."

Jackson's heart soared higher than the mountains that overlooked the cabin. "You've never said anything before."

"No." Ko turned his gaze away and focused on the sky. "You're young, Jackson. I didn't think you wanted to hear those words coming from me. Not yet, anyway."

"Then what do you think I'm doing here?" Jackson snapped. "Biding my time?"

"Jack…"

Ko reached for him but he shoved away the hand.

"No." Jackson exhaled. "Why else do you think I've been so careful in the last month, to give you everything, to make sure you're happy?"

"Jackson, don't be mad. I didn't think you were biding your time. I just thought…"

"What?"

"That you needed more time to pass before I tie you down with these strong feelings raging inside me. I mean, telling someone you love them is heavy and I don't take it lightly."

"So, you carried all that alone?" Jackson asked, still upset, just not as he was a second ago. "Ko, seriously."

Ko cradled his face and sat up for a kiss. "I'm new to this, *koibito*."

"Damn you. You know I melt when you call me that!"

"So I'm closer to being forgiven?"

Jackson crinkled his nose. "Yeah. I'm here, Ko. Here for as long as you want me."

"And what if I want you here forever—beside me. Because one day I will fall to one knee and—"

"The answer will be yes."

"You don't know that." Ko shook his head.

"Yes, I do. It will always be yes."

He kissed Ko again, this time a long, lingering kiss that made Jackson sigh. He rose and took Ko's hand. "Come on. I can't feel my butt."

"I can help you get the feeling back."

"I bet you can." Jackson giggled.

Ko laughed as the two of them trudged through the snow and in through the back door of the cabin. Even with Charlie, Jackson had never had that warmth by a simple thing as holding hands. He'd never had that spark with another man. As they stripped out of their winter clothes, Jackson stopped to watch Ko's body come to life and he couldn't help smiling. He allowed his gaze to travel up Ko's frame, to his beautiful mouth, over his nose and to his eyes.

Yes, Jackson Stark was in love. There was no way around it. He didn't even want to try denying it. He dumped his jacket and snow pants on the floor and rushed over to Ko. For a silent moment, he merely framed Ko's face with his palms and stared into his eyes.

"Baby?" Ko asked, concern filling his gaze.

"I love you," Jackson whispered.

Ko said nothing. He blinked.

"Did you hear me, Ko? I said I…"

Ko fused their lips together, drinking Jackson's words and sending fire through Jackson's veins. They kissed until Jackson tasted the saltiness of tears. At first, he thought they were his but when he lifted his head from their connection, he saw they belonged to Ko.

"Darling?" Jackson asked.

"You've made me happier than I think I should be right now."

Jackson used his thumbs to dry Ko's eyes. "I only hope I can keep doing that—making you happy."

"You will. Don't forget, I'm easy."

Jackson laughed. "I can see that."

They kissed again and Ko reached down to grab his stuff. "Let me hang these up so they can dry out."

"Okay. I'll get us some cider and start a fire?"

"Yes, please." Ko reached for Jackson's clothes, too, then stopped. "I love you."

Jackson beamed. Warmth spread through him like the sun rising on a new day. "I love you, too, Ko."

Ko left him in the kitchen and Jackson turned to the fridge. He poured some cider into a pot and set it on the stove. Ko didn't like the cider heated in the microwave. At first, Jackson didn't understand why then he tasted it and afterward, he was hooked. After turning the stove down to low, he hurried into the living room and hunched before the fireplace. As he removed the front panel and dropped wood in, he reached for a lighter to check the draft.

The sound of Ko whistling from the hall filled the space. Jackson smiled and finished lighting the fire. He set the front panel back in place and held both his palms toward the flames. He thought back to the moment he'd looked up from his photo shoot and had seen the infamous Ko Takao watching him. Primal urges had twisted his insides that day, ones that had scared him. That night, when he had gone home, he'd prayed—at first for forgiveness, then for clarity. But as he'd fallen heedlessly harder for the sexy businessman and designer, Jackson knew forgiveness hadn't been what he should have asked for.

As he stood by the fire, he said another prayer. This time, one of thanks. For as Ko whistled louder and more melodic, Jackson knew that was how their life would be. Sure, as Ko had said, it wouldn't be easy or perfect for everyone, but perfect for the two of them.

Jackson's heart danced. "I'm yours, Ko Takao. Yours..."

FALLEN INTO YOU

Dedication

To everyone who made my intoXication boys so loved
– Thank you.

Chapter One

Mathias Jago started his shadow kickboxing session with a side kick. That was after forty-five minutes on weights, twenty on the indoor track and another ten on the elliptical machine. Though he hadn't wanted to get out, it was a part of his everyday life. He had to keep his body in top shape if he wished to keep working as a stripper at the Thornless Rose. Sure, some guys let themselves go over the years and they couldn't be fired because of employment laws. As time went by, their bosses would begin pushing them out with trumped up reasons—the clients booed or refuse to request them for private sessions.

Those were the ones Mathias hated the most. He'd be stuck in a luxury room, shaking his ass for some in-the-closet pervert who had too much money and way too much time on his hands. Still, it was one of the cards he'd been dealt so he might as well play.

A roundhouse kick gave way to a few jabs followed by an axe kick. Mathias picked up rhythm. Pulling his mind from the depression over how his life had turned out, Mathias tossed himself into getting through the workout.

He imagined his opponent and went in for the kill. Uppercuts, knee and elbow strikes, and sweeping by dipping down to knock his imaginary opponent off his feet — all of it worked together, making Mathias sweat. By the time his routine was over, his T-shirt was soaked all the way through and perspiration slid down the center of his back.

That made Mathias smile as he paced for a few breaths before picking up his water bottle and towel and making his way to the change room. As he sat on the bench in front of his locker, he tilted his head back and squirted water into his mouth from the bottle. But it wasn't satisfying. Mathias loved when it was so cold, simply thinking about it gave him brain freeze. He frowned and snapped the lid back in place then chucked the bottle into his locker. The sooner he could get showered and dressed, the faster he could get out of there and find some that was cold.

Mathias took a quick shower, more to wash the stink off than anything else. He was on his way home anyway and would take a more detailed one there. He grabbed a fresh towel from a pile sitting close to the shower entrance, chucked his dirty one in a nearby bin and walked, naked, to his locker. There he dried himself and redressed in a pair of black track pants and a blue T-shirt. He hauled on a sweater over that and was just shoving his arms into the sleeves of his winter jacket when the door opened behind him.

"Matt!"

Mathias turned and extended a fist. "Hey, Collin. How's it going?"

"It's as cold as balls outside." Collin Mullings touched his fist to Mathias'. "Why do we live in a place where the wind hurts our faces?"

Mathias laughed and continued dressing. "I don't know, man. It's just the way it is. Coming in for your workout?"

"Yeah. I couldn't get out of bed this morning."

"Yeah. It's going around, man."

"Listen, Jackson Stark has a new game coming out soon. He's having a release party for people to test out the beta version of it. You want in?"

Mathias thought about that for a second then arched an eyebrow. "When?"

"Saturday — starts at ten in the evening."

"Sorry. Working that night." Mathias sighed. He rarely got to go out on a Saturday night anymore. "Let me know how that goes, okay? I just got through *Divided We Fall* and lord have mercy, that cat's got talent."

Collin nodded. The two hugged and Mathias pulled his bag from the locker and slammed it shut, making sure the lock clicked in place. Since he had a premium membership, he was assigned his own locker, which was nice. "I'll see you later."

"We need a night at some point."

"For sure. I don't seem to get time to do that kind of stuff anymore."

"You get vacation time from that place, don't you?"

"Eventually. But if I don't work, the bills go unpaid. I'll figure something out."

"Later, man."

Mathias left the gym feeling like the world was conspiring against him. But the thought was banished by the biting cold and the howling winter wind. He growled, tossed the strap of his bag across his body and pulled his hood up over his head. Once his head was as warm as it could be under the present circumstances, he shoved his fingers into his pockets and quickened his steps toward his car. When he was close enough, he hit the small remote and watched as the front lights on his SUV flashed. His engine roared to life and he frowned.

What's the point of having an automatic starter if you forget to use it?

The damn thing was programmed into his cell phone. He could have started the car while he was chitchatting with Collin!

"Ugh!"

Mathias hurried over, tossed his gym back into the back seat then made his way to the driver's side. It wasn't as warm as he would have liked but at least he could only hear the angry wind blowing and it wasn't slicing into his face anymore.

He knew he had to wait until the car warmed up so he played around on his phone, replying to emails and reading through others. Most were advertisements and so-called deals for supplements he knew were super bad for his body. He'd made the mistake of signing up for some newsletters at a fitness expo four years before and it was still haunting him.

Those he marked as spam and hoped they'd stop coming through to his inbox.

He checked Facebook, ignored the one hundred eighty-five friend requests he had. He'd stopped checking them. A few times he went through and deleted most of them but ten minutes later he'd log back in and the numbers would be high again. They were mostly from women and young gay men who'd either seen him at a show or heard from a friend of a friend that he was a stripper. He didn't know any of them.

With a sigh, he replied to a few comments on his status before logging out. Mathias turned on the defroster to ensure his windows cleared, then the heat. The warmth exploded from the small vents, making him moan. Then and only then did he pull on his seatbelt, shift the car into drive and ease from the parking spot.

* * * *

With his day off over, Mathias took a shower, grooming himself carefully, then dressed in a pair of track pants and a sweater. He gathered everything he'd need for the night and headed for his car. The traffic into the city was almost nonexistent so he took his time, taking in the snow-covered trees around him and even sneaking a peek of the snowy mountains. By the time he made it into the Thornless Rose, he was an hour and a half before call time. He bumped fists with security and let himself in through the back. Mathias didn't stop to speak to anyone. Instead he made a straight run for what he'd been using as his dressing room. It was the smallest of all of them but that meant he didn't have to share. He decorated it how he wanted, and could relax on an overstuffed chair he kept there until it was time for him to get dressed. Yet, he hadn't really felt the nervous excitement that would take him over the moment he closed the door behind him.

He exhaled and set about preparing. Once he was dressed in the suit he usually wore on stage, Mathias gave himself a final once over.

"Mathias!"

He turned and smiled. "Hey, Sergei, what's going on?" They bumped fists. "How's the house tonight?"

"Packed," Sergei the DJ said. "I don't know what's happening but I'm not going to complain."

"I hear that. You spinning tonight or is it Jason?"

"I am. Jason is off to Aruba with the fiancé, remember?"

Mathias had forgotten. In all honesty, Mathias had lost track of how many fiancés Jason Plumber had had. It seemed there was a new one every few months or so.

Jason was either the unluckiest man when it came to love or he was just a slut.

"I wanted to know what you were doing tonight."

"I didn't tell you my music again." Mathias sighed. "Old age. I'm sorry. Let's start with *Pony* then go into *First* by Somo and end with *Insatiable* by Darren Hayes."

"Nice." Sergei nodded, patted Mathias on his shoulder and headed back down the hall before stopping. "Oh, and Pat wanted me to let you know that you have a private dance tonight in the Midnight Room."

"Oh yeah? What time?"

"Eleven-thirty."

"Great, thanks," Mathias said. Once the DJ was gone and he was alone, Mathias sighed then frowned. He hadn't been expecting a private show that night. But, luckily, he always kept a few things in his to-go bag just in case.

It took a moment for Mathias to move. But eventually he wandered to the backstage area and into the chaos of other dancers waiting to be called on stage. Though he hated the noise and madness that came with such an environment, he'd forgotten his iPod in his dressing room and was too irritated with himself to go back for it.

Come on, Jago. Pull it together.

One by one, the dancers did their thing on stage and soon it was his turn. Mathias just wanted to go home and sleep. Strange, he wasn't into dancing that night. But the bills weren't going to stop coming if he had an off night.

"Gentlemen, are you ready to be wooed?" Sergei's voice boomed.

Cheers erupted from the other side of the curtains.

"Are you ready to be…catered to?" Sergei pushed.

Whistles were added to the applause and shouting.

"Give it up for the one, and only — The Gentleman!"

Like he usually did, Mathias turned on the charm. He approached the stage, fingers jammed deeply into his pockets. The audience fell silent, almost as if they hadn't been breathing. The moment he moved his head to the right, the venue was filled with shouts and cheers. During his routines, he tended to remain on the stage, but someone caught Mathias' eyes. He'd never seen the man before. The Thornless Rose was a pretty big and swanky place but he knew all the regulars. This man wasn't one of those. As a matter of fact, he seemed a little uncomfortable being there, front and center. He seemed Indian, tall with a mouth that Mathias would like to kiss.

Mathias made his way over to him, stood astride the man's lap and backed up until his ass hit a very hard chest.

Someone from behind the guest touched Mathias but he pushed the stranger's hand away and reached for the object of his dance's hand instead. He lifted it and placed it against his own thigh as he gyrated back on him.

As the dance progressed, Mathias felt the rise in the front of the man's pants. The stranger might not want to be there but Mathias knew he was doing something right. Catching himself, Mathias dropped a chaste kiss to the man's neck before returning to the stage. At the end of his routine, Mathias took his bow, and met the stranger's eyes before exiting.

Backstage, he checked the time. He had twenty minutes before he had to be in the Midnight Room for his private show. Rushing by the other dancers with a smile and a wave, he darted into his change room, grabbed his things and fled the other way down the hall to the showers. He scrubbed, dried his skin, then used unscented cream to moisturize. After dragging a brush through his hair, he wrapped a towel around his hips and returned to his dressing room to haul on his backup suit. Once he was sure he was presentable, with three minutes to spare, Mathias rushed to take position in the Midnight Room, waiting for his guest.

Chapter Two

Abhay didn't want to go to the damn Thornless Rose to begin with. His birthdays hadn't been a big deal ever since he had been a kid. Worse since he had come out of the closet—everyone went along as if he didn't exist, like every other day. Then he'd met the gang—Feng, Darius, Jackson, Thaddeus, Ravi and Ko. They all had conspired against him, even dragging their new friend, Dana, into it. It was with great reluctance that he wandered into the surprisingly fancy building with the beautiful decorations and a stage that reminded him of a concert auditorium. To his further shock, Ko and his fiancé, Jackson, had purchased a private dance for him.

"When was the last time you had a man that close?" Ko asked. "I mean *that* close?"

Abhay frowned. "I don't want a man *that* close!" He lifted his left hand to press his thumb and index fingers mere inches apart to stress his point. "It's not like men are knocking down my door or anything. So, I show them the same respect."

Jackson chuckled. "That's because you're always in business mode. Trust me on this one. You're a good-looking guy."

"Hey!" Ko growled.

"Down, lover," Jackson teased, wrapping his arms about Ko's neck.

Abhay's jealousy at that made him roll his eyes like an insolent child and he left the room. But he'd known getting those two to change their minds, especially when they were in cahoots with the Mastersons, was like bashing one's head into a brick wall.

"Are you ready for your present?" Thaddeus asked in his ear.

Abhay sighed. "I can't believe Ravi allows you to come to a place like this."

"Allows me?" Thaddeus scoffed. "Abi, Ravi and I are married, we don't own each other. And besides, Ravi trusts me. He knows that the men here might be sexy but he's the only one who has control of this body and this heart."

Abhay trembled. He'd always dreamed of a man who would look at him the way Thaddeus looked at Ravinder Raja-Masterson. It was as if there was no one else in the room when the two of them looked at each other across a space. They always had a kiss for each other, a smile, a hug, a soft caress—no matter how mad Thaddeus made Ravinder.

"Mr. Masterson," a man said. "I am here to escort you to the Midnight Room."

"Oh, the dance isn't for me," Thaddeus said with a grin, lifting his ring finger to show the man. "It's for the birthday boy here."

"Right!" the man said. "This way please."

Abhay inhaled and, with a final look at his friend, he followed the man's slender body down the hall, praying this wasn't the dancer. It wasn't that his leader wasn't good-looking — he had been. It was just, the man was too skinny, his suit looked too big for him and he had a nose only a mother could love. When the man stepped aside, Abhay entered the room and the door was closed behind him. The space was dimly lit, but smelled clean. The far wall was backlit white and was bright enough to expose a set of beautiful sofas. With his heart hammering inside his chest, Abhay made his way across the space, unbuttoned his jacket and sat heavily.

"Did you want to start with a drink?" a voice asked.

Abhay whirled around and noticed a man seated there. He'd been so still, Abhay had missed him. "Who are you?"

"Your entertainment for the evening."

"I want to see your face."

"Strange," the man said. "Most men don't want to know what I look like at all. They just want to see my ass."

"I'm not most men." Abhay rested his back into the seat and tilted his head. "And as much as I'm sure I'd love to see your ass, face first."

The man leaned forward and rose. Abhay guessed he was about six foot of muscle. He wasn't bulky muscular but rather sleek, perfect for a designer suit kind of muscular. As he neared, the man hunched down, his pants splaying over some well-defined thighs, Abhay recognized him. "What's your name?"

"The Gentleman."

"Your real name."

"Why is that important?"

Abhay sighed. "I'm Abhay Chetan."

"You've never done one of these before, have you?"

"Is it that obvious?"

The Gentleman smiled, a glorious look that sent shivers pulsing down Abhay's spine. It was the same heat Abhay had felt the moment The Gentleman had pressed up against him earlier. The dancer still smelled divine with a body that made Abhay want to open himself up again to being with someone. But the last time he'd had those dreams they'd crashed and burned.

"Well, Abhay," The Gentleman's voice pulled through his thoughts. "Telling you my name is against the rules."

"And who will know? We are alone in here, aren't we?"

"Yes. We are. But there are cameras."

"What if I said I don't want you to take your clothes off for me? I just want to talk to you."

"Then I'd tell you I'm not your therapist."

Abhay laughed. "Very well. If you don't want to talk and there are cameras in here then I suppose you'd better show me your ass — after you tell me your name."

Something flashed inside The Gentleman's eyes but Abhay could have been mistaken. After all, the room played tricks on one's mind in the dark. He watched, holding his breath as his performer rose again, this time to rest one knee on the sofa between Abhay's legs. He leaned in, smelling like cinnamon and fire. Abhay bit back a moan and forced his hands to remain pressed against the leather surface of the sofa.

"You can call me Matt," The Gentleman whispered into Abhay's ears. "Are you ready to begin?"

"Yes."

"Do you wish to take charge, or do I?"

"Um…" Abhay shook his head to clear it. "What?"

Matt breathed against the side of Abhay's face, before catching Abhay's ear between his teeth. "Some men love it when I'm rough with them. What's your poison?"

"Rough? Are we still talking about dancing?"

Matt laughed, a sexy, guttural sound that had Abhay tenting his pants.

"Stand," Abhay managed after a series of deep breaths. "When you begin, turn your back to me."

Matt did as Abhay instructed, his body swaying from side to side in rhythm to the soft music that was being pumped into the room. Abhay hadn't noticed it before. Matt had put him in a trance, made him blind, deaf and clueless to everything about his surroundings but the arch of Matt's back turning into his ass. Licking his lips, Abhay tried to sit still, to be passive so his arousal would go away, but Matt's suit hit the floor, followed by his shirt, and the tattoo spanning Matt's shoulders made the hardness worse.

"Turn around."

Once again Matt complied, and though Abhay knew the rules, he wanted to swipe his tongue over Matt's hard pink nipples. Abhay sat on his hands, eased into the material of the sofa and allowed his eyes to feast on Matt's body, down his perfectly sculpted abs to where Matt's belt sat unbuckled.

"Slowly," Abhay said. "Zipper down."

Matt's hips gyrated and his abs contracted then loosened. The zipper glided downward under a finger and Matt started easing the pants down his perfect thighs. When he stepped out of them, Abhay smiled. "Now turn around."

This time, he was left speechless. The jockstrap Matt wore left nothing to the imagination in the back. The dancer was perfect in every single way and there was no denying how Abhay felt in that moment. He chewed on his bottom lip. The urge to touch, to fall on his knees and crawl forward for a taste rose inside him like a storm brewing on the horizon. Maybe it was his years of being celibate. Maybe he was just so depraved that every naked man he saw churned this kind of raging wildness in him.

No, the other dancers had done nothing for him. And he hadn't been paying much attention while Matt had been on the stage. He'd been too busy trying to hide the arousal in the front of his pants from the little impromptu dirty dance Matt had given him.

"Damn."

"Does that mean you like what you see, Abhay?" Matt asked cheekily.

"You have no idea how hard it is not to touch you right now," Abhay admitted before he could stop himself. "I think you should get dressed."

"You're a grown man. You can control yourself."

"Yes and it's becoming increasingly difficult. I want you to take a look at what you've done."

Matt spun slowly and his eyes dipped to the front of Abhay's pants. Abhay trembled under his stare. His heart raced faster and harder as Matt looked at him.

"That means I did my job," Matt said.

"Please, get dressed."

Though he hesitated, Matt put his clothes back on and took a seat in the chair he had been sitting in earlier. Only this time, he scooted forward to rest his elbows on his knees and laced his fingers.

"I don't understand you," Matt said. "You came here to see naked men, didn't you?"

"I came here to shut my friends up," Abhay replied. "It's my birthday and they figured the best way to celebrate it is to be here."

"I see. What did you want to do for your birthday?"

"A nice dinner, maybe watch a movie then curl up in front of the fire with a glass of whiskey and a book."

Matt tossed his head back and laughed until he snorted. "Whiskey and a book in front of the fire? Do they even make men like you anymore?"

"Make men like me?"

"Every man I know would rather come to a place like this on their birthday. They want the party and the noise. Yet here you are wanting peace and quiet."

"What's wrong with peace and quiet?"

"Nothing." Matt leaned back. "Nothing is wrong with it. I just didn't think the life machine cranked out any more like you."

"I'm not sure if I should be offended or flattered."

"It's a compliment. Trust me. Are we done here?"

Abhay wanted to tell him they were far from finished. He wanted to tell Matt the only way they'd be finish was if Matt dropped to his knees and…

"Abhay?"

"Yeah? Sorry." Abhay nodded. "Yes, we're finished here."

Matt scooped up his tie from where it was on the floor and rose. "It was nice talking to you, Abhay. Happy birthday, even if it is after midnight."

"Thank you."

Matt headed for the door but stopped. "This might be none of my business, but don't go back into the closet. It's dark and lonely in there."

For a silent moment, Abhay stared at Matt, wondering why he would say that. It seemed Matt had seen through the worries inside Abhay's soul. That irritated Abhay, making him frown. "You're right. It isn't any of your business."

With that, Matt left him alone. The good news was his arousal was gone. The bad news was his mood had been altered so all he wanted to do now was go back to his condo, change and head down to the all-night gym to bash the stuffing out of something or someone...

He didn't care which.

Chapter Three

"Mr. Chetan?"

Abhay turned from the glass of his office and looked down at the phone on his desk. It was a miracle he could still see the oak underneath because the desk was piled high with paperwork and drafts of software he'd written out by hand. With a sigh, he reached across and pressed a button on the phone. "Yes, Beverly?"

"Mr. Raja-Masterson to see you, sir."

"Send him in."

Though he'd tried to get Beverly not to address him like that, she wouldn't hear of it. She was an older lady and it felt weird having her call him sir. Still, she was a career secretary and insisted formalities be adhered to at all times. When a knock came at his door, Abhay reached for his jacket. "Come in."

Ravinder Raja-Masterson entered and closed the door behind him. The smile on his face was refreshing and Abhay welcomed it. He hurried around his desk to hug his friend, a man who had saved both his and his sister Priya's lives a few years back.

"It's good to see you," Abhay said. "Your husband is the devil."

Ravinder laughed. "I heard about the Thornless Rose." He sat on one of the chairs in front of Abhay's desk. "Sorry. We had to think of something to get you out there. I mean, you haven't had a man in years."

"I know. It's not like I don't want one...look, enough about me, how was Italy?"

"Same old," Ravinder sighed. "I managed to get *Protello's* up and in the good graces of the public again. I don't know why it's so hard for people to be faithful to the person they chose."

"I supposed Antonio has learned his lesson," Abhay said. "Not every dark hole needs to be filled."

"Yeah. Some dark holes bite."

Abhay laughed. "Listen, Ravi. I wanted to talk to you about something."

"Sounds serious."

"Um..." Abhay fell into the second chair and twisted it against the wooden floor until he was facing his friend. "Do you think I'm in the closet?"

"Wow." Ravinder exhaled. "You, in the closet? Well, I don't think you're necessarily *in* the closet. I think you're just less experienced than most men your age."

"Less experienced. Why does that sound like another way of saying I'm a closet case?"

"I don't know, Abi. What's going on in that head of yours?"

"The dancer last night..."

"You know he's just a stripper, right?"

"No." Abhay rose and walked over to the window again. The view led to the mountains and he could see skiers and snowboards zipping along. "He's more than that—he has a brain in his head. When he danced for me I was so turned on, almost as if I was going to burst into flames."

"That was the point."

"You don't understand." Abhay turned to face him. "When I was watching all the other dancers, all I felt was bored to tears. Not tenting, no tingling, nothing. Then this man had me alone in a room, and the moment I was near him I…"

"You what?"

"Nothing. Forget I said anything." Abhay shrugged. "It's the blue balls talking."

"And the fact you haven't been with anyone in a while."

"You see, that's what scaring me now." Abhay approached Ravinder and sat on the edge of the desk. He folded his arms and met Ravinder's brown stare. "Last night I was telling him what to do and enjoying every second of it. I've only been with one man. And even then there was no emotion—no feelings. But as I went to bed last night I kept having this dream of holding him down and…I think I've waited too long and now my body…"

"Abi, there's no shame in liking what you like," Ravinder told him. "Rough, soft, loud, quiet—it's all about what turns you on."

"Do you let Thaddeus hold you down?"

Ravinder grinned and wiggled his eyebrows. "As often as possible."

"Really?" Abhay's cheeks heated. "And he likes that?"

"Depends on the day. Sometimes he likes it when I restrain him with his ties." Ravinder shrugged. "It's not always about only giving or only taking. What makes Thaddy and my relationship work is we give and take."

"Are we talking about sex or in general?"

"Both."

"Ravi—would you think any lesser of me if I wanted to see this man again?"

"No," Ravinder said. "But as your friend please don't begrudge me for saying this. He's a stripper. His job is to turn you on. Do not fall for this guy."

"Are you saying he's beneath me?"

"No. Not at all. What I am saying is be cautious. Find out what you're feeling first before you go after him. You need to go in knowing that sometimes you get what you pay for, other times you don't."

Abhay nodded. "This conversation..."

"Stays between us," Ravinder said. "I got your back, Abi. You should know that."

"But if Thaddeus asks..."

"He won't," Ravinder assured him. "No. I haven't seen you in a long time. Feng and I want to take you out for lunch."

"Feng? Where is he?"

"He will be meeting us at Clover in a few minutes," Ravinder said. "Come on, get the lead out."

Abhay laughed. "Wait...this isn't one of those days where I turn up and everyone is a couple except me, is it? I don't know if my soul can take one of those."

"No. It's a me, you and Feng having lunch and talking like old times. Now come on. Grab your shit and let's go!"

* * * *

The day ended and Abhay finally got the chance to sit in front of a fire with a book. But even as he tried reading, none of it was sinking in. His brain kept bringing him back to Matt. Matt's body, Matt's eyes, Matt's lips—Matt's ass. He slammed the book closed and grabbed his keys, phone and wallet. He exited the condo and descended into the underground parking for his car.

'He's a stripper. His job is to turn you on. Do not fall for this guy.'

But even as he sped through the center of Bathsheba, the night glowing around him and horns blaring, Ravinder's words and Matt's body were like a force inside his head. Both collided repeatedly, making him whimper at the pain it caused behind his eyes. Still, he pulled into the parking lot of the Thornless Rose, not even knowing if Matt was working that night. When he entered, the place still radiated elegance. Hell, if a person didn't know it was a strip club they'd just think it was a high-end bar.

Dumping his keys into his pocket, Abhay made his way over to the bar and leaned in to speak with the bartender. "How do I set up a private dance?"

"Talk to Pat," the bartender said, motioning to a woman sitting at a fancy table that was raised above the ground level.

Abhay nodded and made his way through suit-clad men until he could climb the steps to speak with the woman. "Hi there. I want to set up a private dance."

"Sure. Any particular dancer you had in mind?"

"The Gentleman."

"Oh yes. A crowd favorite. Let me see here — he is — oh wait, someone just canceled. He has a spot opened in half an hour in the Midnight Room."

"He is that popular?" The thought that other men were looking at Matt, possibly touching him, made Abhay angrier than he cared to admit.

'He's a stripper. His job is to turn you on. Do not fall for this guy.'

But Abhay was a little too far down the rabbit hole. Though he wasn't in love with Matt, he had to see him to get him out of his system. Hell, he didn't even know if Matt was The Gentleman's real name. After all, Matt did tell Abhay that he wasn't allowed to give his real name — hence the stage name.

"Yes," Pat replied, pulling Abhay's thoughts from the conversation he'd had with Ravinder earlier. "Tonight he doesn't go on stage at all. It's all private dances. One client tried booking him for the whole night. That's not allowed, of course."

"Of course."

"Okay, so for private time, the charge is two fifty an hour. Cash, debit or credit?"

Though it shocked him that it cost so much, Abhay didn't bat an eyelash. He pulled his credit card out and handed it to her. After she swiped it, checked his identification and handed his things back, she smiled. "We will have someone escort you to the Midnight Room when the time has come."

The fact that Abhay knew the route as if it were stamped to the inside of his eyelids didn't leave his lips. Instead, he nodded and said, "Thank you."

Abhay checked his watch. It was just about nine. He didn't care to see any other dancers on stage and he couldn't drink since he'd be driving home, so he went back to the parking lot to wait his turn with Matt.

Time dragged on. Perhaps because he was checking his watch every few seconds or so, but it felt like an eternity before it was almost time. He hurried back inside and was swiftly escorted to the same room he'd been in for his birthday. This time, he knew Matt was there. He expected him. When he entered, Matt smiled and tilted his head, a curious expression on his handsome face. His brown eyes flared with an unknown emotion and he pressed his lips into a thin line.

Abhay noticed the music playing in the room.

"You're back," Matt said. "Do you want to talk or watch?"

"I thought you weren't my therapist." Abhay took a seat in the same sofa. This time, he stretched his feet out before him and relaxed.

"I'm not. But you are a talker, Abhay. This is all on your dime. Whatever you want us to do, we'll do."

"You make it sound like if I wanted…"

Matt laughed. "Except that. Chris Rock was right when he said that there's—"

"No sex in the champagne room—got it."

"You know your pop culture. I'm impressed." Matt eased forward and rested his elbows on his knees, using his palms to prop up his head. "So, do you want to talk, Abhay?"

"Not tonight." Abhay chewed on his bottom lip for a silent breath as he allowed his eyes to drink in the perfection that was Matt's face. "Dance for me."

Mathias rose slowly and walked to stand in front of Abhay. He had to admit, Abhay was one fine-looking man. With thick black hair that fell into his face when he laughed, to perfect white teeth and thick lips to flank them. He had a nice body too. Mathias could tell by the way his Hansamu-designed jacket draped over his wide shoulders and fell on his body. For more than just a second, Mathias found himself wondering if Abhay had hair on his chest. He wondered if it would feel good sliding across his nipples.

Clearing his throat, Mathias dragged a hand down Abhay's chest as he noted that Abhay was a bit taller.

That was always a plus and every time he smiled, something gripped Mathias' groin and held on tight.

Forcing his arousal away, he started by swaying his body from side to side. This dance was different, even as he undid the buttons on his vest and loosened his tie—Mathias knew that. Each time he looked up it was to see that Abhay was watching him almost like a predator. The slow heat in the man's eyes, the tense way he set his jaws and pressed his lips into a determined line—all of it told Mathias that tonight was different from the last time he'd seen Abhay.

The first time, his client had been talkative, demanding he remove his clothes, ordering Mathias to turn around then caressing Mathias with his dark brown eyes. That had been imprinted onto Mathias' mind, leaving him wondering what could have been, leaving him aroused. It was just as hot though Abhay said nothing, nor did he move in an attempt to touch Mathias. That disappointed him, even with the cameras set up to ensure the clients didn't get handsy. He wondered about Abhay's touch—was he rough or did he use the tips of his fingers to caress his lover?

When he met Abhay's eyes, a fire raged inside them. It was almost hotter, having Abhay watching him like that.

When he turned his back to Abhay, the seat creaked beneath the man's body and he glanced over his shoulder to see Abhay was sitting in the same position he had been earlier. There was a slight tent in the front of his pants. Mathias wished he could help Abhay with that, just fall to his knees and…

"Stop."

Mathias paused and turned to face Abhay.

"I have to go," Abhay said.

"Abhay, you paid for two hours," Mathias said. "It's barely been half an hour."

"I know." Abhay bowed his head. "I really have to go."

Abhay rose and was charging past Mathias but Mathias reached out and grabbed his arm.

"Tell me what's wrong," Mathias said. "Let me repay you for the time…"

"You're not my therapist, Matt…"

"Mathias."

Abhay blinked at him. "Mathias. I will see you soon."

With that, Abhay yanked his arm away and barged out of the door. Mathias watched after him, wondering what could have happened. Sure, he knew Abhay was turned on, but that was nothing to be ashamed of. He gathered the few pieces of clothing he'd removed and shoved into them before making his way into the main area. No matter how long he looked, he knew he wouldn't see Abhay. Mathias even checked the parking lot, though he had no idea what kind of vehicle Abhay drove. There was something in Abhay's eyes that Mathias knew very well. It was fear and he couldn't understand it.

* * * *

Two days later, when he sat around with Collin, holding a beer, Mathias was still perplexed.

"So he just told you to stop and left?" Collin asked.

"Yup." Mathias took a long drink from his bottle and set it back on the table. "I've never had that happen before."

"Well, isn't your motto to not get involved with a client?" Collin asked. "Don't think so much into it. You probably won't see him again."

"I don't know how I feel about that."

Collin scratched his chin and leaned back in his seat. "Matt, what is it about this cat that makes you so concerned? It's obvious he's still in the closet."

"He might not be gay."

"Um — why would his friends bring him to a gay strip club if he wasn't?"

Mathias drank some beer and shrugged. He didn't have an answer to that so he said nothing. Their evening ended and he wandered home. After a quick shower, he dropped a load of laundry into the machine then sat back with beer to search the internet for Abhay. It seemed Mr. Chetan was a big deal in the computer software world. He was in the process of helping Jackson Stark with his new game as well as working for a major company on internet security. In that moment, Mathias knew he could never attract a man like Abhay Chetan. Sure, his body may be something Abhay would want, but Mathias had nothing otherwise.

First of all, Mathias wasn't remotely good at anything except dancing. He'd been on the path to becoming an actual dancer but that hadn't been derailed with his mounting bills and a need to not be homeless. There was no room for being a starving artist. He'd tried regular jobs, from bartending to security guard, but he was horrible at all of them. Stripping was the only thing he seemed good at, but for a man like Abhay Chetan he'd walk away from that life in a heartbeat.

Mathias sighed, closed the laptop and climbed the stairs to his bedroom. He flipped on the bedside lamp. With his back against the headboard, he turned on the television and with it on mute, he continued sipping on his beer. No need crying over spilled milk…

'Not tonight. Dance for me.'

There had been a chance in Abhay that night. He'd seemed stronger at first, more in control. Then something had happened and Abhay was running out of the Midnight Room as if Mathias had suggested they go to Vegas and elope then have two point five kids. Mathias sighed. Maybe Collin was right — he should let it go.

After draining his bottle, he set it on the bedside table and shifted down so he was lying on his back. Just before drifting off to sleep, a thought swam through Mathias' mind.

Did Abhay mean what he said when he said 'see you soon'?

Chapter Four

A week passed and though Abhay could focus on work, whenever he made it home, his mind was still on Mathias. He was also stuck on what Ravinder had told him about not falling. He didn't see it as *falling*, just attracted. There was a difference — right?

For the most part he was able to hide it from the guys, but not from Priya. Even over the phone she could tell something was wrong. Though he'd managed to evade the question, Abhay knew there would be a day when Priya returned from her job in the Turks and Caicos before heading to Paris for a little while. Hopefully, he wouldn't have to face her until after that.

He wasn't in love with Mathias — Abhay lusted after him. It was the kind of carnal hunger that kept Abhay up at nights — that made him stand in the shower and touch himself with the sway of Mathias' perfect frame inside his head. Slipping into his jacket, Abhay let himself out of his home and trudged through the snow to his car. The engine had been running due to the automatic starter. The last thing he wanted to do after a long week was go to a pub and sit around shooting the breeze with married couples. *But what excuse would he give?*

The cold air soaked through the exposed skin of his face instantly. During this time of the year, he missed India. The heat was maddening but he'd become used to it. Though he'd been in Bathsheba and numerous countries since Ravinder and Thaddeus had saved him and Priya, Abhay was still not used to the cold.

Disgruntled, he climbed behind the wheel and slammed the door, slipped on his seatbelt and turned the car toward the center of town. By the time he walked into Sliver's his mood had improved with the ride and the music blasting so loud, he thought his brain would explode. Still, he unzipped his coat the moment he stepped through the door. Ko was the first to see him and a big grin spanned the Japanese designer's face. That caused his fiancé, Jackson, to turn and the dominoes began falling. At the table, each man rose to hug him as well as Dana Salazaar, a trans dancer Jackson had met at one audition or another. She was a new addition to the team, one they all welcomed with open arms and hearts because she was such a happy person. Though she was Jackson's friend, Abhay was the closest to her.

"Thought you were going to cancel," Dana said, shoving a French fry into her mouth. "It's freezing outside."

"I thought about it." Abhay hooked his coat on the back of his chair and fell into it. The server hurried over to take his drink order and was off again. "I've been having one of those weeks."

"Tell me about it," Jackson said. "I think, I'm not sure, but I think I sprained a toe."

"I keep telling him to see a doctor but will he listen?" Ko bounced Jackson with his shoulder. "Of course not."

"I told you, don't be too proud to toss him over your shoulder and drag his ass to the doctor." Thaddeus lifted his beer to his lips. "It's for his own good and he can spank you later."

The group erupted in laughter. Even Abhay had to give a chuckle at that as his drink arrived. He ignored it and delved into the conversations around him. Food came, was eaten, plates were cleared and still he found himself engrossed in his friends. Back in India, he'd never thought his life would be anything like this. After being disowned by his family and later managing to get Priya disowned too because he just couldn't turn his back on her, Abhay thought he'd cursed his sister to a life of pain and misery. Now, Priya was on her way to finishing her business degree and was modeling for some of the biggest names out there.

"When I moved here," Dana was saying, "I was a fish out of water. Let's be honest, I was scared to show anyone who I really am. But you guys..." She choked up and Abhay reached over to rub her back since she was closest to him. "You guys embraced me — as corny as this might sound, family isn't just the blood that runs through your veins. Family are those who choose you."

"And we choose you!" Darius said.

The others agreed wholeheartedly.

"To family." Abhay lifted his drink.

"To family!" they chorused.

The night ended, and since Dana didn't have a car, Abhay agreed to give her a ride home. It was freezing and her taking a taxi with some stranger didn't sit well with him. As he settled in for the drive he turned on the heat and was thankful it had warmed up while the car was running in the parking lot.

"You okay?" Dana asked.

"Yeah." He glanced at her. "Why wouldn't I be?"

"Usually, you're the most talkative one of the bunch. Tonight, you barely said anything."

"I just have a lot on my mind, that's all," Abhay said. "I've been thinking of settling down in Bathsheba — rather than contract myself out to companies around the globe."

"Why the sudden change?"

Abhay shrugged. "It's not really sudden. But I look around and everyone is pairing up, everyone is getting married and I wonder why I can't find someone. Then it hit me — you know how they say if you get lost in the woods to stay put and let someone find you?"

"But you're not lost in the woods."

"It feels like it." Abhay stopped at a sign, checked the street then pulled through the intersection.

"And another thing." Dana shifted. "I didn't know you were looking."

"I'm not. I mean, not really." He sighed. "This stays between us, right?"

"Of course."

"I don't want to die alone."

She reached across and caressed his hand on the steering wheel. "You won't die alone. I won't let you. Even if I have to set you up with someone myself."

Abhay chuckled. "I've met your friends from the studio, remember?"

"Oh right — you want a man who can spank you one minute then spin you like a basketball the next — understood."

He blushed. "I just want someone who will love me. I think I'd be satisfied with sleeping in different beds as long as he loved me."

"So you're looking for Prince Charming," Dana said.

"Oh, screw Prince Charming! I want the dragon."

Dana giggled. "Yup. Why is it that the quiet ones are always the freaks in bed?"

"I'm not a freak!" But even as the words left his lips, he remembered the primal urges that had slammed through him watching Mathias dance on stage and in the Midnight Room. He remembered wanting to hold Mathias against the glass wall while he crashed into him from behind, not caring who walked by and saw or stopped to watch. "At least... No, I'm not a freak."

"Whatever, man. There's no shame in it. Now, vanilla sex with a body like yours? That's a shame."

"Focus, Dee. Focus!"

"I am... Is this because your birthday just passed?" Dana asked. "I mean, you're still too young to be going through a midlife crisis, but with all the pollutants in the air and..."

"Oh gawd." Abhay groaned.

Dana sighed. "Seriously, then. Sorry I missed your big night, by the way. But that video was a once in a lifetime opportunity and to be the first openly trans woman in a video of such a big artist—huge A!"

"No need to be sorry, sweetie. I understand. I have to get it together. I'm sure you knew something was wrong so the others did too."

"I wouldn't worry about them."

Abhay pulled up before Dana's apartment building and eased the car into park but didn't turn off the ignition. "Here we are, m'lady."

Dana giggled. "You wanna know something?" she asked, her voice sober.

"What?"

"You were the first person to address me as a female," Dana said. "Everyone else looked at me and still said *he*. That's when I realized in our next life, you'll be mine."

Abhay leaned in and kissed the side of her head. "You are who you are, Dana. You're a beautiful, smart, talented *woman*. And don't let anyone diminish your self-worth because of their closed mindedness. Promise me."

She beamed at him. "I promise."

"Good. Now, are you going to be okay going in?"

"Yes, Abhay. I'm a big girl. I got this."

Abhay laughed then leaned across to drop a kiss to her cheek. "Thanks for coming out tonight, Dee. Sweet dreams of me tonight."

Dana winked at him and pushed from the car. Abhay watched as she hurried across the small space and into the three-floor walkup. He wondered how she could wear such a skimpy dress in the weather they were having, but women were strong. After leaving the apartment he headed home but didn't stay there. Instead, he changed into a pair of sweatpants, a T-shirt that said *I run this* on the front and grabbed his gym bag.

His mind was full again — overflowing with the need to put down some roots, to be loved, to stay put in the forest of life so Mr. Right could find him.

* * * *

Gripping both ends of the rope, Mathias bent his knees, straightened his back and started flapping them up and down, one after the other in quick succession. Sweat poured down his body as he heated and he gritted his teeth. He counted down in his head and though his arms were tired, his legs strained, he pushed through till the end then dropped the ropes. The final stage was a repeat of the burpees. He fell into a push-up before springing into a squat only to push to his feet and reach for the ceiling. His body ached, pulsed, burned — all the wonderful indicators that he was doing a good job. His body had to be in good shape, not just for his work but to remain healthy.

When the set was finished, he paced one way, then the next in order to give his feet some time to get used to the stop in activity. After about a minute, he stopped moving completely. His shoulders still rose and fell but he turned toward the clean towels and grabbed one. As he swiped it over his face then against the back of his neck, he turned and his eyes fell on a familiar face. His breath caught in his throat and he debated if he should go over and say hello to Abhay or stay out of the man's personal life. Then again, he had been worried about Abhay from the way he had all but —

Good lord!

Abhay dipped into a squat, his sweatpants pressing to him and accentuating an ass that threatened to make Mathias choke on air. Unable to stop himself, Mathias strung his towel around his neck and made his way over. He leaned against the mirrored wall and watched until Abhay was finished with his squats before he spoke. "Hello."

"Mathias?" Abhay panted. "I didn't know you came here."

"I have to stay in shape somehow," Mathias said. "I eat way too much chocolate bars."

Abhay smiled.

"I didn't know if I should say hi," Mathias said. "But I wanted to see how you were feeling after...well...you know?"

"Yeah. I'm sorry about that." Abhay reached for a towel and brought it over his face. "I'm not usually such a jackass."

Mathias laughed. "A jackass? I wouldn't say that. Most men aren't comfortable with a place like the Thornless Rose—even if they walk in under their own steam. There's no need to apologize for that."

Abhay glanced over his shoulder then met Mathias' eyes again. "I promise, I'm not usually like that. I just—can I be honest?" He lowered his voice.

"Sure. We're the..." Mathias glanced around. "We're alone."

"It was a little—I mean you were—you turned me on and I felt a little guilty about that."

Mathias tilted his head. Never since he'd been a stripper had a man felt guilty for staring at him as he gyrated on a stage or in one of the private rooms. They would try touching him or propositioning him but none were like Abhay.

"Guilty?"

"You sound surprised." Abhay walked to where his water bottle sat and picked it up. As he unscrewed the cap, he looked rather thoughtful.

"I am." Mathias stood across from him. "Honestly."

"Why?"

"Abhay, men don't usually feel bad for watching me at the Rose. They try touching, or getting me in their beds—but never anything like this. It's not a bad thing. I guess I'm not used to men seeing me as anything than a piece of ass, you know?"

Abhay nodded and drank from the bottle. He recapped it and set it against the ledge on the wall. Once he had his arms crossed and his back pressed into the wall, he licked his lips. "Mathias, you're a good-looking man. Of course they'd want to touch or get you into their beds."

"You think I'm sexy?"

"I said good-looking and that's not the point."

Mathias laughed. "You haven't tried."

"It's not like I didn't want to. Or still do. Trust me. That's one of the reasons I left so abruptly the other night. I didn't want to cross that line. I don't want to be one of *those* men."

Mathias took a step closer. "What if I want you to be one of those men?"

"Do you enjoy these men touching you without permission then?"

"No." Mathias eased closer. "I've never enjoyed it before. But with you—somehow it feels different... Shit, and that sounds like a line."

"And you wouldn't be angry if I did?"

Mathias smiled. "Well, Mr. Chetan—there is only one way to find out, isn't there..."

"Abhay!" A voice called from behind them.

Mathias wanted to scream. He was that close to feeling Abhay's lips on his, to taste this perfect specimen of a man's mouth. Still, he backed up and smiled at Abhay, who was waving. He turned to see who'd been so damn rude as to interrupt. A Japanese male, one Mathias recognized as Ko Takao—the mastermind behind the Hansamu clothing line. Though the Japanese man was as sexy as sin, Mathias still wanted to strangle him.

"Hey, Ko," Abhay said.

"Who's your friend?" Ko asked.

Abhay smiled. "Ko Takao, Mathias. Mathias, Ko."

The two shook hands but Mathias excused himself. Instead of going back to his workout, he watched the two men talk for a while. With a sigh, he headed into the change room but skipped a shower. He dressed, emptied his locker and exited the building through the back door, toward his car.

Chapter Five

Another two days passed and Mathias figured he'd been wrong about Abhay and the moment they'd had at the gym. He couldn't expect Abhay to want anything to do with him. Each night he took the stage, he would take in the faces of the audience, hoping to find Abhay looking at him, watching as intently as he had that night. Every private dance had him running to the room but the disappointment he felt when Abhay wouldn't be his client worried him.

He finished the second night and packed up. He said goodnight to Pat and the others still hanging around the Thornless Rose. When he stepped through the doors into the cold night air, he pulled the neck of his coat together. He'd forgotten his scarf at home and was paying for it as he all but jogged across the lot.

"Mathias."

He stopped. Mathias didn't have to turn to know who had called him. The accent, the soft gasp at the end of the word *Mathias* told him Abhay was there and trying hard not to show his excitement. He counted to ten in his head and spun on his heels. "Abhay."

"I'm not stalking you, I promise," Abhay said, stepping closer.

"Why didn't you come inside?" Mathias said. "It's freezing out here."

"I didn't want to see people," Abhay said. "I only wanted — speaking of cold — can I treat you to a cup of coffee?"

"Are you asking me out, Abhay?"

Abhay smiled, his brown eyes twinkling in the moonlight. "And if I was, would you say yes?"

"Ask me again."

"Mathias, would you have a cup of coffee with me?"

"Yes."

Abhay laughed and nodded. "Okay. Follow me to Sliver's?"

"Sure."

Mathias said nothing else. He managed to keep his smile at bay until he was in the privacy of his own car. He waited until a silver sports car pulled up to his and Abhay pushed his head out of the window. "Ready?" Mathias asked.

Abhay nodded.

On the way to Sliver's, Mathias squirted on some cologne and dragged a brush through his hair. By the time he arrived and parked beside Abhay, he was nervous. Strange, because he'd never felt that way going out with anyone else. And this was just a cup of coffee — not an official date. But he couldn't stop the pounding of his heart. Forcing himself to pay attention, he inhaled and thanked Abhay, who opened his door for him.

"What a gentleman," Mathias teased.

"On the outside, yes," Abhay wiggled his brows. "Come on. It's warmer inside."

Now there's a side of Abhay Chetan I want to explore more.

Instead of voicing what was in his head, Mathias stepped into the warmth of the popular pub slash diner. It was nice yet low key enough to accept anyone—suit or jeans. They found a table in a corner booth and Mathias peeled himself out of his coat. After hanging it on the hook beside their booth and waiting for Abhay to do the same, Mathias fell into the leather and rubbed his frozen hands together while blowing on his fingers.

"I'm not a fan of winter," Mathias admitted. "Well, when I'm outside, that is. If I'm inside, let it snow, baby."

Abhay grinned. "The first time I saw snow was just a few years ago."

"Oh?"

The server arrived for their orders and Mathias frowned at the interruption. He ordered a hot chocolate with his cheeseburger and fries after Abhay ordered a poutine with a hot chocolate and finally they were alone once more.

"So, tell me the reason you hadn't seen snow until a few years ago."

Abhay watched him, his dark eyes intense and unsure. "I was born in India," Abhay said, his voice soft. "Lived there all my life with my parents and things were great. Then I came out…"

"Yeah. Say no more." Mathias sighed. "I'm sorry it was hard for you. I'm still not sure why coming out as gay is such a hassle. I never had to come out to anyone. My father took off the moment he found out my mom was pregnant and my mother—well, she died when I was eight."

"I'm sorry."

"It's okay. It's been a while."

Their hot chocolate arrived, whipped cream, chocolate dusting and all. Mathias grinned as he stared into it. "The one good memory I had when I was little was saving the whole week. On Friday, I would take the little I'd saved and I'd run all the way from school to this small diner at the corner close to the group home. I would order a cinnamon bun and hot chocolate. It was served just like this."

"That's a nice memory."

Mathias met Abhay's eyes and nodded. "It is. Anyway—" He lifted his mug. "To new friendships."

"I can drink to that."

After touching his glass to Abhay's, Mathias took a sip from the mug and moaned. It tasted just like Maggie would make when he was a child.

"Um…" Abhay said.

"Yeah?"

Abhay shifted in his seat. The twitch of his lips curled into a smile that was so damn handsome, Mathias grew hard. His cock forced against the material of his pants.

"You, um…" Abhay stopped speaking and leaned forward. He braced his large palms to the table and drew closer and closer.

Mathias' heart betrayed him. It raced inside his chest as if it wanted to escape. There was a strange excitement that pulsed through him, wanting what was coming, hoping Abhay wished to kiss him yet knowing if that happened he would implode.

Then their mouths collided. Mathias didn't hesitate. He parted his lips, giving Abhay access. Their tongues swirled about each other—twisting and tasting. Mathias moaned and grabbed a fist full of the front of Abhay's shirt. He couldn't allow this connection to be over too fast. He wanted to be wrapped around Abhay, to be consumed by him.

A throat cleared near them and Mathias released Abhay and fell back into the seat. Though his head spun, and his cock throbbed, Mathias found a smile and offered it to the waitress even though all he wanted to do was strangle her.

With their food settled before them and alone again, Mathias shoved a fry into his mouth.

"You had some whipped cream on your lips," Abhay said. He even had the nerve to look bashful about it.

"So you kissed me?"

"Do you want me to apologize?"

"No," Mathias said, picking up another French fry. "Can I be honest?"

"Sure."

"I've wanted you to kiss me since that first night you sat in front of the stage," Mathias admitted. "But I figured one of the guys you were with was your man."

"No. They're all either married or engaged to be. I'm the only one left in my group of friends who are still single—well, aside from Dana."

"You're a good-looking man, Abhay. And from the car you drive I'd say you have a job and you're not homeless…so why are you still single?"

"Fear."

"From your coming out?"

Abhay chewed but nodded. He chuckled. "This is insane. I barely know you yet I'm telling you all my secrets."

"What can I say—I have the face of a siren."

Abhay laughed out loud. As the sound of his mirth floated around him, Mathias realized he could get used to hearing it. He kept that to himself.

"I just feel comfortable around you."

"Look," Mathias said. "Is this going to be one of those things where you play hide the stripper whenever your friends are around?"

"Hide the stripper? I don't understand."

"Men like you don't want to date men like me." Mathias wiped his mouth with a napkin and dropped it beside his plate. "You want lawyers and doctors and bankers —"

Abhay said nothing.

"Fine. We're having a meal and hanging out," Mathias said. "That's all this is and I'm cool with that. But then you kissed me and — right. I had something on my face."

"Mathias. Breathe."

"I *am* breathing. Let's talk about something else. Please? Or I'm going to say something I'll regret. So, what do you do for a living?"

"Computers, software mostly."

"In other words, you're a nerd."

Abhay chuckled. "Sure. I love what I do though."

"I used to love what I do. Now it's just a way of paying the bills." He took another sip from his hot chocolate. "I can't see myself wearing a suit and tie, sitting in an office dealing with people. I'm not remotely good at anything."

"That can't be true." Abhay pushed the last bit of cheese from his poutine into his mouth and chewed in contemplation. "There has to be something you're good at. I mean, sure, you're very good at what you do now. But what are you going to do when you're older?"

"Hopefully, I'll have some money saved up to not have to worry about it."

Abhay nodded. "Listen, I'm the last person to pass judgment on what you do for a living. You're not ripping anyone off or serving kids with drugs so that's fine with me."

"You say that now. None of the men I've been attracted to before wanted the stripper for real—I mean, they wanted to sleep with me and get private dances at home or dress me up to show off to their friends, but nothing more."

"Well, I'm not going to patronize you and tell you I don't want to sleep with you." Abhay lifted his mug toward his lips. "But I understand things don't work like that and I'm under no delusions that you'd want to sleep with some guy from the Thornless Rose."

"What do you mean?"

"How many men—clients from the Thornless Rose have you slept with?"

"Zero. Aside from the fact it's against house rules." Mathias sighed. "When I'm on that stage or private dancing, I don't really look at the men. I imagine I'm with my man and I'm dancing for him."

"You're telling me you want to do that at home too?"

Mathias blushed, his cheeks burned. "Don't you think it's sexy? Think about it this way—you come home after a long day at work. Your man takes your bag, sits you down on the sofa and hands you a drink. Then he turns on the music and dances for you right before he slips to his knees…"

"And?"

"And what?"

"What would he be doing on his knees?"

Mathias smiled. "Use your imagination."

"I was trying not to let my mind fall into the gutter."

Mathias laughed. "Let it fall, Abhay."

"You're right—that is a sexy thought."

"I tell you what," Mathias said. "What are you doing on Friday night?"

"This Friday?" Abhay asked. "The same thing I do every weekend—well, not every weekend. Sometimes I spend it with friends but this weekend I have nothing planned but a good book, in front of the fire."

"Sounds boring."

"Boring—not a reader, right?"

"I love reading," Mathias said. "I actually have a small library in my bedroom. But a man like you deserves someone with you in front of that fire anyway. Let me cook you dinner on Friday—my place."

"Um—Mathias."

"I promise you I don't live in a slum and I do know how to cook."

"I don't know if that's…"

"Just say yes, Abhay, and see what happens," Mathias implored him. "I know you're nervous. Look, if you want, you can bring a friend."

"I thought this was a date."

"I would like it to be." Mathias was shocked at how true that sounded—how true it felt. "But I mentioned it and the fear I saw in your eyes damned near knocked me out. Are you scared of me or of what could happen between us?"

"Neither."

"Then what?"

"I'll come to dinner—one thing, I don't eat beef."

Mathias smiled. "I figured as much. Give me your phone."

Though Abhay looked hesitant, he handed over the cell and Mathias added his phone number and address. Once he was sure the information was correct, he saved it and handed the phone back. "Friday at eight—dinner at my place for us, or you, me and your friend. Either way, I'd like to see you."

Abhay smiled and dropped his phone into his pocket. For that moment, however, Mathias changed the subject. He figured he'd beaten that horse enough for one night. Though he was worried he might have pushed Abhay a little hard, there was no way Abhay could drop a kiss like that on him and not want anything else. Mathias wanted this man — there was no denying it and he was going to do what he could to get into Abhay's bed. Hopefully after that, he could make his way into Abhay's heart.

Chapter Six

With a last bit of coding done, Abhay shut down the computer and reached for his laptop. If he hurried, he could get back to his place, shower and change before heading to drinks with Dana. The others were all busy — Ko and Jackson were on their way to Japan for the opening of one of Ko's stores and Abhay had lost track of where the others were. Priya was busy studying so he would have to see her the next day before he went to dinner at Mathias'.

After slinging on his jacket, he hurried from the building, bag strapped over his shoulder and cell in hand. He climbed into the front seat of his car, started the ignition and sat back to allow the space to warm. While he did that, he looked at his cell's face again, for what had to be the millionth time, with the typed message he was tempted to send to Mathias.

Finally, he held his breath and sent.

I wasn't sure if I should send you this. But I'm going to put myself out there — I've been thinking of you.

When the phone chirped that the message had been sent Abhay let it fall to his lap, peeled his scarf from around his neck and draped it over the back of the passenger seat. His heart hammered as he waited for Mathias to reply—or not. The invite to dinner could have just been something to pass the time—to give them something to talk about. Then again, they'd kissed.

Abhay was hard all over again thinking about it.

The phone chimed.

Aww sweet talker. I bet you say that to all the guys.

Mathias had replied with a smiley face.

All the guys? You're assuming way too much, my friend.

I don't think so—are we still on for dinner tomorrow night?

Abhay paused to think about it. He wondered what Dana would say if he asked her what he should do. He figured he'd save himself the lecture since he already knew.

Of course. Want me to bring anything?

Condoms.

Abhay choked. He hadn't expected that answer. He'd thought Mathias would have said wine or dessert. How could a man be so open about his sexuality? Sure, he had been hanging around Thaddeus and Ravinder then Jackson and Ko for a while. They held hands in public, kissed in public, touched each other — yet was still self-conscious to let himself be sexual, be attracted.

Abhay, I'm joking – partially. I know how you feel about – intimacy.

Abhay sighed.

Sorry. I'm in the car and about to drive. I'll message you again once I get home – I have drinks with a friend so it might be late.

I'll be here.

Abhay placed the phone in his lap and was about to shift the car into drive when he thought of something and opened Mathias' messages again.

Only partially, huh??

Exactly. I'll see you tomorrow.

And what if I don't want you partially?

Then we'll just have to work something out.

Abhay laughed, did put away his phone and drove to where he would be meeting Dana. They hugged then hurried inside where it was warm. The indoor fair happened every year and though Abhay had been in Bathsheba a while, he'd never once had time to visit.

"So, what's up with you?" Dana asked as she looped her arm through the crook of his elbow and strolled with him. "You've been strangely silent."

"Remember that guy? The one I told you about."

"From the strip club?"

Abhay nodded. "We went out for coffee the other night and one thing led to another and I kissed him."

"Oh yes!" Dana fist pumped. "Then why do you look so nervous?"

"Well, he asked me to dinner tomorrow."

"Oh!"

"At his place."

"Ooo."

"Yeah." Abhay sighed as they stopped before a basketball kiosk. He held up two fingers to the attendant, handed the young man money then accepted the ball. With a sigh, he positioned himself and made the shot. The ball sailed through the air then landed in the hoop with that familiar, distinct *swoosh*. When it rolled back to him, he took aim again. "I said I'd go. I want to go. I mean, I'm attracted to him and he seemed attracted to me. But I'm terrified."

"Of?"

Abhay made two more shots before replying. "Does he want me, or my money? I mean, he is a stripper."

Dana sighed.

"What?" Abhay made the final basket and turned to Dana. "Pick a prize."

"For me?"

He nodded.

Of course she picked the biggest teddy bear in the place and grinned as they walked off to something else. "Sure, he's a stripper. But they have feelings too. They want the same love and mutual respect we do. And I can't believe you said that."

"Ravinder said something—never mind."

"Forget what Ravinder said for a second." Dana set the bear down before her. "Wasn't Thaddeus in trouble with the law at some point?"

Abhay nodded.

"So, Ravinder shouldn't be judging."

"I don't think that's what he was doing," Abhay said. "He didn't say not to date the guy. He just said I should be careful."

"As well you should. You're the one who is attracted to this man. You're going to have to go into it with an open mind and see how things play out." Dana hefted her prize. "That's all you can do."

"Maybe."

"So you are going to this dinner. Does he want you to bring anything?"

Abhay chuckled. "I asked that same question earlier. He said condoms."

"Condoms?" Dana laughed. "I like this guy already."

After stopping for funnel cakes, the two found an empty bench close to back of the establishment and sat. "It's not like I wouldn't want to sleep with the guy. He's sexy as hell. But the thought of being naked for a man, of being that intimate, scares me. It's been a while. Hell, I've only slept with one guy and it wasn't the most ideal situation."

"How so?"

"We were young—it was my first time. It wasn't like anyone taught me anything about straight sex, much less gay sex, so I had *no* clue. Add to that the fact that I was terrified of being caught—or of him telling someone what we'd done. I kept messing up, slipping out, pushing in too hard, moving too fast or too slow. He was frustrated that I wasn't *doing it right*. He did come but I didn't. I didn't enjoy it."

"And you never tried again?"

Abhay shook his head. "With whom?"

"Well, sweetie, maybe now is the time for you to let someone in. Do you even know if you're a bottom—top—versatile?"

Abhay cringed. "I topped him—but I figured for the right guy I'd be versatile. It's pathetic, isn't it? At my age, I should know what I want. I feel like, like—my parents ruined me for every man out there."

"Only if you let them." Dana finished the last of her funnel cake and faced him. "Listen, you go to dinner with your sex-pot tomorrow. You talk to him. You laugh. And if at any point in the night you feel like you want to give yourself to him, you do that. There's no judgement on my part and this conversation stays between us."

"Dana…"

"And besides, you shouldn't allow anyone to guilt you because you crave pleasure like the rest of us."

"How did you get so smart?"

She grinned then leaned over to drop a kiss to his nose. "I'm not. When it comes to my life, I'm a hot mess. Everyone else's, I'm a fucking genius. I've been single a while too—men hear trans and think plague."

"Well, I have this friend…"

"No, no!"

"Dana, come on—hear me out. He's employed, kind, funny, educated…and not bad looking. He's looking for someone to settle down with."

"And what's going to happen when I tell him I'm trans?"

"His ex was trans—well, Zayna hadn't fully transitioned yet, but he won't freak. Look, Leon will be in town next week. All you have to do is say the word."

Dana nodded and stood. "Let me think about it. I'll let you know tomorrow after you call me to tell me about how your night went with the sexy stud. And don't think you have to call me so you need to end your night early."

Abhay laughed. After he finished his night out with Dana, Abhay made his way home, took a shower then, lying naked in his bed, he grabbed his phone.

Are you awake?

Yes… Call me?

Abhay didn't even hesitate. He rolled to his back while hitting send on Mathias' name. The phone rang twice before Mathias picked up but those were the longest two seconds of his life. When Mathias' voice came over the line, Abhay's cock perked up immediately. He moaned. "You know, I'm trying to behave."

"Behave? That's boring."

"Mathias—you don't understand."

"Then make me. Can I be honest with you?"

"Sure." Abhay reached a hand down to stroke his cock, massaging the head after each pull. "What's on your mind?"

"You're a sexy man, Abhay. And I would love to have you fuck me—but any man I allow in my bed can't be afraid. The word *behave* shouldn't even be in his vocabulary. I don't know what it is about you but I feel this wildness when I think about you, when you look at me that excites me."

Abhay exhaled while sliding a finger in circular pattern. "You're not making this up?"

"Wait, you think because I'm a stripper my feelings aren't valid?"

"Mathias. Of course not. I've never had a man tell me he wants me before."

Mathias sighed. "I want to be marked by you—Abhay. And that scares me but I still want you. There's no pressure tomorrow, okay? We're going to have a nice dinner, drink a glass of wine, have some dessert and then you go home — an old-fashioned date."

"How about this..." Abhay massaged his balls and moaned. "How about — we just see where the night takes us?"

"I like the sound of that — Abhay?"

"Mmm?"

"What're you doing now?"

"Touching myself." Abhay couldn't stop the words pouring from his lips. And even after they were out, he should have felt ashamed for his admission. But the fire that raged through him didn't give way to guilt.

"I wish I was there to watch," Mathias said.

"And you don't feel bad for thinking that?"

Mathias laughed, a smoky sound that made Abhay's dick pulse harder. "Not even a little bit. If I were with you now — what would you tell me to do?"

"Tell you to do?"

"Yes," Mathias replied. "Where would you want my hands — my mouth, my tongue..."

"Oh." Abhay squeezed his cock tighter. "You're that kind of lover."

"Yes."

"Well, your mouth on my cock as you play with my nipples," Abhay admitted. "I find I love when my nipples are pinched — bitten — sucked."

"Mmm." Mathias moaned. "Then you definitely have to let me cater to you one day — no rush."

"Damn," Abhay whispered. "I have to go."

"Why?"

"I'm going to come soon and I don't want you to hear."

Mathias laughed. "Come on, Abhay. I want to have sweet dreams tonight too, you know? Now, be a good boy..."

"Matt..."

"And come for me."

There was no staving off the climax that burned a path through Abhay's core. Though it had been a while since he'd experienced one, he knew it was coming for certain when it curled the pit of his stomach and his pre-cum streamed from the slit of his dick like a waterfall.

"You can't mean to— To— Oh shit!"

"Come for me, Abhay," Mathias cooed, his voice low like the rumble of an impending storm. "I want you to come for me."

Unable to control himself, Abhay allowed himself to get lost in the words coming to him from Mathias. He flung himself headfirst into the vulgarity of it and roared as his cock exploded, spurting hot, white jizz everywhere. His ragged breathing, the sweet ache in his shoulder from the exertion and the quiet lullaby of Mathias' voice soothed him.

"I'll see you tomorrow, Abhay," Mathias said. "And remember, no guilt, just pleasure."

"Okay."

The dial tone caused Abhay to pull the phone from his ear and drop it to the bed. He remained like that, fingers tight around his cock, for what felt like an eternity afterward. There was something about Mathias, something so innately forbidden that Abhay wondered if that was the reason he was so conflicted with the new and exciting sensations flowing through him. But whatever caused them, Abhay didn't care. Dana had been right. He was an adult and it was time he either fuck or be fucked.

Chapter Seven

All day, Mathias was beside himself. Ever since he'd hung up the phone from Abhay the night before, he'd been sporting a raging hard-on. It was an amazing sound hearing a man truly let go and allow himself pleasure. Abhay had roared for him. The only downside, it had been over the phone. What Mathias wouldn't give to be sitting across the room watching Abhay on the bed, his caramel thighs wide, his fingers around his dick. He wondered if Abhay had tossed his head back. Did I close my eyes? Did I imagine Mathias with me?

Somehow, Mathias managed to get through his day without any bodily injuries. He even drove to a local Indian bakery and picked up some desserts without incident. By the time lunch rolled around, Mathias had gathered everything he needed for dinner and began watching the clock. Abhay wasn't due until eight so he couldn't start cooking. Instead, he went to the gym, then after a shower he stopped for coffee with Collin. For a long time, he sat there, stirring his coffee even though he hadn't added anything to it.

"Okay, seriously," Collin said. "You're going to stir a hole in the bottom of your mug. What's going on?"

"I have dinner with Abhay tonight."

"Right—your Indian raja."

"Raja? What?"

Collin sighed dramatically. "Raja—king?"

"Oh…right. I'm nervous, Col. Remember when we came back to this city you said one day I was going to find a man who will make me want to settle down?"

Collin nodded.

"This is going to sound stupid, but I want to settle down with this man." Mathias sighed, realizing how dumb and needy that sounded. "Of course, I'm not going to tell him that yet. We've only kissed once. But every time I think about it my whole body reacts."

"Well, it's worth exploring."

"What does he tell his family and friends if this works out?" Mathias asked. "'This is Mathias, my boyfriend—he's a stripper.' That'll go over real well."

"You've never been ashamed of what you do before."

Mathias sighed. "I was dreaming to think a respectable man like Abhay would want…"

"Stop it!" Collin snapped. "Stop it right now. The only worry you should have is if he's going to be okay with strange men touching you. When it comes to that time, if he says anything like 'you should quit your job because I can't date a stripper' or anything like that you call me and I will shoot him. If he gets jealous of other men touching you, you might want to reconsider your career path. He's not going to ask you to quit and even though it hurts him, a good man would rather you be happy than ask you to find another job."

Mathias checked the time and sighed. "I should go." He took a quick sip from his coffee then slid out of the booth. He stopped long enough to hug Collin before hurrying out the door.

By the time he got home, it was just after six. He dumped his gym bag at the foot of the stairs and rushed into the kitchen. He began by frying the chicken breasts — not to cook them but to give them a little color. Once that was finished, he set them in a large Pyrex dish, covered it and put it in the oven. Mathias set the timer, then focused on the potatoes. Those took longer since he had to peel and slice them up before rinsing.

He set them in a large pot on the stove to cook and turned the heat down to medium. It was a mad dash afterward — first to find an outfit that didn't look like he was trying too hard and then to fix his hair to look just right. Between all of that and the time he stepped in the shower, he must have darted up and down the stairs a million times. At seven-fifteen, he set a bottle of medium bodied red into the fridge to chill, poured some spaghetti sauce over the chicken and squeezed half a lemon in. He covered it again and set it back into the oven. After mashing the potatoes with butter, ground pepper and milk, he covered it on the stove, added parmesan cheese to the chicken and turned the oven down low.

Abhay was right on time and the moment Mathias opened the door and took one look at him, all thoughts of behaving floated out of the window. Still, Mathias settled for kissing his cheek then stepped aside to allow him in.

"I brought you a bottle of wine," Abhay said, handing Mathias a decorative bag. "It's not condoms but I suppose it will have to do."

Mathias laughed. "Thank you." Mathias closed the door and locked it while Abhay removed his shoes. Mathias had to set the bag down to accept Abhay's jacket and store it in the closet then led his guest into the dining room.

"You didn't have to go through all of this for me." Abhay motioned to the table.

"Yeah, I did." Mathias turned immediately for the kitchen. He'd been trying to hide his embarrassment at saying that out loud but Abhay's footsteps followed him. "Do you want a glass of wine?"

"Maybe with dinner," Abhay said.

The softness of his voice caused Mathias to face him. Abhay was now seated on the far side of the island, his dark eyes shimmering in the kitchen light. There was something there, something that made Mathias tremble. Forget the fact Abhay was dressed in all black, a gold necklace being the only color in his ensemble. And forget his beautiful hair was brushed back away from his handsome face, exposing perfection and the creases at the corners of his eyes. Mathias could scarcely breathe. To save face, he slipped on his oven mitts and pulled the chicken out. He carried the Pyrex to the table and set it on heat pads. His next trip was to scoop some mashed potatoes into a bowl. That he handed it to Abhay who accepted with a wink and carried it off. The hardness in the front of Mathias' pants made it difficult for him to maneuver to get the salad but he somehow managed.

Once they were seated across from each other, Mathias spread his legs to alleviate the pressure.

This was insane. There was no way he should be so affected by a man already. They'd only shared a kiss and heavy breathing over the phone!

"This is delicious, Mathias, thank you."

"Thank me? For what?"

"The only other person who's cooked for me has been my sister."

"You have a sister?"

"Yes." Abhay wiped his mouth and fingers in his napkin before pulling out his phone. After tapping away for a few seconds, he turned it to Mathias. "Priya."

"She's gorgeous."

"Yeah. She models for Ko now while going to university. She is taking business."

"You're very lucky. No siblings—that I know of."

"That you know of?"

Mathias tilted his head. "The world is a very strange place, my friend. You never know what might pop out of the woodwork."

"Oh, Matt…"

"It's all right," Mathias said. "I don't even know why I said that."

"I don't feel sorry for you," Abhay said, setting his fork down and reaching for his wine. "I'm actually really proud. Even though life kept giving you lemons, you've done really well, you know? You own this house, right?"

Mathias nodded.

"See? You've come a long way from a scared little boy, Mathias. There's nothing to be ashamed of."

"How do you feel about what I do?"

"Well." Abhay sipped his wine. "If you were my man, the thoughts of others touching you would drive me crazy. But, it's a job, nothing else, right?"

"Right."

"Then…" Abhay shrugged. "It is what it is."

Mathias ate the last piece of chicken on his plate and wiped his mouth. "Tell me about your childhood."

"It was okay—I was brought up in India. Started university, came out to my parents and was disowned, had to drop out of school." Abhay finished his wine and set the glass delicately on the table. "But, I met a couple of friends who wouldn't give up on me. They got me here, I finished school and here I am."

"I'm glad you're here," Mathias said with a smile. "Trust me. Okay, are you ready for dessert or did you want to give your stomach a little time to digest?"

"Digest please." Abhay rubbed his stomach. "That was amazing."

Mathias grinned. "Come on. I'll give you the tour."

They rose and Mathias led Abhay through the house. From time to time they'd stop as Abhay inspected a picture. Mathias hadn't realized how many pictures of Collin he had in the house until Abhay asked who he was.

"My best friend," Mathias said. "He's Bathsheba police. No, before you ask, we've never slept together. He's not my type."

"And what is your type?" Abhay reached out to catch Mathias around the hips and pressed him to the wall.

"You."

Abhay moaned and kissed Mathias' shoulder. He dragged his mouth up Mathias' neck and across his jaw. It was as if Abhay was dragging a trail of fire over his flesh. Mathias' body pulsed in anticipation. He relived their first kiss over in his head and knew Abhay knew how to use his tongue to make Mathias moan. Mathias closed his eyes, waiting for his mouth to be conquered, plundered, owned.

Abhay exhaled, the heat of his breath searing Mathias' lips so sweetly.

"I've wanted to kiss you again since that night out," Abhay confessed. "I go to bed at night wondering what it would feel like to hold you against the wall and devour your lips. Would you kiss me back if I allowed you to see the fire raging inside my head? Would you slap me for being too rough with you? Or would you want more — more of me?"

"I'm right here," Mathias said. "Why don't you find out?

"Do you really want me to kiss you?"

"What happened to the man who ordered me around that night in the private room?" Mathias asked. "Where is he? He was aroused by me. He wanted me."

"And you think I don't?"

Mathias said nothing. *What could I say in reply to that without offending Abhay?* Instead he sighed.

"I asked you a question, Mathias." Abhay's voice now a low rumble. "Do you want me to kiss you?"

In reply, Mathias pushed his hips forward, grinding his cock into Abhay's, and watched the way Abhay's eyes rolled back. "I want more than a kiss, Abhay. But I promised I wouldn't push you. Don't tease me unless you want me to break that promise. I'm not as strong as you think I am." Mathias extricated himself from under Abhay's body and continued toward the office. "And this is my library slash office slash party room."

When he turned, Abhay was still standing where he'd left him. "Abhay?"

"Sorry." Abhay jogged over. He squeezed by Mathias into the room then proceeded to walk around, looking at the books. From time to time, Abhay would stop and run a finger against the spine of a particular book as if he was touching a lover. "You have some good books here."

"I know. A book doesn't get a place on these shelves unless I've read them."

Abhay glanced at him over a shoulder. "That's the sexiest thing a man has ever said to me."

"What? That I read?"

Abhay nodded and faced the books again. "This is my favorite book of all time."

"Which one is that?"

"*Shantaram.*"

"Yes—it took me a while to get through but I did enjoy it." Mathias sighed. "Abhay."

"Mmm."

"Look at me."

Abhay set the book back on the shelf and turned. He pushed a wayward strand of hair behind his ear and lifted brown eyes to meet Mathias. "I want you. No pressure but I…" Exhaling, Mathias shoved his fingers into his pockets and left the room. He could hardly breathe he was so turned on. He had to leave—he had to get out of there or he was going to die.

Chapter Eight

Abhay followed in silence. He couldn't understand what was happening. Not having much experience with men and intimacy, he couldn't be sure if it was desire he'd seen in Mathias' eyes or fear. Deep down, Abhay knew Mathias wanted something from him that he wasn't sure he was capable of. At the door leading to the kitchen, Abhay leaned his shoulder against the doorframe and watched. Mathias was nervous— Abhay sensed from the way Mathias moved around the space, the busy work he found to do. In that moment, Abhay wanted to see Mathias smile again.

"At my age, I've only been with one man," Abhay said.

"And how old is your age?"

"Thirty-five. It's not because I didn't want to be with others—you see, the man I—he never claimed me. Being with me was a rebellion. His parents never approved and he knew there was nothing they could do about it. You see, his grandfather had already given him his inheritance. But he was ashamed of what we were to each other — or rather what I wanted us to be for each other."

"Are you a virgin, Abhay?"

"I wish." Abhay rubbed his face then sighed. "I mean I've never bottomed for anyone and only topped him."

"Why are you telling me this?"

"Um — Mathias, I don't understand intimacy," he admitted. "I know, with the right man I'd enjoy it. But I don't get it. I want to…"

"There is nothing to really understand." Mathias put away the dish he'd been drying then turned to face Abhay. "You want or you don't. You crave or you don't. Abhay, I've been with a few men. I'm not going to lie. I've been searching, waiting — for the right man, but after a while I think, I don't deserve a good man. I mean, look what I do for a living."

"That doesn't define you."

"No?"

"No. I'd still want to feel you even if you weren't a stripper," Abhay said.

Mathias smiled. "When I said we didn't have to do anything tonight, I meant it."

"I know."

Mathias picked up a silver dome and set it to the side before lifting a plate and turning to face Abhay. "Surprise!"

Abhay laughed and stepped farther into the room. "Mathias…"

"Did I do good?" Mathias asked.

Abhay leaned over the plate with his favorite dessert and kissed Mathias. "You did perfectly." He picked up one of the Pinni and pushed it into his mouth. The flavor brought back nothing but good memories for him. "Where did you even find Pinni?"

"I have my secrets." Mathias set the plate on the island and leaned forward. He bit into one and smiled. "Do you like it?"

"It's my favorite. My sister used to make them for me."

"Not anymore?"

Abhay reached for another while shaking his head. "She doesn't have the time. Between school and work and traveling for work..." He chewed, all the while watching Mathias. "I was nervous to come here tonight. Hypothetically — if I asked you to make love to me, what would you say?"

"I'd ask you if you were sure — hypothetically, of course."

"Of course. And if I said I'd never been more sure about anything in my life?"

"Then, hypothetically, I'd say — I'd say — come around this counter and kiss me."

Abhay allowed his feet to carry him to Mathias. He cradled Mathias' face and allowed his eyes to drift closed. When their lips met, Abhay moaned. It was almost as if he couldn't control his body anymore.

"Damn, Abhay." Mathias panted. "Where did you learn to do that?"

"I'm not sure." Abhay nipped at Mathias' shoulder then his ear. "I think of the things I want to do to you."

"Okay, Abhay. Right here — right now."

"But we don't have any — lube and..."

Mathias smiled. "Wait here."

With Mathias gone, Abhay figured he would have changed his mind. The wait should have made him scared. But when Mathias returned, shirtless and carrying tube of lube and a box of condoms, Abhay was more turned on than he ever thought possible.

"You're still fully clothed, Abhay."

Smiling, Abhay removed his clothes slowly. Mathias never looked away once and when Abhay was naked, Mathias licked his lips. Abhay wasn't sure what came over him but he wrapped his fingers around his own dick and stroked it. Having Mathias' eyes on him made the sensation even more wonderful. Instead of being disgusted, Mathias leaned in and flicked Abhay's nipples with his tongue.

"Oh yes," Abhay whispered. "Suck them."

The suction of Mathias' mouth was unlike anything Abhay had ever experienced. He clutched at the back of Mathias' head, pressing his mouth even closer. They stumbled from the kitchen and into the living room where Mathias pushed him to the sofa. Abhay stared up at Mathias, watching the way his body became bare. Seeing Mathias naked did everything for him. Every part of him pulsed. Abhay licked his lips. "Come here, Mathias."

"Why?"

"I want to suck your cock."

Mathias played with himself as he walked closer. He climbed onto the sofa, astride Abhay's body, and presented his beautiful dick. Without questioning, Abhay pulled it into his mouth. Though he wasn't sure what to do, he moved as his body demanded him to. He sucked on Mathias, slurping, passing his tongue over the head. Mathias dripped onto his tongue, hot and tangy. Abhay looked up to see Mathias playing with his own nipples, twisting then pulling on them.

He sucked on Mathias, loving the sounds that escaped his throat. Mathias moaned for him, growled, whimpered.

"You have to stop," Mathias whispered. "You're gonna — make me come."

Abhay didn't stop. He grabbed Mathias' balls and massaged them with one hand while his other snaked around and played with Mathias' quivering hole. Mathias moaned, reached down to pinch at Abhay's nipples.

"Do you want me to come for you?" Mathias asked.

Abhay lifted his eyes but said nothing.

"Ab—hay!" Mathias panted. "Shit!"

That was the only warning Abhay received. A few seconds later, his mouth was full of Mathias' release. Without thinking, Abhay swallowed then pulled Mathias' dick back into his mouth for more. Mathias moaned, eased his hips back and hopped off the sofa. He fell to his knees, panting even as he wrapped his fingers around Abhay's dick.

"Your turn, sexy," Mathias whispered.

Mathias went down on Abhay, taking his beautiful, dark dick down his throat. He relished the feel of it pulsing against his lips. He couldn't wait to have Abhay fuck him. "Hold my head," Mathias said.

Abhay grabbed both sides.

"Fuck my mouth."

Relaxing his throat, Mathias accepted Abhay's dick. He braced his palms on both sides of Abhay's thigh and took it all. He moaned each time Abhay's cock breached his throat. When he couldn't breathe, he pulled his head away and fell to his ass on the floor. He couldn't help smiling. Abhay made him feel primal and he didn't care.

Rolling to his knees, Mathias arched his ass in the air. "You know what I want."

"Mathias, I was never any good at this part," Abhay said, caressing Mathias' ass.

"Don't think about it," Mathias said. "Put a condom on and lube me up."

He waited until Abhay was finished before spreading his legs and arching his back. He was rewarded with the perfect, mushroom head of Abhay's dick breaching his hole. Mathias moaned and tapped his palm on the floor. "Deeper," Mathias pleaded. "I need you deeper."

Abhay gripped his hips and pushed farther. Mathias held his breath as Abhay filled him and withdrew only to punch in again. His body arched as if it had a mind of his own. His toes curled in on themselves.

"Oh fuck, Abhay! Fuck me!"

"Brace yourself, baby."

He wasn't kidding. Mathias chewed on his bottom lip as Abhay gave him what he asked for. He trembled each time Abhay slammed home. He slipped forward and Abhay released him and moved back to the sofa. "I've always wanted a man to ride me," Abhay confessed. "Climb on."

"As you wish."

Mathias gripped his shoulders and took Abhay deep. This time he rose up and down on the dick he knew he'd have to have again. He threw his head back and enjoyed Abhay's body while he allowed his hands to travel Abhay's chest, flicking at his nipples then massaging the muscles. He rode him hard and fast. Then Abhay gripped his cock and Mathias lost his mind. He leaned in and slammed his mouth over Abhay's. He plunged his tongue in and growled as his cock erupted.

How is this even possible? He'd just climaxed and he already wanted Abhay again. Reluctantly, he climbed off Abhay's cock and went down on his back on the floor. He spread his legs wide then winked at Abhay. He didn't have long to wait as Abhay seemed to have gotten the idea. When Abhay slid into him again, Mathias was so far gone all he could do was whimper Abhay's name and grind his hips to meet Abhay's thrusts.

"Please," Mathias pleaded. "Please, fuck me harder."

Abhay cradled both sides of Mathias' neck and rode him. Mathias lost track of everything except the force of Abhay's body. He allowed himself to get caught up in the pleasure of the fire surging through his being. Without warning, the condom expanded inside him. He looked up to see Abhay's head was tossed back with sweat slicked on his beautiful frame. A low growl rumbled from Abhay's chest that that made Mathias' cock pulse harder.

It was so strange just how sexy Abhay looked in that moment. But he couldn't think for very long because Abhay took his dick to the back of Abhay's throat. Mathias didn't think it was possible but once again, he climaxed roughly down Abhay's throat.

Chapter Nine

At some point, they'd gotten to Mathias' bedroom at round two or three of making love. Abhay couldn't believe the feelings that raged through him every time Mathias turned those beautiful, brown eyes on him. He'd taken Mathias so many times he'd lost count, but he didn't regret any of it. As his eyes caught the clock and it flashed four in the morning, he settled into the bed and pulled Mathias closer to his chest. The truth was, Abhay knew he had to leave. He couldn't stay the night but, so help him, the last thing he wanted to do was let Mathias go.

How is this possible?

He closed his eyes once more and when he opened them, it was well past six. This time, he eased away from Mathias' body to use the bathroom. Once finished, he collected his clothes and made his way back to the bedroom. Abhay sat on the side of Mathias' bed and checked his phone. He'd missed a few calls from Dana and Priya. Instead of calling back, he turned, dropped the phone into his pocket then leaned over to nibble at Mathias' nipples.

Mathias moaned. "Abhay, you're going to have to take me to get a massage."

"Why is that?" Abhay eased upward to lick Mathias' chin.

"I've never been fucked this good before." Mathias cradled the side of Abhay's head. "And I enjoyed every second of it but I'm sore."

"I'm sorry," Abhay whispered. "I never meant to hurt you."

Mathias sat up and pressed his back into the headboard, the sheets falling to his waist. "You didn't hurt me. It's been a while since I've bottomed anyone. I'm not complaining, darling. Give me a few hours and try me again."

"You got it. I have to go anyway," Abhay said. "I have a date with Dana. I'm pretty sure she's going to drill me all about my night with you."

Mathias smiled. "Well, can I call you?"

"I'm counting on it." Abhay said softly, leaning in to drop a kiss to Mathias' lips. "I don't want to go, but if I don't—"

Mathias caressed the side of his face before kissing him again. "I'll call you tonight. I'm going to call out of work so I can spend some time with you—is that all right?"

"My sister comes back tonight," Abhay said. "You can come by my place, have a glass of wine with us."

"Meet your sister?" Mathias asked. "Don't you think that's a little fast? Once I meet the family…"

"You could be right." Abhay kissed him again. "I can take Sunday and give you all of me."

"Can I think about meeting your sister and give you a call later?"

"Sure." Abhay stood.

"Before you go—kiss me again."

Abhay braced his palms on the bed and gave Mathias what he wanted, sucking Mathias' tongue into his mouth then allowing it to battle with his own. Soon his cock got involved and Abhay knew he had to back off. Licking his lips, he picked up his sweater where it was lying on the side of the bed and pulled it over his head. "Walk me to the door?"

Mathias climbed from the bed and reached for a black robe. He wrapped himself in it then walked ahead of Abhay. Abhay held on to Mathias' hip and drew his chest into his lover's back as they moved closer and closer to say goodbye. At the door, Abhay activated the automatic starter to his car. Ravinder had insisted Abhay get it because it defrosted the vehicle while warming the inside. Abhay pushed his feet into his boots and was amazed when Mathias slipped to his knees to lace them.

He locked eyes with Mathias and smiled then extended a hand to help him up. Mathias pulled Abhay's jacket from the cupboard and Abhay slipped his arms in.

"I don't want to go," Abhay confessed.

"But you have to. The truth is, it takes time to build anything and we also need time apart." Mathias snuggled into Abhay's chest. "I need to give you time to miss me."

Abhay laughed. "Call me later."

"Is that an order, Abhay?"

"Yes."

"And what happens if I don't call?"

Abhay smiled. "I know where you live and I'm not above giving you a spanking."

It took everything in him to leave. Yet, he gave Mathias a quick kiss then stepped out into the biting cold. He pulled up his collar, hurried through the snow and let himself into his vehicle. It wasn't quite as warm as he'd have liked but it was better than it could have been. After a minute, he grabbed the brush and climbed out to clear the snow off the front of his car. With that done, he got back in and drove away. He could still feel the heat of Mathias' mouth against his lips and wondered if Mathias was serious about calling him later. At the first stop light his phone chimed and he checked it.

I will call you later, Abhay.

Abhay laughed. This man could already read him better than he could himself. He activated the hands-free and called Dana. She answered, her voice sleepy.

"You were supposed to call me last night," Dana said. "I mean, after your date."

"I am calling you after my date," Abhay said. He checked his mirrors and switched lanes to go around a slow-moving van. "I'm just heading home."

"Darling, leave all the juicy deets until we meet!" she said. "Can you pick me up in an hour?"

"Sure, let me go home and shower first?"

Dana agreed. He turned the car off and ran into the condo. It took him no time at all to shower, change, grab an apple and be out of the door again. He found he was very excited to tell Dana all about his night with Mathias. The moment she got into the car and kissed his cheek, she wanted to know everything. Abhay left nothing out and by the end of it all he wanted to do was head right back to Mathias' arms.

"Wow," Dana gasped.

"I know, right?" Abhay said, pulling into the parking lot of Sliver's. "I never thought being with a man could be that good. I mean he was — wow."

Dana giggled. "Well, that's because the ass you were with before had no clue what he wanted. A man or woman has to tell their lover what they want, what makes them go gaga. Mathias demanded your body and it turned out great."

"You know what got me though?" Abhay asked, climbing from the car then closing the door. He turned to extend a hand to Dana.

"What's that?"

"I was vocal — once I got over the initial nervousness that is. I was just as demanding as he was and he didn't shy away from it. In fact, it seemed to turn him on even more."

"Like I said," Dana said as they entered. A waitress walked them to their booth and Dana removed her jacket and hung it up with Abhay. "Sex doesn't have to be shameful or taboo. I don't know how you went so long without experiencing that. So, what now?"

Abhay waited until the waitress took their drink orders and was gone before he replied. "Well, he's supposed to call me later. I'm waiting to see if that happens."

"You said you left him sore." Dana wiggled her brows. "He's definitely gonna call."

Abhay's cheeks heated. "I really like him, Dana. I figured I should go into this with an open mind."

"As so you should."

"I'm just afraid of what the others will say."

The waitress returned and after they placed their meal orders without looking at the menu, they were left alone once more.

"What do you mean? Because he's a stripper?" Dana asked. "I'm sure they won't have an issue with his job per se. They might be worried he'll hurt you but I don't think that's unexpected."

"It's not. Don't you just love it? I've spent this entire time trying to stay away from men and the first one that gets me is a stripper."

Dana laughed. "Well, I think it's divine intervention. I mean, you were almost a..." Dana glanced around then leaned in as if she was about to impart some wisdom. "A v-i-r-g-i-n and Mathias sounds like a certified freak. It's the perfect combination."

"He is. He likes to touch himself while I watch," Abhay whispered. "And lord have mercy, do I love to watch."

"My point." Dana smirked as she lifted her coffee to her lips.

Abhay dropped a couple of sugar cubes into his and stirred.

Is that the kind of lover I am? Can I be as wild as Mathias in bed? Will I – should I – let Mathias top me?

There were so many questions swirling about his head. They were ones that had vanished the moment Mathias' beautiful ass was hiked in the air for him. There was no thinking when seeing that hole pucker and his palms imprinted on Mathias' ass from grabbing it hard.

"Hello? Earth to Abi?" Dana snapped her fingers in front of his eyes. "Where did you go just now?"

"Mathias' bedroom."

Dana giggled. "Well, sweetie, I bet he's one hot stud, but focus on me for a second."

"Okay, beautiful. What's on your mind?"

She laughed and gave his shoulder a playful smack before setting her coffee mug on the table. Their food arrived but she didn't focus on it. Instead she met Abhay's eyes and smiled. "Remember you offered to set me up with your friend?"

"Leon."

"Yeah."

"Let's do it," Dana said. "I can't seem to find a good man on my own to save my damn life and I'd like someone special by my side. So, yes. I'm game."

"Okay, cool. I'll call him later and set something up. I figure I could invite him to my place for dinner and you could be there. That way, you can meet him and see for yourself if you want a one-on-one date."

"Do you have a picture of him?"

Abhay nodded and pulled out his phone. He scanned through a slew of Dana's selfies before he reached one of Leon with his big gray eyes and dark hair. He handed the phone to his friend before picking up his fork to eat.

"Damn, Abi!"

"Good damn?"

"This man is gorgeous!" She sighed. "Are you sure…"

"Dana, you're beautiful," Abhay said. "He'd be lucky to have you look at him."

She giggled and handed the cell back. "You're a sweet talker. He just seems — very straight, that's all."

"Ugh, labels. Hang on, let me call him." Abhay wiped his hands in his napkin before scrolling through his phone to find Leon's number. It rang a couple of times before his friend picked up.

"Hey, Abi!" Leon answered, his Spanish accent evident. "How's it going?"

"Pretty good. I don't have a lot of time to talk but I wanted to know if you're still single."

Leon laughed. "Are you trying to set me up?"

"Actually, yes."

"Oh?"

"Her name is Dana."

"Your friend Dana?" Leon asked. "I thought she wasn't looking."

"Well, she's ready now. I told her I'd have a dinner at my place and the two of you can meet and talk to see if you like each other enough to go on a date."

"And her reply?"

"She's down for it."

Leon chuckled. "Then by all means. I'll be a perfect gentleman."

"Sure you will be." Abhay laughed. "Send me your flight info and I'll pick you up at the airport."

"Thank you, my friend…"

He chatted for a little while longer before Abhay hung up and smiled at Dana.

"So?" she asked. "What'd he say?"

"He said he's down."

Dana flailed. "And he knows I'm…"

"He knows." Abhay assured her. "Trust me — he's seen your videos. And I think he might have a little crush. He'll be here next Wednesday."

"He's staying with you?"

Abhay shook his head. "Nope. Hotel. I tried getting him to stay by me but he wants to be closer to the slopes."

Dana nodded and they continued with their morning date. By the time he dropped Dana off at her audition and was on his way home, he couldn't wait to lie in bed and text or call Mathias. But he slowed down when he remembered he was the one waiting to hear from Mathias. He couldn't call.

He got home and parked his car in the underground garage. Exhaustion kicked in so all Abhay did was send his sister a quick text telling her to call him when she arrived at the airport, plugged the phone in and set it on the bedside table. He removed his shirt and socks then fell face first onto the bed.

For the first time since being with Mathias the night before, he realized just how tired he was. His shoulders ached, right along with the backs of his thighs. He'd sunk his fingers into Mathias' thighs to use them as leverage to fuck him as deep as possible.

Every muscle had been used, strained and stretched. Perhaps a shower would be good, but for the next few hours he had no intentions of moving—except to roll over. For the time being, Abhay was going to bask in his soreness, wear it like a badge of honor and take a nap.

Chapter Ten

Calling off work hadn't been possible and after texting Abhay to let him know, Mathias walked into the Rose feeling as if the world was ending. He said hello to the usual people but pretty much hid out until he had to take the stage. His one private dance that night canceled and he was able to leave early at around ten. After taking a quick shower in the back, he changed into a fresh pair of jeans and a black shirt then sat in his car texting Abhay. The first text went unanswered for a while and he began panicking.

What if canceling on Abhay had been the wrong thing to do?

What if Abhay realized the job would always get in the way?

What if I wasn't enough in Abhay's bed last night?

Ding!

He grabbed the phone.

Sorry I took so long. Priya was regaling me with stories of her trip to Bora Bora. What's up?

Mathias exhaled long and hard.

I know it's late but can I still see you tonight?

Really? I thought you had to work?

My last dance canceled so I took off early. If it's too late I understand. We can see each other tomorrow.

No — it's not too late. 3215 Brigada Lane. Text me when you get here and I'll give you access to the penthouse elevator.

Okay. See you soon. Is your sister still around?

Yes. She's gonna be here for a little while then a friend is coming to pick her up.

Do you still want me to meet her?

Yes.

Okay. See you soon.

Mathias exhaled, tested his breath by blowing into his palm then reached into the side of his bag to grab a stick of gum. With that set, he turned on the heater, checked his mirrors and pulled out of the spot. Though he was still nervous about meeting Priya, Mathias figured there was nowhere to go but up. After all the things he and Abhay had done to each other — He sighed. With a shake of his head, Mathias refocused as he sped through the core of Bathsheba, the mountains running along his right before veering off onto Pasternack Avenue and then onto Brigada. This was where the super wealthy lived, in condos that towered into the heavens and houses that overlooked the beautiful mountains. Mathias always felt out of place whenever he ventured there. He'd gone out of his way not to. After an ex-boyfriend had moved there and they had broken up, Mathias had no reason to visit. Now Abhay was there and he found himself back among the rich and famous.

At the gatehouse he was stopped, and the guard had him sign in. Apparently, Abhay had called down telling them to expect him. Once he was allowed through the large gates, he followed the guard's directions to the visitors' parking and found a spot close to the entrance of the luxurious building. The lobby was beautiful with works of art on the wall. *No doubt generic.*

He stopped at the elevators to text Abhay, who replied.

The code is 1452.

Repeating the numbers to himself, he stepped in. Once the doors closed he followed the directions on the small screen above the numbers and soon the elevator was sliding smoothly upward. When he stepped from the elevator it dawned on him that he hadn't gotten directions to Abhay's unit, but thankfully the sexy stud was leaning against the wall as the door opened. Without thinking, Mathias rushed across and pressed into Abhay's chest. He buried his face into Abhay's neck and inhaled.

"Hey," Abhay whispered, tangling his arms around Mathias' back. "Hey, come on now. I'm right here."

Mathias spoke, but even he heard his voice was being muffled by Abhay's skin, so he lifted his head. "Sorry. I didn't mean to act so needy."

"Really? You think I'm offended because you missed me?"

Mathias' cheeks heated. "Some guys don't like that kind of thing."

"Well, I'm not some guy. I wanted to meet you out here to give you a little time before meeting Priya. And to do this…"

Abhay framed Mathias' face in his palms and gave him a deep yet tender kiss. Mathis sighed and melted into Abhay's chest, still amazed he'd been the second man Abhay had kissed. *How is that possible when Abhay knows how to use that tongue?*

"If you want, we can stay here a little longer," Abhay whispered.

"No. Let's do this."

But as confident as Mathias hoped he sounded, his heart raced inside him like a drum. He stole another kiss just before they stepped into the warmth of the unit. Abhay took his coat and hung it up while Mathias removed his shoes, then they walked together into the living room where the television was going.

"Yes!" A dark-haired woman punched the air. "Yes! Yes! Yes!"

"Are you gambling again?" Abhay asked, laughter in his voice.

"I don't gam—" She whirled around. "Oh! Hello. Sorry, I'm not usually this crazy."

She was beautiful—big eyes, gorgeous lips—then again, she looked like Abhay. How could she not? Mathias had to pull himself from his head to realize she had her hand extended to him. With a smile, he accepted it. "You must be Priya."

"I am. I'm the beautiful one." She wiggled her eyebrows at Mathias.

Abhay groaned. "That's what she thinks."

"He's just jealous," Priya said, taking her hand back. "It's nice to meet you, Mathias. My brother has told me about you. "

"I didn't mean to interrupt your time together," Mathias said. "I know you've been away. I just wanted to say hello."

"Oh, no trouble a-tall. I thought you were imaginary at first," Priya pretended to whisper.

"Ooo-kay. All right," Abhay cut in, taking Mathias' shoulder. "This conversation is over."

"No, no." Mathias grinned, stepping from Abhay's arms and toward Priya. "Tell me more."

Priya giggled. "My brother isn't a dater. We've labeled him the Hermit. I'm happy he's found someone."

"Even if that someone is a stripper?"

"I've learned a long time ago, Mathias," Priya said, her eyes serious now. "Never judge a book by its cover. When my brother came out, our parents judged him. They never gave him a chance to show the kind of man he is. I see what it did to him and I never want to do that to anyone else. So, as long as my brother is happy, and you make him happy, I have no reason to object."

Mathias nodded. "I can respect that."

"Good. Now, I must get ready." She patted Mathias' shoulder then stepped by to drop a kiss to Abhay's cheek. "Feel free to um — kiss and make out. But if you're taking it any further, please hang a sock on the door or something."

Mathias laughed out loud but when he turned to Abhay, Abhay had his face buried in his hands. Mathias didn't speak until after Priya left the room. "She's amazing."

"Yeah. She's not your sister," Abhay said.

Mathias could still hear love in Abhay's voice. With a sigh, he stepped forward and wrapped his arms around Abhay's hips. "She did, however, make some valid suggestions."

"We both know if we start kissing now it won't stop at that and I don't want her walking in on us," Abhay said. "So, in the meantime, let me feed you."

Mathias moaned. "Yes, you can."

"Food, Mathias Jago! Food." Abhay laughed but kissed Mathias anyway.

"Now who's being a tease?"

They left the living room and spilled into the open-concept area that was the kitchen. Mathias took a seat in one of the stools and watched Abhay move around the kitchen as if he knew what he was doing. There was something even sexier about Abhay then—his shoulder-length dark hair pushed back, his wide shoulders, his very delectable ass. Mathias breath caught in his throat.

"Try this." Abhay set a place before him.

"What is it?"

"Couscous with chicken tandoori," Abhay said. "Priya and I made it earlier. Let me get you a glass of wine."

"I can't. I'm driving."

"Um—I was kind of hoping you'd stay the night...too soon?"

Mathias grinned. He couldn't have stopped that emotion from spreading his face. In that moment, he knew for sure he looked like the Grinch who'd just gotten an idea but he didn't care. Instead of replying, he leaned in and kissed Abhay deeply. "I'd love to—but, darling, I have no clothes."

"You're not going to need any."

Before Mathias could reply to that, Abhay turned away from him to open the fridge. He then sat beside Mathias with a bowl of grapes. "How was your night?"

"Weird. I didn't want to go to work. I usually enjoy dancing but tonight I couldn't..." Mathias put some food in his mouth and paused as the flavors exploded on his tongue. He moaned and chewed. "Tonight was different."

"Why do you think that is?"

Mathias shrugged. "Damned if I know." But that was a lie. Mathias knew why it had been different on that stage. He didn't feel right having other men look at what he knew in his heart belonged to Abhay. It was too soon to admit that, though, so the lie would stand. "Maybe it's time I did something else. I mean, my body can't hold out like this forever."

"Mathias, this isn't because of me, is it?"

"No. I'm twenty-seven years old and I have no future," Mathias said. "I suddenly realize it—that's all."

"Well." Abhay rubbed his back gently. "If you need some help deciding, I can offer whatever you need."

Mathias turned to look into Abhay's eyes. For a moment all he did was stare into them, feeling the truth in those words. He nodded, kissed Abhay then went back to his meal. "It's not bad that I want to settle down and rejoin the mortals, is it?"

"No." Abhay's voice cracked.

"Okay, lovers!" Priya floated into the room, looking like a version of Aphrodite. "Jeremy is here. I shall bid you two..." She kissed Abhay's cheek then Mathias'. "Adieu."

Abhay laughed. "Be safe."

"I will. Love you."

"Love you too, sister."

When the condo was quiet again, Mathias looked over at Abhay and cleared his throat. "Friend?"

"He's her boyfriend. I'm just waiting for her to admit it."

Mathias laughed.

Abhay left Mathias to finish eating. He straightened up his bedroom, tossed a load of laundry into the machine then showered. When he returned, Mathias was curled onto the sofa watching some boxing match or the other. Though he had no interest in the sport, Abhay crawled onto the sofa in front of Mathias and snuggled into his body. He was relieved when Mathias wrapped an arm around him and began kissing the back of his neck. His body reacted immediately but he loved the peace he felt being like that with a man. Though his mind veered off course a few times to what the future might hold, Abhay reined it in and tried to focus on the heat of Mathias' body, the softness of his lips and the fire of his breath against his skin.

"I could get used to this," Mathias whispered.

"This?"

"Yes. Coming home and holding you on the sofa. This."

Abhay laughed. "I travel a lot for work. I think it's only fair that I warn you."

"I didn't know that," Mathias said.

The change in his voice was evident. Though Abhay didn't know what it meant, he knew something was wrong. Shifting, he turned so he now faced Mathias. Their eyes locked and the spark he'd felt that first time returned. He caressed the side of Mathias' face and smiled. "I always come back," he said. "And if you're mine I will always be thinking about you — even if you weren't."

"Okay," Mathias said. "Then let's set those labels right now. I know they're dumb and most men don't want them but I—"

"Want them."

"Good." Mathias licked his lips. "I want to be your boyfriend. I want to be able to come home to you. Too soon?"

Abhay smiled and kissed him. "No. Not too soon. I've never been anyone's boyfriend before. I think I'm going to like it."

"I'm glad your sister didn't think me unworthy of you."

"Priya isn't hard to please," Abhay said. "She likes seeing me smile."

"Yes. She's your sister."

"I'm so glad you're staying the night," Abhay whispered, inching closer. "It was so peaceful sleeping in your arms last night, I didn't want to leave but I couldn't cancel on Dana. She's been there for me so much. I always like to make sure I return the favor."

"I'll have to meet her sometime," Mathias said. "How about we watch a movie and cuddle?"

Abhay laughed. "Cuddle. You want to cuddle?"

"After I make you come."

"I thought so." Abhay laughed. "I'm hip to your games, Mathias Jago."

"Whatever you say, grandpa!"

"Grandpa?" Abhay groaned.

"No one says 'hip to your game' anymore." Mathias climbed over Abhay and stood. "I'm just waiting to hear you call me a 'jive turkey'."

Abhay laughed. "Come on." He extended a hand to Mathias, who accepted it. They walked silently down the hall to the large bedroom, and when the lights came on, Mathias stared out at the city. For a moment, Abhay remained silent, watching the way Mathias looked up at the mountains.

Eventually, he removed his shirt and when he reached for his belt buckle, the jangle pulled Mathias to turn around. "Don't mind me," Abhay said. He walked into his closet and returned with a pair of track pants.

"What're those for?" Mathias asked.

"Bed? You seem tired."

Mathias smiled. "No, no, no, Mr. Chetan. There's one rule tonight…"

"Let me guess." Abhay dropped the pants onto the chair closest to him and met Mathias' gaze. "No clothes?"

Mathias undid the buttons on his shirt and hurled it to the same chair. "Ding! Ding! Ding!"

They stripped together, until nothing but air caressed their flesh. Mathias sat Abhay on the edge of the trunk at the foot of the bed then slid to his knees before him. Abhay's brown eyes narrowed but he said nothing. Mathias took that as permission to kiss at his knees then up to the inside of his thighs. He moaned and rested a large palm on the back of Mathias' head but didn't add pressure.

Mathias took his time, enjoying the heat of Abhay's body and the way Abhay sighed and trembled. Abhay's legs were covered in soft, dark hairs that felt amazing against Mathias' lips. He dwelled on that, relishing the situation.

"You're so beautiful," Mathias whispered before he could stop himself. "Abhay."

Abhay framed Mathias' neck and slipped down to his knees. For a moment, they stared into each other's eyes. Weak from the feelings throbbing through him,

Mathias fell against Abhay's hair-covered chest and sighed when Abhay's arms snaked around him.

"Did you want to do this another time?" Abhay asked.

"No." Mathias shifted and moaned when his nipples traversed the hairs on Abhay's chest. "I want you so bad. I feel overwhelmed with it."

After that confession, Mathias thought for sure Abhay would freak out. Instead, Abhay held him tighter while pushing to his feet. He was further surprised when Abhay picked him up and carried him to the bed. For the first time ever, Mathias felt like one of the sexiest beings on the face of the earth. Abhay stroked him, touched him, kissed every part of him. He trembled in Abhay's arms, sighed each time Abhay's tender fingertips traversed his body.

Abhay slipped down Mathias' frame, dragging his tongue along the way. Then his hot, wet mouth engulfed the head of Mathias' cock and he lost his mind. For a man who hadn't had sex with anyone in years, Abhay sure knew how to make a man's eyes cross.

"Oh, baby," Mathias sighed, burying his fingers in Abhay's hair. "Take it deeper — how far can it go?"

He watched in stunned delirium as his cock disappeared, inch by glorious inch, down Abhay's throat. *How can being with a man feel so good?* Mathias tried focusing, tried keeping control, but all he could manage was to throw his head back and whimper. Abhay was good — so damn good that repeatedly, Mathias had to hold his breath to stave off the orgasm he knew would surge through him.

"I need you to fuck me." Mathias panted, gripping Abhay's shoulders. "Please. Now."

Abhay crawled upward but walked away to the bedside table. Mathias touched himself as he waited impatiently. He stood, braced his palms on the trunk and hiked his ass in the air. When he glanced over his shoulder, Abhay was standing behind him, his fit body looking so perfect, Mathias' knees shook.

Abhay touched him then, tracing Mathias' cheeks with a tender hand. He spread Mathias and squirted a cold dollop of lube on his hole. To add to his pleasure, Abhay used a large finger to work the lubricant in. Mathias moaned and licked his lips, all the while riding back onto the digit.

"Please," Mathias begged.

"Okay, darling," Abhay whispered, his voice brimming with restrained control.

Abhay pressed a hand against the small of Mathias' back and pushed downward. Mathias was rewarded with a large, stiff cock sliding deep into his hole. He chewed on his bottom lip and held his breath as his eyes crossed. Mathias wanted to scream, to shout his happiness, but no sound would leave him. Instead, he rode back onto Abhay, loving the way his man purred for him.

It was better this time and Mathias didn't know why that was. Abhay slammed home and Mathias suddenly didn't care. "Yes!" Mathias cried. "Fuck me, Abhay!"

Abhay gripped his shoulders and did as he was told. He crashed forward, their bodies slapping together louder and louder. The rising tide of Mathias' orgasm edged repeatedly, dancing to the ebb and flow of Abhay's whim.

"Mathias…"

Abhay flipped him around and pushed him against the hardness of the trunk. Mathias tried crawling backward across it to the bed, but the carnal madness in Abhay's eyes made him tremble. Still, he pushed, sliding across the sheets until his back hit the headboard. He glanced down to see his juices mixed with lube glistening against the condom over Abhay's dark dick.

Instead of walking around the side, Abhay climbed across the trunk to the bed. He grabbed a pillow with one hand while reaching for Mathias' ankle with the other and pulled. Mathias moaned as his ass eased across the Egyptian cotton of Abhay's sheets. Abhay tossed the pillow aside, picked up Mathias' ankle and spread him.

"Don't. Move." Abhay growled. "I want to fuck you until you come for me."

"Damn."

"Don't like the side of me, Mathias?"

"Damn!" Mathias sighed. "Give it to me."

Mathias licked his lips but shouted when Abhay's hard cock slammed home once more. This time he had the pleasure of seeing Abhay's eyes as he dug deep. Abhay's pupils dilated. Mathias' orgasm swam along the edges.

Abhay must have seen it because he wrapped his fingers around Mathias' dick and stroked tightly. It didn't take long.

"Come for me, Matt."

"Abhay." Mathias was breathless, arching upward, eyes wide as he did as he was told. He bucked hard but Abhay held on, riding Mathias like a trained jockey.

To Mathias' pleasure, the moment he thought the fire would end, Abhay roared for him. His lover's body tensed for what was a silent eternity. Abhay trembled as the condom expanded inside Mathias' body. It was impossible not to come again. Abhay's fingers were still trapped around Mathias' dick, stroking it to life and making him explode once more. This time, Mathias kept his eyes on Abhay's beautiful face, even as his pleasure stormed through him.

Chapter Eleven

"You two are dating now?"

Mathias rolled over and reached for Abhay but the bed was empty.

"Yes," Abhay's voice said with finality. "And would you not yell?"

"Look, I'm know it's none of my business but—you do realize he's a stripper."

"You're right. It is none of your business." Abhay didn't sound impressed and Mathias was quickly losing his patience.

"Abi, listen. I'm not trying to be in your business but are you sure you know what you're doing?" the other voice asked. "Have you spoken to Priya?"

"Ko, seriously. I am not a child and please don't say shit like this around him. Things are new between us and I don't want to ruin what we're trying to build here."

Mathias climbed out of the bed and rummaged around for his clothes. His shirt was still on the chair, only now it was folded. He picked up his boxers from the side of the bed and his pants from the dresser. He couldn't stay. His thoughts had been right. As much as he wanted to build a life with Abhay, to see what they could be to each other, Abhay's friends would never approve. Sure, he shouldn't care — hell, he should be riding out of that damn condo with both his middle fingers in the air — but Abhay didn't deserve that. He'd always known his job wouldn't win him any favors.

With a sigh, he shoved his feet into his pants and zipped up. He pulled on his shirt, latched the buttons then dragged a hand over his head. He hadn't come in with anything but his wallet and cell and once he was sure those were still in his pockets, Mathias took a breath and headed out the door.

"Matt," Abhay called. "I didn't know you were awake."

"Obviously," Mathias said. He didn't even acknowledge Ko. "Look, um, thanks for last night, but I should go."

"Why?"

"Seriously?" Mathias asked. "Look, I know my work isn't ideal. I get it. But I'm not out ripping anyone off or asking for handouts. I've lived my life without parents, without a family and without a wealthy boyfriend. I own my car and my house and I did that all on my own. I've never once begged anyone for anything. I've never asked a man to take care of me. I really like you, Abhay, but I'll be damned if I'm going to have your friends or anyone talk down at me because of my job."

"Matt…"

"I have to go."

He headed out the door, stopping only to slide his feet into his boots. Abhay caught his arm and pulled away. "I'm sorry, Abhay."

"Don't leave like this," Abhay said.

Mathias said nothing. He stepped into the elevator once the doors slid open then eased all the way into the back. He watched Abhay until the doors closed then buried his face in his hands. *How did I let everything move so fast?*

When he hit the first floor, he rushed to his car and peeled from the gated community as if he was being chased. His phone rang and when he looked down, Abhay's name flashed at him. Mathias declined the call and dropped the phone on the passenger seat. But he didn't go home. He pulled over to fix his clothes then made his way to the station and let himself into Collin's office.

"What happened?" Collin asked, hurrying around his desk to close the door while Mathias fell into one of his chairs. "Matt?"

"Abhay is a great guy. And his sister is amazing."

"But?"

"But his friends hate me."

"Matt, you're not dating his friends," Collin said. He sat on the edge of his desk and folded his arms. "If Abhay is good with you then who cares what anyone else thinks?"

"You don't understand. He needs his friends. They've been good to him."

"And he doesn't need you?"

"No." Mathias exhaled. His cell began ringing. This time when he saw Abhay's name he turned off the phone. "All I'm going to bring to his life is unnecessary drama."

Collin sighed. "Tell me this. Does Abhay have anything to say about your work?"

"He said if that's what I want to do he will accept it," Mathias explained. "He said he'd go crazy knowing other men were looking at me and I get it. Last night I was at the Rose and I just didn't have the same adrenaline it used to give me. Deep down, I knew I was giving away what belonged to him. And I know you're going to say I'm going too fast but I can't help the way I feel."

"Well, maybe you need to fight a little harder for him."

"Are you saying I should quit my job?"

"No." Collin shook his head. "What I'm saying is maybe you should stand by his side despite what a few closed-minded dopes think. Give Abhay a chance to defend you. You can't live your whole life alone, Mathias. You can't do it all yourself. Sooner or later masturbation will stop working."

Mathias crinkled his forehead at his friend but managed a smile. "I wish I was someone else, you know? Someone who has an education and a respectable job—someone he didn't have to hide."

"Hide? You said his sister was nice—that means you've met her. Did she have anything bad to say?"

Mathias shook his head.

"If you've met his sister then he's not hiding you. You don't have to make the decision today. But think about it before you do something you'll regret. I know that was him calling earlier. You can't hide from him forever."

Mathias knew Collin was right but he didn't admit it. Instead he grunted and they went out for breakfast. When he made it home, it was in time to bathe and crawl into bed. But he hadn't changed the sheets since Abhay had been there and now everything smelled like him.

Abhay dropped the phone on the counter and dragged frustrated fingers through his hair. He'd been calling Mathias for two hours and still nothing. The rage he felt in that moment pulsed behind his eyes. He swore he was going blind.

"He's not picking up?" Ko asked.

"No. It's going directly to voicemail."

"I'm sorr—"

"Don't!" Abhay snarled. "I told you he was here, Ko. But you didn't care because you had to say what you had to say and to hell with everyone else!"

"I didn't mean to hurt his feelings!"

"Yes you did. I know you, remember? But I didn't think you'd do anything like this. When did you become an elitist?"

"I am not an elitist! I was just looking out for you." Ko sighed. "I know you don't want to hear this but I really didn't mean to hurt him or you. I only wanted to make sure you were going into this with both eyes open."

"I'm done taking advice from you today," Abhay said, walking toward the bedroom.

"Abhay…"

"Go," Abhay said. "Please."

"Abhay, seriously…"

"I liked him, Ko." Abhay turned to look at his friend. "For the first time I had a man in my bed who reads, who cooks, who wanted me—not because I had a few dollars and not because he thought I was an easy mark but because he genuinely liked spending time with me. The fire I feel for this man surpassed everything. He put my desires ahead of his and didn't run away when he found out I was basically a forty-year-old virgin. And now, he's gone. And I have to figure out a way to get that back. If you're not going to help me then you're in my way so get out."

"I'm not leaving you like this."

Abhay frowned and stormed into his bedroom. He was in the process of hauling on some clothes when Ko entered.

"Give him some time to breathe." Ko leaned against the doorframe.

"What'd I tell you about giving me advice today?"

"Abhay, I'm sorry. Okay? I fucked up. I get it."

But Abhay had no words. He walked around Ko and stopped at the door to grab his coat and boots. It was then he realized Mathias had left his jacket. He could bring it to him, but maybe Ko had been right. Mathias needed some time to breathe. Abhay left it where it hung and exited his condo.

To keep from going to Mathias' house, he wandered the street until he wound up at Dana's dance studio. He sat in the back on one of the benches, watching her stretch and wondering how anyone could be against her. She was peace — there was no other way to describe watching her move across the dance floor as if it pumped in her blood. It took another hour before she got a break and hurried over to sit beside him while drinking from a bottle of water.

"Well, this is a surprise," Dana said. "I always love seeing you, but you hate just sitting here."

"Mathias is gone," Abhay reported. "I think we've broken up but I'm not sure."

"Wait — this has to be the shortest dating session ever. What do you mean he's gone?"

"He — uh — stayed over at my place last night." Abhay picked at the corners of his fingers. "We ate, watched a movie, made love — it was perfect. We decided we wanted to date, be boyfriends…"

"Awww!"

"Then Ko came over and ruined everything."

"How do you mean?" Dana asked.

"He was trying to warn me off Mathias because he's a stripper. Mathias heard and stormed out—after giving us a piece of his mind, that is."

"Damn."

"Yeah." Abhay rubbed his eyes. "Now he's not picking up his phone and I'm trying to give him breathing room but I need to know there is something to go back to."

Dana went silent for a second then reached over to rub Abhay's back. "I'll cut practice short and you come home with me."

"Dana…"

"Nope. I'll make you some soup. We'll cuddle on the sofa and watch a movie. I know I'm no Mathias, but until you figure this out I shall be your shadow—your beautiful, flawless shadow."

Abhay groaned.

Dana excused herself to pack up her things and soon he was driving them toward her place. He parked and they made their way up to her apartment. While she showered he tried watching television but wound up calling Mathias again. Still, Mathias didn't answer.

The sinking feeling that filled Abhay's chest was enough to make him ill. He charged into the bathroom, with Dana still trying to dry herself, flipped the toilet lid up and vomited.

"Something you ate?" Dana asked.

"No. Called Mathias again." Abhay panted. "He didn't answer."

"Giving him space is good and all, but you know where he lives."

Abhay flushed the toilet, rose and rinsed his mouth in the sink. Though he considered her suggestion, he didn't say anything. For the rest of the evening and the night, he tried being a good guest. Even after Dana fell asleep with her head on his chest, he muted the television and remained awake. A few times his phone vibrated and he was disappointed to see it was text messages from either Ko or Priya. He ignored them both.

The next morning, Abhay rolled out of bed, exhausted and sore. He made Dana breakfast then brought her a tray. He kissed her forehead to wake her before setting the tray on the side of the bed. "I made you breakfast," he said. "I have to head home then to the office. There is some work I need to get done before Leon gets here."

"Are you going to be okay?" Dana asked, wrapping her fingers around her coffee mug.

"I think so." Abhay smiled. "Enjoy your breakfast."

After placing another kiss to her forehead, Abhay gathered his things and locked the door behind him. He did as he'd told Dana and when he arrived at the office and opened his emails, the world seemed to have imploded because he'd taken the weekend off.

Grunting, Abhay picked up the phone and dialed the number to the client with the biggest issue.

"It's Abhay Chetan," he said into the receiver. "What did you do to the software?"

"I don't know," his client said. "All I know is the system went down sometime Friday night. We got it back up but the security tag is blinking red so we had to shut down to protect the data. How soon can you get here?"

The last thing Abhay wanted to do was head to Hong Kong at that moment but he had a contract with this firm for the next five months. He sighed. "I'll be on the next flight."

"Good. I'll make sure your suite is ready and a car is available to take care of you."

"Yeah."

Chapter Twelve

Mathias listened to all the messages. Three of them were from Abhay and after two days Abhay had stopped calling. He'd spoken to Collin a couple more times since their first conversation and Mathias had realized he'd acted like a moron. As he sped through the late afternoon traffic toward Brigada, Mathias had some time to think over what had happened between him and Abhay. Though Ko was worried about Abhay's relationship with Mathias, Abhay hadn't been. He'd stood up for Mathias.

'Things are new between us and I don't want to ruin what we're trying to build here.'

That was what Abhay had said. He hadn't agreed with Ko and he hadn't remained silent. Yet, Mathias had been offended. Maybe this whole thing had nothing to do with Abhay. Maybe it was Mathias' heart's way of telling him it was time to get off that stage and put some damn clothes on.

When he arrived at the building, the guard at the gate remembered him and let him in. When he got out of the car, he knew he couldn't get into the building without

Abhay's code and he couldn't remember it from the last time. Since he'd been upset, he'd deleted all of Abhay's texts. He climbed from his car so he could cool down.

No answer.

He hung up and called again.

Still no response.

"Mathias, right?"

He turned to see a woman standing there. She was dark-skinned with big brown eyes. With her black hair tied back she looked like a model. "Um, do I know you?"

"Dana — Dana Salazaar."

"Abhay's friend."

"You've heard of me," Dana said. "Good. Why are you here?"

"To see Abhay."

She folded her arms across her chest. "Abhay isn't here. I'm here to check on his unit."

"Check on the unit? Why?"

"He's in Hong Kong at the moment," Dana explained.

Mathias' heart raced inside his chest. "When is he coming back?"

She shrugged. "I don't know. He had a bit of an emergency and flew out pretty quickly. But the last time I checked, you broke up with him. So, why are you really here?"

"I was an idiot, okay? I thought his friend was — look, it doesn't matter. Do you know where he's staying?"

"Maybe."

"I know you are trying to protect him but I need to talk to him and he's not picking up his phone."

"Mathias, you really hurt him. I mean, I know it's only been a few days and a couple of dates but Abhay doesn't date. He's not the type. I've known him a while and he's never let a man get as close as you did. He tries so hard to stay away from men, from intimacy and then here you come. Then just when he's opening up, there you went."

"I panicked."

"And who's to say this isn't going to happen again?" Dana snapped. "He's a great guy and he's been through hell to get to this mountain top. People are always going to talk, Mathias. They're always going to stick their noses in where it doesn't belong. If every time someone is an asshole about what the two of you have you run, then leave now."

Mathias nodded. He deserved that too. Hearing Ko speak, Mathias had been blinded by the fury of the man's words. But Dana was right — people would say what they wanted. What Mathias always had to remember was that he was in a relationship with Abhay — or wanted to be in a relationship with Abhay, not Ko.

"Please. I have to —"

"Dana! Have you seen — oh, hello."

Mathias frowned. "What are *you* doing here?" Mathias glared at Ko. "Haven't you caused enough trouble?"

"I'm sorry you took what I said the wrong way but I was only looking out for a friend," Ko said, resting his hands akimbo. "You get that, don't you?"

Mathias turned from him. Had he not, he knew there would have been a brawl in the parking lot. "Dana..."

The woman titled her head, contemplation rich in her eyes. After a silent eternity, she reached into her purse and pulled out a pen and a small notebook. She scribbled on it. "I don't give second chances easily, Mathias. Pray Abhay is not a stubborn mule like I am." She ripped the paper out and handed it to Mathias.

"Thank you."

"Mhmm." She cocked a hip.

While Mathias had a smile for her, he shoved past Ko and climbed back into his car. As he sped back toward his place he glanced at the paper. Dana had written a hotel name and room number on it. He clung to that paper as if it was his lifeline.

At his house, he placed it under his cell phone on the island in the kitchen then darted for his laptop. He couldn't believe just how expensive it was to fly to Hong Kong. In any case, he dug into his savings and paid for it. Mathias then called in to work to book time off for a 'family emergency' and tossed some clothes into a bag. He had to be patient until the next day before he could leave and Mathias thought he'd go crazy. Mathias passed the time pacing his home, trying to call Abhay again and worrying.

First thing the next morning, he called a cab and was on his way. It would be fifteen hours before he reached Hong Kong — after a stop in Shanghai. He climbed into the back seat of a taxi and tried his best to relax while the car hurtled through the street toward central Hong Kong.

The hotel stood before him soon enough, towering to the sky. It was a glass monstrosity that resembled something from a futuristic movie. But Mathias took a second to admire it before jogging up the front steps and into the luxurious lobby. A doorman tipped his hat at Mathias, who smiled and nodded a greeting. It took him a little while to find the elevators. The last thing Mathias wanted to do was ask a worker. He didn't want questions about who he was and he didn't want them calling Abhay's room and warning him.

Exhausted, he waited for the door to open then checked the paper Dana had given him again.

Thankfully, the walls had number plaques and soon he was standing before Abhay's suite. He knocked.

No answer.

He knocked again.

Still no answer.

What had he been thinking? He'd just dropped his life and jetted off to a foreign country without telling anyone where he was going. Abhay wasn't at the hotel and Mathias had no place to sleep. After trying to call Abhay a few more times, and failing, Mathias figured he'd rest for a little bit, find somewhere to eat then head back to the airport. With his open ticket, he was sure he'd be able to get on a plane for home.

But he was so — damn — tired.

* * * *

After a long day, Abhay left his clients' office and made his way back to the hotel. He stopped at the front desk to grab his messages then made his way up to his suite. When he got close, someone was sitting on the floor, leaning against Abhay's door. At first he thought the person was either drunk or high. He inched closer and almost fainted when he realized it was Mathias and he was fast asleep. With a sigh, Abhay hunched down in front of Mathias and touched his cheek.

"Matt?" Abhay called. He tapped Mathias' cheeks. "Mathias. Mathias, wake up."

"Just five more minutes, baby," Mathias moaned.

Abhay smiled. Going down on his knees, Abhay set his bag on the floor, braced his palms on either side of Mathias' body and kissed Mathias. He didn't move until Mathias was kissing him and moaning.

"Hi," Abhay said.

"I'm sorry," Mathias whispered as he rubbed the back of a hand against his lips. "I didn't mean to just show up but I was driving myself crazy."

"Come inside," Abhay said, rising and grabbing his bag. Though he was happy to see Mathias, he knew they had to talk. They had to get some things out in the open then deal with the fallout that would come afterward.

He helped Mathias up then let himself into the luxury unit with Mathias close behind him. He set his bag down, plugged his phone in to charge then walked into the kitchen area. After pouring them both a glass of wine, he handed one to Mathias. Instead of sipping, Mathias set the glass aside. He seemed tired, drained. Abhay hated that expression on Mathias so he took the man's hand and led him into the large bathroom.

"Strip," Abhay said.

"We have to talk," Mathias said.

"Yes, I know. But you're tired. The flight from Bathsheba to Hong Kong is a very long one. Come on, we can talk later. Take your clothes off."

Mathias was hesitant but began doing as Abhay had instructed. Abhay wanted to enjoy watching Mathias' beautiful body coming bare but, instead, he focused on the Jacuzzi tub and turned the water on. He tested the temperature of it and once he was satisfied, he undressed. He then got into the large tub and extended his hand to Mathias, who accepted and climbed in. Abhay then sat and pulled Mathias' back against his chest. He wrapped his arms around Mathias and settled in, feeling the jets massage both of them.

Mathias trembled in his arms and Abhay dropped his lips to Mathias' shoulder. After a little while, Abhay couldn't resist using his lips to skim Mathias' shoulder, to trace Mathias' flesh, up the side of his neck to kiss behind Mathias' ear.

"I never wanted to hurt you," Mathias said, his voice sleepy. "I just didn't want to embarrass you. You had everything—friends, wealthy, a good job—and here I was… Ko's words struck a nerve and I've learned my lesson. I'd be with you, not others."

Abhay kissed his head. "How'd you find me?"

"I met Dana." Mathias sighed and cuddled closer.

Abhay laughed. "I'm sorry about that."

"She loves you, you know."

"I know." Abhay sighed. "Matt, you didn't have to come all this way. I was coming home."

"You don't understand. I couldn't let you go on thinking I didn't want you," Mathias said, shifting around to meet Abhay's eyes. "I'm not ashamed of what I do. This wasn't the dream. I wanted to get married, have kids, do a job that was respectable and honest. Life was never easy for me. I grew up alone. I'm not telling you any of this for pity. But I have nothing left. All I can offer you is my independence, my promise that another man will never put his hand on this body and that—"

Abhay kissed away the rest of his words. He tangled his arms around Mathias, pulling him into his chest and deepening the kiss. In that moment, the memory of the things they'd done to each other swarmed in on Abhay, hardening his cock. He tugged his mouth back and framed Mathias' face with his wet palms.

"Make love to me," Mathias whispered. "Forgive me."

"Darling, there's nothing to forgive." Abhay brushed his lips against Mathias' forehead. He said nothing else. Silently, he climbed from the tub to grab a condom and lube. When he returned, he drew Mathias into his arms and merged their lips again. This time, he exhaled and threw himself into the kiss, allowing Mathias to find his tongue. But Abhay wanted more—he needed to taste Mathias, to feel him grow hard and throbbing on his tongue. Even so, Abhay behaved. He sat with Mathias in the tub, making out, trailing his fingers across Mathias' flesh.

Mathias sighed and Abhay took that to mean he was doing the right thing. He dragged his mouth against the back of Mathias' neck before letting water drain through his fingers against the intertwined thorns that were carved into Mathias' back. When the water began getting cooler, he rose and climbed out. He wrapped a towel around his own hips before extending another to Mathias. His lover accepted it and after Mathias exited the tub and wrapped himself in his towel, Abhay took a second to drain the tub then led Mathias to the bed.

"Are you hungry?" Abhay asked.

"Yes."

"Climb into bed. I'll order room service."

"Abhay—we really should talk."

Abhay said nothing. Instead he called the front desk and ordered food then turned to face Mathias. "Okay—let's talk."

For a long time, Mathias said nothing. He sat on the side of the bed then walked over to the window to stare out. Abhay folded his arms and waited.

"I'm not used to men who want me for me," Mathias said. "I'm not used to men who take me to meet their families—their sister, their friends. All the men I've been with treated me like a dirty little secret. And I vowed never to let that happen again. Then come the men who always believed I wanted their souls. And after I heard Ko talking, the memories, the hurt—all of that came flooding back and I ran. I didn't mean to hurt you. But I had to get away. I didn't want you to think I wanted your money."

"Do you?"

Mathias whirled to face him. The anger Abhay saw in that gaze paralyzed him.

"Don't you dare!" Mathias snapped. "Don't you *ever* — Of course I don't want your money! I don't want anything from you but — I just want to be the kind of man you can one day love. I don't need you to take care of me — financially at least. I've been on my own ever since I was a kid and no, my job may not be the one parents dream of for their kids, but it's a job and it affords me the chance to do for myself."

"You're angry," Abhay said. "That question wasn't because I think that's what you're doing. I asked so you will get mad — get it out of your system so we can get past this."

Abhay stepped closer. "I'm looking for love, Mathias. A few years ago I thought that was soft, that it made me weak, but I look around at my friends and they love their men like the earth was on fire. Sure, they're not perfect but you see it every time they look at each other. And I crave that. So let's agree on a few things."

"Okay."

"Let's agree that we're both here for the right reasons," Abhay continued. "That we both feel this almost supernatural pull toward each other. That we're in this together and all decisions having to do with us be made by *us*, not our friends. Can you do that?"

"Deal."

"Good." Abhay kissed Mathias. He'd been patient, waiting for that. When he finally couldn't breathe, he lifted his head. "We're going to eat so you can regain some strength. But afterward, Mathias, your body — all of it — is mine."

"Anytime you want it."

Chapter Thirteen

The next morning, Mathias was on top of the world. With Abhay still asleep, he took a shower, ordered room service then, while waiting, called Collin. He stared down over central Hong Kong, wondering if there was a more beautiful sight in the world.

"Hello?" Collin's sleepy voice came over the phone.

"Sorry to wake you," Mathias said. "But I didn't want you to worry."

"Worry? Mathias?"

"Yeah. I'm in Hong Kong."

"Wait…" There was shuffling on the other end before Collin spoke again. "I could have sworn you said you were in Hong Kong."

"That's what I said."

"I know I probably shouldn't ask because I might regret it. But why are you in Hong Kong?"

"Abhay had a business trip and I had to make things right," Mathias said.

"Wasn't he coming back?"

"Yeah. But it was driving me crazy. Look, check on the house for me, okay?"

"Matt, when are you coming back?"

"Soon—I can't stay away from work too long." Mathias dragged a hand over his head. "And don't worry about me. Abhay and I have talked and we're good."

"And you sure this guy is worth all of this?"

"Definitely."

With the conversation over, Mathias found a plug to charge his phone. He was going to crawl back into bed when the doorbell rang. The food was delivered and he rolled the cart into the bedroom where Abhay was still sleeping. After pouring two cups of coffee, Mathias set them on the tray and eased into the bed with Abhay. He dragged his mouth from Abhay's ear, down along his jawline to his lips. Abhay moaned and reached for the back of Mathias' head to keep his mouth there for a kiss.

"Good morning—"

"Mmm."

"I ordered breakfast," Mathias told him. "Coffee?"

"Yes please." Abhay nuzzled Mathias' neck with his lips. "First I must use the bathroom."

With a smile, Mathias let his lover go. Abhay wasn't long and soon they were sitting, facing each other on the large bed, eating breakfast with their fingers. It was the simplest thing Mathias had ever done with a man but it felt real. Between bites and stolen kisses, Mathias was flying so high, a few times his heart lurched as if the other shoe was about to drop.

With breakfast done, they showered together and wrangled over what they had to get done that day. Mathias knew Abhay had work but when Abhay insisted on spending the time with him, Mathias gave in and decided to enjoy whatever they had to do.

"A temple?" Abhay asked. "You've come all this way and all you want to do is see a temple?"

"You asked about the one thing I had to see while I'm here."

Abhay pressed his lips into a thin line before dropping a kiss to Mathias's. "Okay, baby. You're the boss."

Mathias laughed.

It took them half an hour and soon Mathias was left in stunned silence. Never in a million years had Mathias thought he'd be standing in front of one of the most beautiful buildings in the world, looking up and marveling at its greatness. The Man Mo Temple was breathtaking and so very different from anything he'd ever witnessed. *A stripper from some small city shouldn't have access to any of this – that isn't how it works.* But, there he was, Abhay clutching his hand and waiting by his side while Mathias tried not to cry at how insignificant he felt in the presence of such history.

"I've always loved history," Mathias confided. "My history marks were higher than my English grades, which stunned my teachers. I could read something and be able to remember it months later. They couldn't understand how."

"Maybe that's your calling."

"You think?" Mathias turned to look at Abhay. "You might be right. You know, this temple is a tribute to the god of literature and the god of war?"

"I did not know that." Abhay released his hand and lifted his eyes to the building. "Strange those two gods would be worshipped in the same place."

"Not really when you look back throughout China's history. It makes perfect sense — can we go in?"

Abhay nodded and they climbed the staircase at the front then dipped thorough the red door leading inside.

"Thanks for taking time off work to do this with me," Mathias said. "I didn't want to leave without seeing at least the outside."

"Any time."

Mathias roamed the interior with Abhay, who walked like a silent guardian angel either by his side or just behind him. From time to time he stopped, glanced to see if anyone was around them, then he stole a quick kiss from Abhay, just because he could. After a while, they exited the temple and stopped at a gift shop nearby. Abhay insisted on buying Mathias a gift to remember the trip. Mathias picked a red and gold, handmade trinket that he could hang back at his house.

They took another few hours to travel around Hong Kong, from Victoria Peak to Lantau Island. By the time they made it back to the hotel, Mathias was exhausted. He kissed Abhay and left him to contend with the barrage of calls he'd have to return. After a while, Abhay had turned off his phone. Mathias had felt guilty when he'd seen that but he'd remained silent. He placed his bags at the foot of the bed then peeled his shirt over his head. Mathias was undoing his belt buckle when warm hands snaked around his midsection. He turned his head just as Abhay rested his chin to Mathias' shoulder.

"I thought you had work?" Mathias sighed. He melted into Abhay's hard body.

"I do," Abhay whispered. "But there will always be work. I was thinking as I turned on my laptop that you'd be in the tub, naked, water flowing down your perfect body. How could I ignore those thoughts?"

Mathias trembled. "Would you like to watch or join me?"

"Join."

Reluctantly, Mathias peeled his body from Abhay's hold and backed toward the bathroom. "Well, Mr. Chetan, as you wish."

Mathias stripped and turned on the water. All the while, Abhay's gaze traced his frame. To give his lover something to look at, Mathias did everything sexier than it needed to be. As he tested the water, he bent over, bracing one hand against the rim of the tub. To his pleasure, Abhay slid a finger down his crack. Mathias glanced back at Abhay then righted himself and stepped under the downpour.

"You're still dressed, Abhay," Mathias cooed. "I thought you wanted me."

Abhay smiled and joined Mathias under the water, fully clothed. Pressed into the cool wall, Mathias accepted Abhay's kiss and the lust that he knew was flowing through Abhay's body. He spread his legs to give his lover more access and was rewarded with Abhay's long fingers wrapped around his dick.

Mathias managed to get Abhay's wet clothes off him and on the floor of the tub or wherever the pieces had fallen. This time, as he turned and offered his ass to Abhay, Mathias knew there was no maybe about falling in love with him. He was already more than halfway there.

He gave himself to Abhay that night so many times he lost count. Somehow, at some point they wound up in the bed, sheets being crumbled in his palms as Abhay licked every inch of Mathias' body. When they finally slumped together in the dark, they were both panting hard.

Chapter Fourteen

On the fourth night Mathias had joined him in Hong Kong, Abhay got around to calling his sister. She'd been worried about him, her message buried under the mountain of others he'd received. He chatted with her for about an hour. The last few minutes of their conversation were a fight to keep his mind straight because Mathias had been nibbling on his body. When he was off the phone with Priya, he'd made love to Mathias again.

Now, as they lay in the darkness of their room, their bodies tangled together, Abhay couldn't help smiling. He turned and dropped a kiss to Mathias' head.

"I've been thinking of going back to school," Mathias said out of the blue.

Abhay thought he'd been sleeping. "Oh yeah? To do what?"

"History." Mathias replied. "I figured once I have the bachelor's degree I could then decide what to do with it. At least I'll have the formal training."

"That is true," Abhay agreed. "You're not doing this because of what Ko said, are you?"

"No."

"Will going back to school make you happy?"

Mathias nodded against Abhay's chest. "I'd of course have to quit my job. I could actually start dancing legit because I do have the skills for that. I just don't know how I'd go about any of that."

"I could help."

"Abha—"

"Look, you dropped everything to come all the way here for me," Abhay said. "You feel it too, don't you? That inexplicable pull that is happening—please, tell me I'm not alone."

Mathias shifted. "You're not alone."

"Then let me help. I can't get you jobs but I can open a door or two for you. Jackson Stark is a dancer. He has connections."

"As in Ko's fiancé? No, I don't think so."

"Mathias…"

"I said no." Mathias rose and climbed from the bed. He exited the room, leaving Abhay sitting up, staring after him.

Frustrated, Abhay flopped back to the pillows. He understood why Mathias wouldn't want Ko's help but Jackson hadn't even met the guy. After a few minutes of waiting to see if Mathias would return, Abhay climbed out of the bed, grabbed a nearby pair of jeans and pulled them on. He exited the bedroom to find Mathias staring out at the city moving along beneath them like a lighted trail. He snuck up behind Mathias, wrapped his arms around his lover's body and drew him close. "I'm sorry, darling," Abhay whispered. "I just thought if I could help you, you wouldn't have to do this alone."

"I won't be alone." Mathias' voice was soft. "I'll have you. I'm used to doing it all by myself. I now have to learn to lean on you but I don't want to do it and have your friends believe I'm using you. Things are going to be rough—this will *not* be easy. All you can do is be there when I need a shoulder."

"That's it? Don't ask me to turn a blind eye when…"

"When what?"

"You're struggling."

Mathias turned to frame his face. "That's a part of life. You've told me the story of your life—you know how bad it can get."

"I do."

"Then trust that if or when I need help, I'll ask for it."

Abhay nodded. "I'm so glad you came here," Abhay said. "I thought I was going to lose my mind and I just couldn't understand it."

"This is the most out of the box thing I've ever done— well, aside from taking the job at the Rose. I never thought I'd run after a man, much less to the other side of the world. But you, Abhay—I feel like you're worth it."

Abhay had no words. Instead, he kissed Mathias softly, enjoying the slide of their tongues together and the naked firmness of Mathias' body.

"I'm starving," Mathias whispered. "Did we have any of that cake left?"

"Cake isn't a meal."

Mathias crinkled his nose and kissed Abhay again before walking away to look under the domes on their room service cart. "You're not my father." Mathias winked. "You can't tell me what to do."

"Can't I?" Abhay played along. "I may not be your father, Mathias. But after you have your cake, I'll show you I aim to be your daddy."

Mathias looked up and caught his bottom lip between his teeth. When Abhay glanced down Mathias' body, he noticed just how hard Mathias had become.

"I see you like the idea," Abhay said with a smirk. "Enjoy."

He turned on his heels for the bedroom, having every intention of showing Mathias just how naughty he could truly be.

* * * *

It took them another week before they returned to Bathsheba. After the long flight all Mathias wanted to do was find food, shower then crawl into a bed — his, Abhay's, Mathias didn't care. But the moment they entered Abhay's place, they were bombarded with visits from all Abhay's friends — even Darius and Feng Stark with their two sons and Dana. Apparently Feng and Darius' daughter was off to some school dance but would visit at a later time. The introductions took a while and he'd forgotten a few names by the time they were over but the motley crew seemed to adore Abhay.

After a potluck dinner, put together by everyone and Priya, the group sat around to talk and laugh. It was amazing to watch the interaction. They went from eyeing him — probably wondering what his motives were — to telling him embarrassing stories about Abhay.

During it all, Abhay sat with a palm resting against Mathias' thigh. Between the stories, the mirth and the kisses, Mathias was positively giddy. But as happy as he was to be in the midst of all of that, it soon became too much for Mathias and his tired brain.

"Baby, I have to go to the bathroom." Mathias leaned in to whisper to Abhay.

"You okay?"

"Oh yeah. But I'm human and need to pee."

Abhay laughed and kissed him. "You're human?"

After crinkling his nose at Abhay, who chuckled, Mathias rose, excused himself and headed to the bathroom. Afterward, he grabbed a beer and retreated to the balcony. His butt was in the seat before the footsteps drew him around. Ko stood there and instantly, Mathias' back went up.

"Look, if you've come for a fight," Mathias said. "I'm not in the mood."

"I'm not here to fight," Ko replied. He stepped through the door and leaned against the railing, leveling his brown eyes at Mathias. His silver engagement ring glistened in the moonlight. "I only wanted to make sure Abi was going into this with both eyes open. It was nothing against you. Abhay is my friend and I know what he's been through…"

"And you thought I was going to ruin his life."

"Not ruin his life — break his heart. Come on, Mathias, you would have done the same damn thing if you were in my shoes."

"Man, you rich folks really suck at your apologies."

Ko's muscular shoulders rose and fell. "I'll apologize for hurting your feelings but I won't for having Abi's back. He's never once betrayed me or disappointed me so I'm not about to feel bad for wanting to make sure he's okay."

Mathias inhaled, held the breath then exhaled. He knew Abhay would like him to get along with Ko and the guy didn't seem like a horrible person. Mathias was just the kind of son of a bitch who could hold a grudge. "I get it. But you have to know that this is not a joke for me. I've spent my whole adult life looking for a man who could see beyond the fact that I take my clothes off for a living. I'm not about to fuck this up."

Ko nodded.

"I mean it. I've worked hard to make sure I was stable so that when I did find him he'd see I didn't want anything from him but his heart. Abhay is willing to give me that so I'm a very happy man."

"I know how that is." Ko moved to take the seat beside Mathias. "Honestly, if Kent and Darius had freaked out when Jackson and I had first started dating I don't know what I'd have done. I shouldn't have said what I said. I'm really sorry, man."

"Don't worry about it."

"Abi told me you're going back to school."

Mathias smiled and took a drink from the bottle. "I'm going to look into applying on Monday. I'll go back if they'll have me."

"They will."

"Hopefully. I'll have to quit my job. I figure since dancing was the only thing I've ever really been good at, I'd try and do the whole audition-for-things thing."

"Jackson has connections. I'm sure —"

"No." Mathias shook his head. "I don't want any handouts."

"It wouldn't be a handout. Look, I have a warehouse space that I'm not using at the moment. It'll be the new Bathsheba design space once I get around to making all the changes but that won't be for another year. You can use it as a rehearsal space until you either find something more permanent or it's time for construction to start. I know how expensive studio space is."

Mathias tilted his head. "You'd do that? For me?"

"Once you become a part of this family, Mathias, you do nothing on your own." Ko rose. "Abhay sees something in you. He obviously feels something for you because—well, you two made love. He's not the type to give up his body. So if he's chosen you, that means you're here for as long as you want to be here."

"I'm here—all of me."

"Good. Then the space is yours for as long as necessary."

Mathias rose and extended a hand to thank Ko. Instead of shaking, Ko pulled him into a hug.

"Well, neither of you require bail." Abhay's voice had laughter in it. "I take it you've worked things out?"

Mathias stepped from Ko's embrace. "Yeah. More lessons for me to learn when it comes to your friends."

"We had to clear the air," Ko said. He moved past Abhay into the house but didn't leave until after patting Abhay's shoulder.

Alone with his lover, Mathias set his beer down and eased into Abhay's arms. He tangled his arms around Abhay's neck and looked up into his face. "I think, Abhay, that life is about to become a whole lot better."

"Oh?"

"Mhmm. According to Ko, I'm a part of a family now. I never had one of those before. The group home wasn't really—it was just a roof and food. It's going to take some adjustments but I'm sure I can swing it. I've always wanted a family."

Abhay grinned.

"I think I'm going to like being a part of a family. I look at Darius and Feng with their kids. And I listen to how he talks about Emily, their daughter, and see the way they are around the boys, and I want that."

"That's great to hear." Abhay slid his palms up and down Mathias' back. "Because Priya just cornered me in the kitchen asking when she can expect to be an aunty."

Mathias tossed his head back and laughed. "Well, she's going to have to wait a little bit longer. I would like some more time to get to know my man."

"Your man..." Abhay moaned. "I do so love the sound of that."

Epilogue

Eight months later...

Abhay frowned at the screen. He was pretty sure he'd written the code properly, but he still couldn't get the damn software to behave. He'd been trying to create his own security software for online shopping carts. It'd been a dream since he graduated university. If he could get it perfected, Thaddeus had agreed to purchase the program under his line of software for a healthy price. Abhay would stay on as the top tech for the program. Abhay's new company would be Bollywood software.

"Abi?" Mathias called from the door of Abhay's home office. "I can't believe this."

"What's going on?" Abhay looked up from the algorithms he'd been fussing over and lounged in his chair.

"I got in!" Mathias exclaimed, waving a letter. "I scored the highest marks in the entrance exam and so they're offering me a full scholarship."

Abhay ran around the desk and hugged Mathias. "Congratulations! See? I told you."

"Thank you," Mathias whispered, returning the embrace. "I know it hasn't been easy for you with all my studying and the late nights—the lack of intimacy."

Abhay leaned back to meet Mathias' eyes. "You were going for your dreams. How could I step in the way of that? And besides, remember when you first met me I hadn't been with anyone since my late teens. I'm used to it."

"You shouldn't have to get *used* to it anymore." Mathias looked upset. "You have me and how am I supposed to show you that I want to be with you if I don't—well—you know?"

Abhay laughed. He framed Mathias' face. "Do you remember a couple of months ago I was having issues with the construction workers at the new space? You came into the office, sat in my lap, wrapped your arms around me and kissed the side of my head."

"Yeah."

"That is oftentimes better than sex."

Mathias' cheeks pinkened. "You sure?"

"I'm sure. Besides, your program is going to be four years long—it's going to get worse before it gets better."

"I won't let school interfere with our lives." Mathias lifted his chin. "Sure, there's going to be times when I'll be all weird about it but I'll work hard to make sure I carve out time for you. You're important to me, Abhay. You know that, right?"

"I know." Abhay kissed him. "What do you say we celebrate?"

"What do you have in mind?"

"Well, we can start out with a date," Abhay suggested. "Tonight."

"Don't forget, we have the gang coming over," Mathias said. He glanced at his watch. "Like—now."

Abhay sighed. He'd forgotten. After another kiss, he led Mathias over to the sofa and they fell onto it together. "Okay — tomorrow we'll go on a date. I'll set it all up."

"And when the date is over, do we get to sit in the back seat of my car and make out?"

Abhay grinned. "Is that a rhetorical question?"

"Touché."

Abhay took a moment and kissed his boyfriend. He cradled Mathias' neck and inhaled while their tongues danced around each other. He would enjoy the few silent moments with Mathias before everyone else descended on the house. Everyone except Darius and Feng's kids would be there. Ko, Jackson, Ravinder, Thaddeus, Dana, Priya, Darius, Feng and Dana's new boyfriend, Leon — all of them would be in Mathias' small house and it was about to be chaos. He sighed while Mathias dragged his mouth down Abhay's neck. In that instant, he realized just how much he's missed Mathias. They saw each other every day, but for two months after they had started dating, Mathias had been in study mode and auditioning mode.

From one book to another, from one audition to another, they hadn't found time to be together as they should. It hadn't been easy and a few times Abhay had been tempted to call it quits. He was dating someone and he'd been lonely. It hadn't always been Mathias' doing. Abhay was focused on building Bollywood Software. But he'd soldiered on, until Mathias had scored a major dance contract. He would be dancing backup for a major musician, performing for a year-long stint in Bathsheba.

The contract was coming to an end but Mathias hadn't seemed worried about it. Abhay pushed those thoughts to the back of his head and enjoyed Mathias' hands on him. He locked eyes with Mathias then tilted his head to take Mathias' earlobe between his teeth. Mathias growled.

"Hon, we can't start this now." Mathias panted. "They'll be here soon."

"I know but I just want to feel you naked against me." Abhay moaned with disappointment. "Is that so bad?"

"No — never bad. We don't have time right now."

"Time." Abhay growled. "Don't tell me about time. I just want —"

The doorbell rang though he didn't want to answer it. "Let it ring again," Abhay whispered, dragging his mouth along Mathias' jawline. "I'm not ready to let you go."

"I know, Abi. But the sooner we let them in, the sooner we can get them to go home."

"You obviously don't know them very well," Abhay muttered, pouting.

Mathias kissed him one final time and stood. Together, they fixed their clothing and Mathias turned for the door.

"I love you," Abhay called.

Mathias stopped and shifted to face him. "I love you too."

"Are you sure?" Abhay asked.

Mathias returned and kissed him deeply. "I'm positive. Now, let's entertain our family and then I can show you how much."

"Show me how —" Abhay smirked. "Bad boy."

Mathias stole another kiss before darting from the room. Soon, voices filled the home as, couple by couple, their friends showed up.

All throughout the get together that morphed into a celebration, Abhay couldn't imagine how happy he'd become. He kept his eyes on Priya, listening to her laughter, and on Mathias, loving the way he was hugged by Dana and fist bumped by Ko and Jackson. Abhay's heart was full. He was in love and for the first time since he had become an adult, he knew what it was like to have a man love him back.

Ciro

Excerpt

Chapter One

Ciro sat before his mother in the Hall of Winds and tilted his head. She grinned at him and patted her hair gently.

"Do you like it?" she questioned. "I thought I should change it up a bit after so many years."

He smiled. "It is very becoming, Mother," he replied, reaching over to touch her hand gently. "I truly like it."

"And yet you seem unhappy."

"I am." He couldn't hide anything from her. Though her wrath could be devastating to anyone who tested her, Thýella was a loving mother. Perhaps she was too kind, for now most of her children ran amok among the very people she cherished so dearly. "There is something unpleasant I wish to speak with you about."

"I think I know what it is."

"In the coming days, I will have to hunt more of my brothers," Ciro began, swallowing a lump rising in his throat. "They have posed unnecessary risk to Terra. Gaia is not pleased and has tasked me in setting my brothers straight. But you and I both know they would rather die than be kind to humans. What should I do?"

"You know what must be done, Ciro. You are the eldest."

"Mother—they will not stop with just a mere defeat. It has been proven repeatedly in the past. They keep right on coming."

"Then they must die..." Thýella lifted her head, elongating her neck, a stern look filling her eyes. "They are my children, and though I love them fiercely, they have disappointed me so desperately. I cannot deal with Gaia's wrath. And she would be right in being angry and seeking retribution for their damage."

"Ciro!" The second eldest ran into the room. "We have trouble."

"Who is it?"

"Gala."

Ciro's heart broke. He gritted his teeth and stood. "I was hoping to reason with him but the more I think about it, the more I know that will never work."

"You cannot reason with a mad man," Koi said sternly. "You were the one who taught me that, brother."

Ciro nodded, gave himself a moment to pull himself together then offered his mother a sorrowful look. "I must go, Mother."

"I will come with you," Koi told him. "Two is always better than being alone."

"No," Ciro said. "Stay here with Mother. If he gets past me, he may show up here. I need someone I trust to protect her."

"I assure you I can protect myself." Thýella raised her chin.

Koi continued as if Thýella hadn't spoken. "You trust me?" he asked in a soft voice.

He touched Koi's cheek then patted it. "We will talk later. Please stay here."

Koi did not look impressed, and after pressing his lips into a thin line, he nodded stiffly.

Accepting a kiss to his cheek from his mother, Ciro took a moment to breathe. With a final look at Thýella, he exited the luxurious room and began his descent to Earth.

Once he landed, Ciro knew something was about to happen. There wasn't much time to look around and take stock of anything, or even call for assistance. Usually, he had a little leeway to get Ares, Adrestia and Hygeia to help him clear cities and towns. In this instance, he had no such luxury.

Ciro bent his knees, digging his feet into the ground just before pushing upward. He flew through the air with his arms by his sides and his chest mere inches away from the tall structure before him. He climbed higher, up the side of the tallest building in the city bordered by two small towns. Darkness swarmed above, as though Hades had risen and tossed a blanket over everything.

He felt it then — the charge of lightning flashing from his eyes caused by the stench of evil carried on the wind. The breeze howled, surging from the north, and Ciro knew it was going to be bad if he didn't figure out what to do — and fast. With his coat flopping behind him in the breeze, Ciro stood atop the one-hundred-and-eighty-story building. He tried figuring out where the attack would come from. Tracking had not been easy. When he was led to one of the small towns in the east, it almost broke his heart. The town was quiet, lovely, perfect.

Children ran along the streets calling to one another. A little boy kicked a ball so hard it flew over a fence, hitting an old man on the side of the head. The man only laughed and handed the ball back.

A couple of dogs chased each other down a back road, barking happily at their game. Lovers lay on towels and blankets on what the locals called the beach, which was merely a lake with a sandy shore.

On the far side, workers had used heavy equipment to pile large rocks into the water so people could sit on them to watch the sunset. Ciro knew if something was to happen there, the place would be devastated. The citizens would lose everything and the town would be wiped off the map. In order to stop it, the only idea he could see was to lead his prey away from the perfection he now watched to somewhere larger, to somewhere he would have more room to navigate and stop the attack.

Something pulled Ciro from his thoughts, snapping his head upward. Though it was dark, a scent filled the air that he instantly recognized — danger. Suddenly, it was there before him. He saw it the moment the funnel shape started forming. Pressing his thumb and forefinger of his right hand together, he then dragged his thumb down his index finger. A white streak of lightning followed his thumb while he frowned. He shoved his left hand out, sending a ball of lightning from his palm that disappeared within the funnel. A growl of pain followed, but it didn't stop the turmoil.

Ciro made a face then looked down. Below him, he discerned the panic. People were running, trying desperately to get out of the way. But the funnel cloud simply grew bigger. The larger it got, the more fear Ciro detected from the crowd beneath him, making him slightly ill. He tried shocking it a second time, which only slowed it before it sped up again.

That was precisely what his foe wanted — to see the humans running around, scattering like headless chickens in their fright. Gala fed from their misery, which made no sense since he was not a god of pain. He wasn't even a god, but a tributary of one. Ciro was instantly sick and disappointed. His brothers were powerful beings but they were weak from their cruelty.

Gala didn't care how harming the humans made his mother feel. Ciro knew that for certain.

"I see Mother sent her favorite son," Gala spat. "Predictable—as always."

"That is not how it is and you know it."

"And how do I know that, Ciro? Whenever something goes wrong, she sends you—as if you are god and creator of us all."

"That is because you act like a child. You do things— these things…" Ciro motioned around him furiously. "Then you expect her to welcome you with open arms."

"She does not welcome me at all," Gala snapped.

"I am not in the mood for these games, Gala," Ciro thundered, his voice echoing through the heavens. "Your pity party is not one I wish to attend."

Gala's anger sent a jolt of lightning downward. When it hit the ground, the earth shook slightly and a gaping hole appeared at the landing sight.

"That is enough," Ciro yelled. "Stop this madness *now*!"

"But I am having so much fun," Gala teased. "Why should I give that up?" A face pushed out from the side of the twister and smirked at Ciro. "Because you love the humans? Why do you think it so important to protect them? When are you going to learn we are better than they are? When are you going to accept that they are merely insects in our paths? Crush them like the insignificant beings they are."

"That decision is not your call. They are Mother's prized people and what you do breaks her heart. Do you not care?"

"Mother is weak. Is that not why we are here? Her weakness to fight Zeus? Come now, brother, surely you see that as clearly as I do."

Ciro growled. "She is your mother. What you do puts us all in jeopardy with Gaia. Now either stop this madness, or—"

"Or what?"

"Be destroyed."

"You wouldn't. Mother will not allow it."

"Oh, Gala, so young and so naïve. Mother has made her choice. She chooses her people. But with or without her blessings, I know you have to die."

"You do not scare me, Ciro. Your bark is worse than your bite. Besides, you love family too much to harm me."

Why do they always tempt me so?

Ciro lowered his head slightly but kept his gaze on the funnel before him. Gala's face had disappeared into his creation again. Brother or not, Gala was a threat and Ciro would be damned if he allowed this joker to destroy another town or city because of his god complex.

Raking his hair from his face, he looked down one last time at the people scurrying back and forth. Pieces of concrete were breaking off structures and hitting the ground. Ciro watched as a chunk struck someone and they fell, to lie still.

"Hygeia—I seek your assistance," he called to the Goddess of Health.

She instantly appeared, beautiful and glowing in white. He smiled sadly at her before pointing downward. Hygeia nodded.

"I shall try and limit your work," Ciro promised. "In the meantime, please help them."

"I will, my friend. Go and do what you have to do."

With those words, Ciro jumped from his perch. He disappeared then reappeared in the center of the funnel. True to form, Gala emerged out of thin air and instantly attacked. Vanishing, Ciro came into view again behind Gala, sending a kick to his back. Gala fell forward and vanished. Inhaling, Ciro turned in time to slam a foot into Gala's chest right as he reappeared. Gala flew across the space and fell out of his funnel. Soon he was back. His powers hadn't developed as strongly as Ciro's, so he couldn't shimmer out of view as fast as Ciro.

"I warned you," Ciro said between gritted teeth. "Now you pay the price."

The fight was fierce like a strange yet beautifully choreographed dance. The power of their exchanged blows caused the twister to grow stronger, and lightning charged across the space a little too close to the ground. Ciro knew if he didn't end the battle soon, his worse fears would come to pass — another town would be swallowed by the spinning inferno and there would be nothing Hygeia could do to help. Defeating Gala seemed impossible. He countered each of Ciro's blows, following them with attempts of his own, but Ciro was becoming impatient.

A wise friend's voice swam through his mind. *"When it comes to fighting, my friend, patience is a virtue."*

Ciro took a fist to the chest and staggered backward. Gala didn't seem to want to give him time to recover, for he attacked again. Turning away, Ciro grabbed Gala's arm, spun him around and slammed his palm into Gala's back. He pushed forward slightly, sending a bolt of lightning through Gala, who stiffened in Ciro's arms, jolted, then slumped in the air. Ciro hovered over him, watching him twitch before he finally faded from view. A low hum filled the air and he recognized it as Gala's soul leaving his body. It sparkled with blue light but only for an instant before turning black and slipping through the earth.

Ciro took no pleasure in his enemy's demise. He knew each time he destroyed a Shiver, there were still more out there, ready to take his place. Gala was right. This battle he was waging to protect the humans was becoming more and more futile with each opponent. Rising higher than the funnel, he opened his palms toward it, forcing it to heed him. Bowing his head, he watched as Gala's creation dissipated and calm was restored. The dark gave way to light and people began making their way outside once more. Homes weren't badly damaged, but a few things had toppled over. Most of the carnage was relegated to the higher buildings.

Hygeia had changed herself into a human woman and was assisting people on the ground. Ciro couldn't land and lend a hand, for humans were easily spooked and unpredictable. He took a breath and shook his head, hungering for peace and rest. Even as he vanished, Ciro knew the rest he craved would never come to him.

About the Author

Multi-published Remmy Duchene was born in St. Anns, Jamaica and moved to Canada at a young age. When not working or writing, Remmy loves dabbling in photography, travelling and spending time with friends and family.

Remmy loves to hear from readers. You can find their contact information, website details and author profile page at http://www.pride-publishing.com.